# The Bad Luck Nickel

# the BAD LUCK NICKEL

## MATTHEW LESLIE

AUSABLE BOOKS

MONTREAL

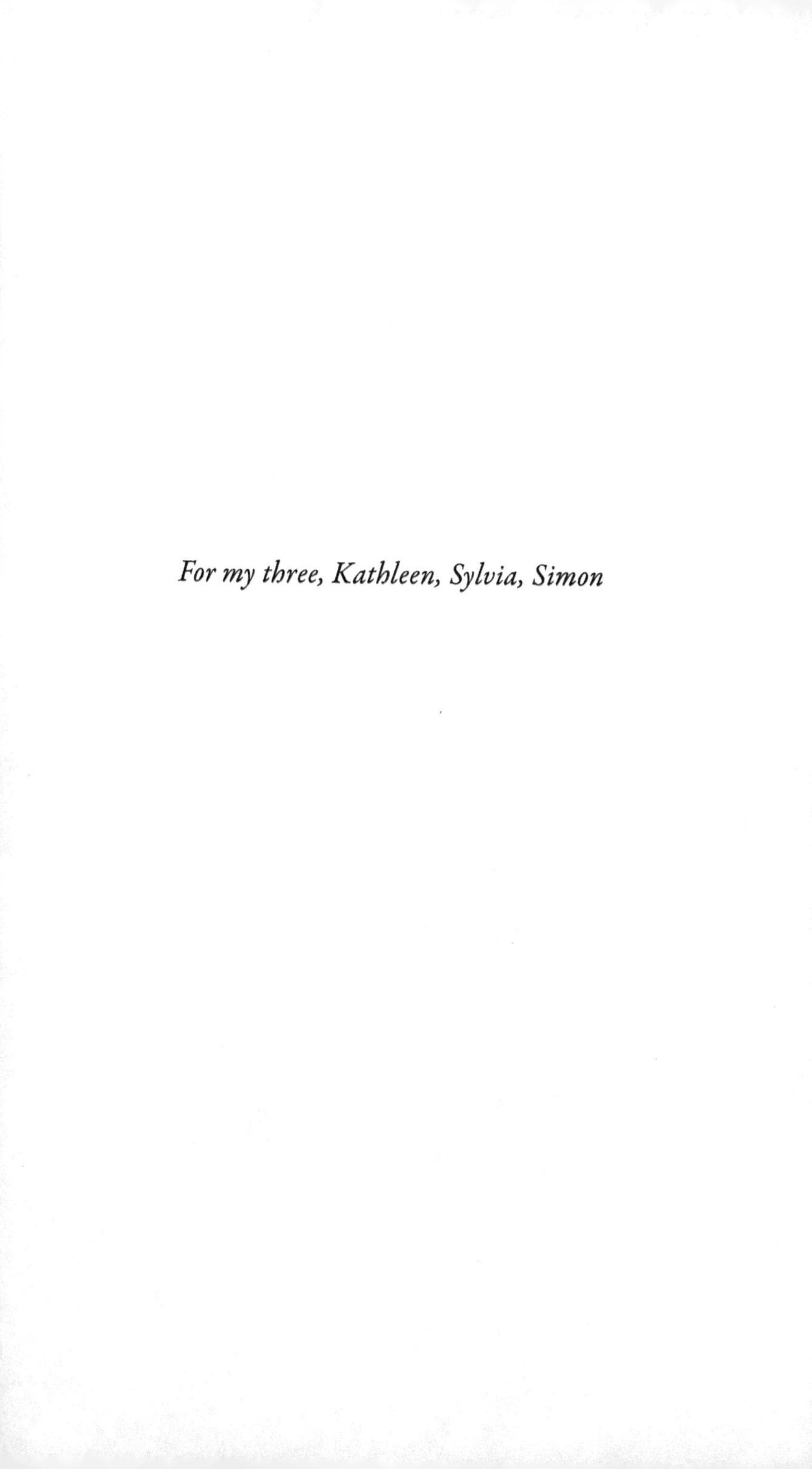

*For my three, Kathleen, Sylvia, Simon*

# PART I

# MARCO

We're supposed to be playing a gig tonight, but Randy's drum set is in shambles because things got out of hand during our show last weekend at Acapulco Delight, and Tank's amp is making this awful buzzing sound because someone knocked it over and spilled beer on it.

Plus, we haven't practiced any of our new songs, and we know that bailing on the show will piss Blair off, and all three of us really feel like pissing Blair off.

And plus plus, it's a freezing Friday night in Montreal, it's been snowing sideways all day, and we're lazy and cold and just want to get messed up. So a few hours before the show, we decide to blow it off and hang in the Henri-Bourassa Tunnels instead.

"I got my brother's ID so I can grab beer if you spot me some cash," Tank says, as we tramp through the drifting snow on the sidewalk outside his house. Tank is always broke and never has any smokes or weed unless girls are involved. But throw a girl in the mix and suddenly a joint will pop out of a hidden pocket or a twenty-dollar bill will materialize out of thin air like he's doing a card trick or something.

Tank's the only one of us who looks old enough to buy beer, so we take advantage of it. We don't call him

Tank for nothing. Tank is a beast among bros. Makes me and Randy look like little squirts. He's sixteen but can easily pass for twenty-five. Probably because he's 6 foot 3 and can grow a beard in a week.

I dig into the back pocket of my jeans and pull out a ten and Randy gives Tank a twenty. Tank's eyes light up as he sees the cash.

"Got paid yesterday," Randy says. "Can you buy me a pack of smokes too?"

We walk a couple blocks to the depanneur on the corner and huddle outside while Tank goes in to get our supplies. I look up at a streetlight and watch the snow swirl and Randy ducks into the alley behind the store to check out the graffiti.

After a few seconds Randy starts shouting: "Holy shit, Marco! Get over here, dude! Hurry, hurry!"

I run into the alley to find out what he's going off about and I see him standing next to a man lying in the snow. The man's on his back and there's a dried-up Christmas tree at his feet. A sensor light above the back door of the store is shining directly on the guy, making the whole scene looked staged.

"What happened?" I ask.

"I dunno. He was dragging the tree over to that dumpster and then he grabbed his chest and passed the fuck out! He was looking at me straight in the eyes as he fell over! So trippy, Marco! D'you think he's dead?" Randy asks, bouncing up and down on his heels, totally freaking out.

"Of course not," I say, slowly walking up to the guy. "Hello, *ça va?* Are you okay?" I ask, nudging him with my boot.

"He looks like he's dead, Marco!" Randy shouts.

"Calm down! Just because he's passed out, doesn't mean he's dead!" I say, leaning over to check out the guy's face in the soft glow of the light. He looks like he's smiling. Sleeping peacefully. But he also looks kinda pasty and gross.

"Check his pulse," Randy says.

"Why don't you check his pulse?"

"Cause you're already right next to him!"

"Fine. Fuck." I crouch down and give the guy a little shove on the shoulder. "Hellooo, sir? Can you hear me?"

Nothing. I take off my glove and reach across to touch the guy's neck, convinced that this is just some weird prank, and that his eyes will pop open, and he'll grab me and start choking me as soon as I touch him. My hand shakes as I place two fingers to his neck. He's warm, but I can't feel a pulse.

I shiver. "Dude, I can't feel anything!"

"I knew it! He's dead, Marco!"

Tank comes around the corner smiling with a 12-pack of cans under his arm. "What the hell?" he says when he sees the scene. He drops the beer in the snow and runs over. "What happened?"

"Fuckin' guy grabbed his chest and passed out right in front of me! Marco can't find a pulse . . . I think he's dead, Tank!"

Tank crouches down next to me and without fear or hesitation grabs the guy's wrist to check for a pulse.

"Should we do CPR, Marco?"

Tank and I had to take a First Aid course as part of our gym class in the fall, but it was the same week I got dumped by my girlfriend, so I was pretty out of it.

"I don't know if I can do it, Tank . . ."

"Randy you're a lifeguard, you know artificial respiration or whatever, right?"

"Eww, no way, man. I'm not giving a dead guy mouth to mouth, are you kiddin' me?"

Tank shakes his head in annoyance at Randy, digs in his pocket for his phone and dials 911. "Yes, hello ma'am, I'm in the alley behind Dépanneur 365 on the corner of Lajeunesse and Fleury. Um, we just saw a guy pass out in the snow and we think he might've had a heart attack . . ."

While Tank handles the conversation with the 911 Lady like a boss, I take a step back and again can't believe how beautiful the scene looks with the gleam of the light and the snow falling on the guy and the silhouettes of Tank and Randy around him. The Christmas tree still has some tinsel on it and it's shimmering. You can even see his footsteps a bit farther down the alley, quickly being erased by the falling snow. I gaze up at the sky and it's this soft pink colour that only happens during winter storms. It makes the night so much brighter.

It's oddly perfect. I have to fight the urge to grab my phone and take a picture. Instead, I watch as Randy continues to pace and dance around the guy, and Tank always fearless, tilts the guy's head back to make sure his airway isn't blocked.

The guy is wearing a pair of clunky winter boots and I notice his laces aren't even tied up, as if he'd just slipped them on to quickly run to the store for a bag of Doritos or a couple of beers to drink while he watches the hockey game.

"She says we have to start CPR, Marco!" Tank says, snapping me back to reality. "Paramedics might take longer than usual because of the snow!"

"I dunno know if I can do it, Tank—"

"Of course you can, dude! C'mon, get over here!" he says, as he unzips the man's jacket. I walk over and crouch down next to Tank and the man in the snow.

"You do the compressions and I'll do the breaths, all right?" Tank asks me, but it's not really a question.

"She says thirty chest compressions to two breaths," Tank says, as I kneel in the snow next to the guy and try to remember what our First Aid instructor, Mr. Campeau said: *"Aim for a 100 beats per minute, guys! Hard and fast in the centre of the chest, hard and fast in the centre of the chest, hard and fast in the centre of the chest . . ."*

As I undo the buttons on the man's shirt, I notice a cell phone sticking out of his pocket, and I grab it and hand it to Randy.

"We got this, Marco! Let's go!" Tank says, as I clasp my hands together and place them on the man's hairy chest.

"OK, count it out for me," I say, as I begin pressing down on the man's sternum.

*"Hard and fast in the centre of the chest, hard and fast in the centre of the chest! Easiest way to remember is to hum the Bee Gees song "Staying Alive", it's the exact same rhythm . . ."*

While Tank counts to thirty, I hear Mr. Campeau singing: *"Feel the city breakin' and everybody shakin', and we're stayin' alive, stayin' alive, ahh, ahh, ahh, ahh!"*

"Twenty-nine, thirty!" Tank shouts, and then he leans in, pinches the guy's nose and gives him two big puffs on the lips. "OK, next round!" he says, and Mr. Campeau starts singing the Bee Gees again.

"Holy shit!" Randy shouts, in between Tank saying twelve and thirteen.

"What is it?" Tank asks.

Randy's looking at the guy's phone, which he's clicked on. "Marco, have you seen this guy before?"

"No, I don't think so," I say, still pumping away on his chest.

"Are you sure?" he asks, turning the phone so we can see what he's looking at.

It's a picture of my ex-girlfriend Bianca, wearing the Batman T-shirt she stole from me, and smiling her super cute, crooked teeth grin.

# JULIANNA

"Your brother is such a dick!" Blair says, as Marco's phone goes to voicemail for the third time. "We're supposed to be at The Coach for sound check in like a half an hour. Will you try calling him? Maybe he'll answer if it's you."

I grab my phone off the nightstand and call him but he doesn't answer. I shake my head at Blair. "Maybe try Tank again?"

"This is such bullshit, Jules. They ditched jamming yesterday and now none of them are answering their phones? What the hell's going on?"

I love it when Blair gets angry. Not angry at me, but like, angry at the world. It makes him look older and gives his pretty boy features an edge that is sooo sexy.

"You should grow out your facial hair for a couple weeks," I tell him. "I think you'd look really good with some scruff."

"Are you even listening to me?" he asks. He runs a hand through his dark hair, and I can see the veins practically popping out of his forearms. I want to kiss him. His tongue is pierced and the novelty of kissing a guy with a tongue ring still hasn't worn off.

"Of course I'm listening, babe," I say. "But I'm also thinking about how hot you look when you get pissed off."

"This is our most important gig yet! Will you try calling him again?"

"Honestly, I think they're all still ticked with you from last weekend—"

"Why? That show was amazing. People are still buzzing from it, and we need to keep that momentum rolling . . ."

"I agree, the show was totally amazing. *You* were totally amazing. But their gear got messed up when you let everyone on the stage."

"Oh whatever, Tank's amp got knocked over, big deal."

"Yeah but someone spilled beer on it. And two of Randy's drum skins got smashed. That's why they ditched jamming last night."

"Why didn't you tell me this earlier?"

"I dunno. 'Cause it's boring, and I thought you knew already? I mean, you were literally on the stage when it was happening."

"Yeah but I was performing, and you know how I lose myself in the moment."

"Blah. I don't wanna talk about The Bad Luck Nickel right now, okay? I wanna talk about you and me and how cute we are together."

"Do you really think they're gonna bail on the show?"

"There's a blizzard out, Blair. And their gear is messed up. And they blame you. C'mon, let's go downtown and do something crazy, like get tattoos." I stand up off my bed and walk over to him. "This'll blow over. And there'll be other shows. You're Blair Matthews and a cancelled show will just create more of a reason for the kids to show up to the next one. It's a total punk rock move. It's perfect. Now kiss me."

He does, and after a second I feel his tongue ring knock against my teeth. I gently bite his bottom lip and embrace him as tight as I can.

"All right, all right, screw the gig," Blair says, grabbing my face in both hands and kissing me harder. And the longer we kiss, the lighter I feel. I get so light I start floating, and I have to hang on to Blair so I won't sail up up up to the ceiling. It feels so good, this floaty feeling, it makes me tingly and graceful and dizzy and drunk. After a little while, Blair pulls away with a laugh, and he kisses my neck and squeezes my ass.

"Tattoos? Are you serious?" he says. "What would you even get?"

"I always thought it would be cool to get f-holes on my back like Man Ray's violin woman. You know what I'm talking about?"

"Oh yeah, I've seen that image. You'd be super hot as a human violin," he says. "But your mom would go ape-shit."

"I just won't tell her . . ."

"Speaking of which, isn't she gonna be home soon?"

"Nope, not for another hour or so."

"Well, we should probably spend that time wisely, don't ya think?" he says, gently pulling me towards my bed.

Blair has this amazing tattoo of a raven on his chest, and I become wild with the need to see it and run my fingers over it and kiss its inky black wings. So I grab at his T-shirt and pull it over his head with a grin . . .

# MARCO

"Holy crap, is this Bianca's Dad?" Tank asks.

"I'm not sure," I say, my hands resting on his chest. Tank has stopped counting and I feel frozen in time and place. I start shaking all over. My toes go numb. Just seeing Bianca's photo makes my stomach hurt. But thinking about her dad possibly being dead makes me almost puke. "He does lives around here," I say, thinking of the nights I dropped Bianca off at his apartment building just a block or so north.

I never actually met him, but Bianca stays at his place a couple weekends a month, which was awesome when we were together, because she didn't have a curfew when she was there. Her mom and stepdad barely let her stay out past midnight.

"Ho-lee crap! We just found Bianca's dead dad in a fucking alley!" Randy shouts.

"Will you shut up?" Tank says. "Go stash the beer somewhere before the cops get here!"

"Fine, but I'm drinking one," Randy says.

Tank looks at me and squeezes my shoulder hard. "Listen, you just gotta fuckin' forget about everything right now, OK? We gotta start over. C'mon, hit him with thirty more!"

As I pound on Bianca's dad's heart, my own heart cramps in my chest. I imagine Bianca at her dad's funeral, trying to be tough because she thinks she's so tough, but being unable to keep her tears inside. Bianca puts on this show of being indifferent to everything, like she can just end any conversation with "whatever" and carry on like it ain't no thang, but it's all an act, none of it's true. She actually cares too much.

"Twenty nine and thirty!" Tank shouts, but he sounds like he's a mile away. I stop and he gives Bianca's dad two big breaths and I start again.

Even though I kind of hate my dad, I don't know what I'd do if he died. I think I'd probably wanna die too. I mean, sure, there was a period there after he left when I wished he would get hit by a fuckin' truck, but I'm over that now, even though we still definitely have our issues. And I know Bianca loves her dad a ton, even if she says she's embarrassed to be seen with him because he swears too much and asks her to do dumb stuff like pull his finger and barely makes enough money to pay child support.

Because family sticks, ya know? I mean it has too, right? I'm lucky because I have Jules, but Bianca is an only child, she's got no one else except her mom, and I know for a fact that her mom hates her dad big time. She'll probably be happy he's dead.

I make it to thirty compressions. "I gotta call her," I say.

"No way, man. What the hell would you even say?" Tank asks after giving him two puffs of air.

"I dunno, maybe that her dad just had a fucking heart attack!" I scream, looking down at his face. Snow has started collecting on his beard and eyebrows.

A flash of red light begins to strobe the street. *Thank God! The ambulance is here.* It pulls into the alley, and two paramedics, one male and one female, hop out.

"Hi. He's over here!" Tank yells. "We started CPR and gave him five rounds of compressions."

Before I even know what I'm doing, I grab my phone out of my pocket and start filming the scene. The paramedics run towards me, pushing a stretcher through the snow as the red light flashes ominously in the background. I follow them with my camera as they reach Bianca's dad and watch as they nod to each other and hoist him up on the gurney.

"What the hell are you doing?" Tank asks. But I ignore him, I ignore everything, and move a bit closer, zooming in to get a better shot. The paramedics have headlamps, which they flick on, giving me the perfect amount of light to keep filming.

The female paramedic presses down on Bianca's dad's neck to check for a pulse, but after a few seconds she shakes her head. "Negative," she says, as she starts pumping down on his chest. "Throw in an OPA and start bagging him."

The male paramedic jams a plastic tube in Bianca's dad's mouth so it'll stay open and places an oxygen mask over his face. "OK, let's get him in the bus, we gotta defib him," he says, as they push the stretcher back towards the ambulance while still performing CPR. I keep filming. They lift him inside the ambulance, and the male paramedic grabs the defibrillator.

"Make sure you wipe him down. I got snow on his chest," she says, as I creep right up to the back door of the ambulance. Tank tells me to stop but they're not looking at me at all.

They brought him in feet first, so I have a great shot of his bald head and the paramedics standing over top of him. The woman paramedic sticks the pads on his chest and the defibrillator machine makes a bunch of beeping sounds as it turns on. After the beeping stops the male paramedic actually says: "clear", but it's not like on TV, where they scream it and everything is over-dramatic and in slo-motion, nope, this guy is all business, a real pro. He calmly says: "All right, clear", and as soon as they both back away, he zaps him.

Bianca's dad's body lurches in the air and he kind of looks like a zombie, but he immediately turns his head, coughs wildly as he chokes on the tube they stuck down his throat, and then he pukes all over the male paramedic's boots.

And I got the whole thing on video.

# JULIANNA

Sometimes after I'm with Blair, I feel total bliss. I can think about all the shitty stuff in my life and shrug it all off with a laugh, because none of it seems to matter at all. The only thing that matters is me and him, and I can listen to the faint thrumming of my body as my heartbeat slowly returns to normal and feel perfectly content.

But other times, I feel sort of emotional and weird afterwards. Or I'll start to feel really vulnerable or even a little bit paranoid. I get this way when I drink sometimes too. And bad news for Blair, because it feels like right now is going to be one of those times. Which sucks, because it had been super romantic with the blizzard happening outside and all the candles flickering around the room, so I hate that I'm going to ruin the vibe.

I'm lying in his arms and he's tracing figure eights on my stomach with his finger. His breathing is slow and steady, like he might fall asleep at any moment.

"Is the rumor true, Blair?" I ask in a whisper.

"Hmmm?" he mumbles.

"Is the rumor really true?"

"Oh c'mon, Jules, not this again. How many times do I have to tell you the same thing?"

"I'm sorry, it's just everyone is talking about it at school . . ."

"Yeah and it's a different bullshit story every frickin' time you hear it! I don't get you, Jules. Two nights ago, the whole idea got you all hot and turned on and you couldn't keep your hands off me. You even wanted to role play—"

"Yeah, I know. But now I feel weird about it, okay?" I say, as I watch the flare of a candle cast a shadow on the wall. "Just tell me if it's true—"

"Like I said before. It's not true, okay?"

"But even The Blade mentions it in his latest interview," I say, knowing I shouldn't bring it up, but Blair is so defensive, I can't help but think he's hiding something from me.

"And I told you, my dad is a fucking liar!" he says, pushing me off him and getting out of the bed. Blair grabs his pants off the floor and starts pulling them on. "But it sure makes a hell of a better story than The Blade not wanting to live with his own kid anymore!"

"Don't get mad, Blair," I say, pissed with myself for even mentioning it. He grabs his phone and clicks it on, looking at the screen. "C'mon, let's just forget it, all right?"

It feels like my heart is pumping in reverse, and all my thoughts flip upside down. Two seconds earlier, I was ready to call him on his bullshit, but now I just want him back in bed with me, our bodies entwined, his hands on my skin . . .

"Marco still hasn't replied," he says, turning his back to me as he angrily thumbs out a text.

"Come back to bed, Blair," I say quietly, hating the meekness in my voice.

He shakes his head at me. "Sorry Jules, but I don't need this negativity right now," he says, grabbing his shirt and hoodie off the bed. "It's bad enough I'm getting ditched by your brother and Tank. You can believe whatever the hell you want. I'm outta here," he says, looking down at his phone, not meeting my eyes.

I pinch myself to stop from begging him to stay, and he leaves the room without even glancing back at me.

I like it when Blair gets angry at the world, but not at me.

# MARCO

Oh man, when Bianca's dad comes back to life, I almost can't believe it! An incredible sense of relief rips through me, but it also totally gives me the shivers. I turn to Tank to be like: "Did you see that? He's alive!" but it's obvious he did because he's dry heaving in the snow. Tank is a beast and a boss but he cannot handle vomit. He just can't. It's his kryptonite.

"I can't believe it," I say. My voice sounds strange to my ears. I'm not sure whether I can't believe he's alive or that I can't believe I recorded the whole thing. I guess it's a mix of the two. "Are you all right?" I ask Tank, shoving my phone in my pocket.

"Yeah, man. I'm good. You know me and puke though," he says with a laugh, spitting in the snow. "That was fucking crazy, Marco! You didn't see it, but I musta jumped a foot in the air when they shocked him. He looked like Frankenstein's monster, the way his arms shot up like that. Holy shit, what a trip."

We hear the quick whoop of a siren and see a police car pull up. I take a look around and notice a few bystanders huddling about in the snow.

"Hey, where's Randy?" I ask.

"Dunno," Tank says. "But he sure ain't showing up now that the cops are here. Perfect time to steal one of his smokes," he says, pulling out the pack he bought for him. He opens it and hands me one. We light them and smoke in silence for a couple minutes, watching the two officers talk with the paramedics. They've hooked Bianca's dad up to an oxygen tank, and it looks like he's passed out again, but he's alive, he's still alive.

*Ahh, ahh, ahh, ahh, stayin' alive! Stayin' alive!*

An officer begins walking towards us, after the paramedic points in our direction. This guy is enormous. He's built like a sasquatch. A total beast. He even makes Tank look like a little squirt.

In general, I hate cops. I don't trust them, I don't like them, I don't even want to be near them. But this gentle giant is totally cool. He's got no attitude, there's nothing threatening in his voice, and he treats us with respect.

"Hey boys, how's it going? I'm Officer Blanchard from 39th division," he says, shaking our hands with his bear paw. "Are you guys okay? It must've been pretty scary finding that man unconscious in the snow."

"Just doing our civic duty, officer," Tank says.

Officer Blanchard laughs and pats Tank on the back. "Well, you did the right thing by calling 911 and starting CPR on him," he says.

"Did he have a heart attack?" Tank asks.

"Looks like it," he says.

"Is he gonna be okay?"

"Well, to be honest, he's not in the clear yet. They'll take him to Hotel-Dieu hospital and run some tests to get a better sense of how serious things are. But it's a good thing you boys spotted him when you did and were brave enough to give him CPR. You may have helped save his life," he says to us with a serious look on his face.

"Holy shit, Marco," Tank whispers in disbelief. More lines from Mr. Campeau's First Aid class come swirling back to me: *Basically when someone has no pulse, they're already clinically dead. Flatlined. Ka-put. But by giving them CPR you keep their brain alive, pumping jussst enough blood up there to stop them from buggin' out completely.*

"I really hope he's gonna be all right," I say.

We all stand there quietly for a moment as the ambulance begins to pull away. I realize I've forgotten all about the cold and the snow even though my toes are like ice cubes.

Officer Blanchard takes our names and statements and me and Tank both leave out the fact that originally there was three of us. *Like, where the hell is Randy?*

"You did a good thing tonight," he tells us. "So treat yourselves, hell, go have a beer, you deserve it," he says with a smile.

"Really?" I ask incredulously. "A cop is telling us to go get drunk?"

"I said *one* beer not ten. Everything in moderation, boys. But lay off the smokes, all right? Especially you," he says to Tank. "You play football?"

"Yes sir. Offensive Tackle for The Cougars."

"Cigs will kill your speed, I'm sure your coach has already told you that."

Tank nods. "I know, I know, but it's the off-season."

Officer Blanchard shrugs his cinderblock shoulders at him and says: "Your choice. All right boys, we're outta here. Thanks for your help tonight."

"No sweat," Tank says, as Officer Blanchard leaves us in the alley.

I can already see the shock on Bianca's face when she finds out we helped save her dad's life. I picture her hugging me, kissing me, and whispering all sorts of sweet somethings in my ear, and me, I'll try to say something smooth back, but I know I'll be lost in her embrace and the amazing aroma of her skin. *Goddammit, I miss her!*

"Can you believe we just gave Bianca Marcuzzi's father CPR in an alley during a fucking snowstorm?" Tank asks with a laugh.

"No way, man. It feels like a dream," I say.

"You were a boss, Marco! Pumping away on his chest like a real pro!"

"Haha, no way, you were the pro, Tank! You gave him mouth to mouth!"

"I even slipped him the tongue," Tank says, and we both laugh.

"I guess it's a good thing Randy came back here to check out the shitty graffiti," I say.

"Yeah, where the hell is that guy?" Tank asks, looking down the alley. He pulls out his phone to give him a call. "Oh man, Blair's called me like three times . . ."

"Shit, I wonder if he called me too," I say, grabbing my phone to check, but the video is still on the screen. I hit play and start watching it.

"I can't believe you recorded that, Marco," Tank says, but I shush him, and he huddles next to me, and we watch the whole thing in silence until the end where Bianca's dad pukes and then we roar in laughter, and Tank dry heaves again, and we walk down the alley looking for Randy.

# JULIANNA

Blair was my first and once we hooked up I decided I was going to let myself go with the flow of our relationship wherever it may. I'd be reckless, I'd take risks. Bust out of my comfort zone. Fall for him hard but not too hard. Just because he's Blair Matthews doesn't mean I have to get stupid about it.

But of course, I'm starting to get stupid about it.

Sometimes it feels like he fills up my mind so much there's no room for anything else.

And in case you're wondering, yes, it's *that* Blair Matthews: son of rock legend The Blade, and child model for The Gap, and star of that "Mmm, *je t'aime*", Tim Horton's Christmas commercial they play every year in French and English that makes everyone cry.

I still remember the first time I saw that commercial four Christmases ago, and thinking he was so damn cute. Me and my best friend Vicky became obsessed with him after that and found his old Gap ads online and started following him on all his social media. This was back in the early Justin Bieber heydays, so of course, Blair had that messy side-sweep hairdo à la young Biebs. It was such a great hairstyle because even though it was an innocent look, it could still be a bit badass, depending on the person. And like his dad, Blair's always had an edge. So even though the commercial is as wholesome as can be and everyone gets that warm and fuzzy holiday twinge in their stomach when Blair says his famous "Mmm, *je t'aime*" line, there's a faint smugness in his shit-eating, cocoa-sipping grin that made me crazy about him even way back then.

So the "rumor" that's been going around as to why Blair showed up at Trudeau High in the fall, was that his dad, aka The Blade, found Blair in a hotel room, completely naked and doing coke with a Hesher groupie ten years older than him. And The Blade, who's a total straight edge, apparently went nutso on Blair, and decided his life in the rock and roll limelight was finished.

It's the perfect punk rock story to go with Blair's perfect punk rock look, and yeah, sometimes the whole idea of his life in L.A. totally turns me on. He already has so much experience in life and love and sex and now he's sharing it with me. That's hot. That's special. And I want him to show me everything everything everything, I really do. But sometimes I get insanely jealous of all those experiences and sometimes I don't like the fact that I slept with him as fast as I did, mainly because I felt like if I didn't, he was going to move on to someone who would . . .

But now, being with him feels like it's all I've ever wanted. Which is weird because I've never felt like this before. I'm not sure if it's love or infatuation, and I can't tell if I am obsessed with him or with who he is . . . all I know is I feel like if he asked me to kill someone for him, I'd do it without question. Is that normal? Is that what love is? I feel so messed up sometimes.

I see the way every girl looks at him in the halls at school and it drives me crazy. They flirt with him constantly. They do it right in front of me. Vicky tells me to just ignore it and revel in the fact that I am the one he's with, and usually I'm a pretty confident person, but it's hard to be confident all the time, ya know? Especially when there's so many beautiful girls out there with bigger boobs and tighter butts and better skin and nicer hair than me, that all want to have sex with my boyfriend.

Even some girls that I've been friends with since elementary school seem to hate me now that I'm with him. They say it's just because he's in a band with Marco that we hooked up. And that he was drunk and I seduced him, which is hilarious, because I seriously have no idea how to be sexy or seductive. And of course, they say I'm a total slut, even though before Blair I'd barely let a boy touch my boobs!

Vicky says they're just jealous and that I need to ignore all the gossip and she's totally right, but like I said, it's hard to be chill all the time, especially when I've suddenly become someone who second guesses herself every chance she gets.

Well guess what? I know what I'm doing tonight. No second guesses *ce soir, tabarnak* . . . I'm going to meet up with Vicky and then find Marco and the boys and get my drink on. And I won't text or call Blair or look at my phone all night.

But do you want to know what the funny part is? At first, I really didn't like the idea of having a "celebrity" at our school, even if he was my pre-teen crush and so goddamn sexy. Celebrity culture seems so fake and vapid and pathetic to me, despite the fact that their lives are supposed to be way better than yours or mine. So I just thought that even though he was super hot, Blair would be a spoiled, narcissistic, pretty boy.

And I probably would've been happy to just keep checking him out in the hallway all year if Marco hadn't brought him home on the first day of school in September.

# MARCO

Two seconds after me and Tank finish watching the video, my phone rings. I show Tank the screen. It's Blair.

"Just answer it," he says.

"Yello?" I say, putting the phone on speaker.

"Where the hell have you been, man?" Blair shouts. "Are you guys showing up to the gig or not?" I don't reply. "So fucking childish, Marco. We can't just bail on a show, dude. We have to treat it like work. If we're going to make it, we have to be serious!"

"Is that what The Blade would say?" Tank asks.

"Tank, is that you? Where are you guys?"

"In an alley near Henri-Bourassa. We just saved a guy's life!"

"Fuck off."

"It's true!" I shout.

"Well, good for you guys," he says, not believing us. "Listen, are you coming or not?"

"My amp is fucked," Tank tells him. "As soon as I turn it on it makes this annoying buzzing sound. I think maybe the tubes need to be changed."

"I'm sure Brendan or Graham will have an amp you can use," Blair tries.

"Forget it, dude. Until our shit is fixed we ain't playing any more shows," Tank says, and he taps the End Call button with his thumb. "I'm starting to miss the days when it was just me, you, and Randy jamming in the basement, Marco. It was so much more fun. Just get stoned and start messing around until we hit the groove and play until your mom made us stop. That's all I want. Blair and his wannabe rock star bullshit is killing what The Bad Luck Nickel is all about."

"You're totally right," I say. "But at the same time, with him in the band we can actually get gigs."

"Yeah, but that's just because his dad is The Blade," Tank says.

Tank isn't a Hesher fan and doesn't give a leaping turd who Blair's dad is. But me and Randy, we fuckin' loooove Hesher and once we found out Blair was going to be a student at Trudeau High, we were secretly like: "Holy shit, his dad is Thee Mother Fucking Blade!"

And Randy was like: "Remember that time we went camping at The Pinery and got super high on that hash we bought off your sketchball neighbour Brad, and we listened to the hidden track at the end of *Reverse Black Hole*?"

"Of course I remember," I said with a laugh.

"Well, The Blade's guitar sounded so trippy it made me have an out of body experience, Marco! It was amazing! I hovered above the campfire and looked down at everything, at you, at Jules, at the campsite, even at my own self! And I felt so peaceful. It was like an epiphany for me. It changed my whole perception, man! And the sound of The Blade's guitar is seared into my brain now, it's like tattooed on there, so I can hear it any time I want. And whenever I'm upset or choked about something I just think about the way his guitar sounded while I was floating above that fire and *boom*, I'm all good, bro, I'm fuckin' smiling. Best song of life!"

I chuckle as I remember Randy's rant and call his cell but it goes straight to voicemail. I do our secret whistle and listen for a reply but there's nothing. "Yo Randy!" I shout. Still nothing.

"Well, he's gotta be here somewhere," Tank says. "And he has the beer!"

So we start trudging down the alley. The snow has slowed and even though my feet are frozen I don't really feel too cold.

"What a crazy night so far, eh?" I say to Tank.

He laughs. "Yeah, man. The weekend is off to an epic start and it's not even eight o'clock."

EXCERPT FROM *Distortion Magazine*,
issue 17, volume 9, Winter 2018


"A Double-Edged Blade: Hesher's frontman talks teenage rebellion, getting older and wiser, and the band's return to form, with their tenth studio album, *Bow Down To The Bull God*."


*The Blade*: Yeah man, when it comes to Blair, I totally blame myself. I pushed him into show biz and doing those damn commercials so early that he never got to be a kid at all, ya know? He never got to play baseball or have a paper route or cheat on his math test or cut class to go hang out at the mall with his age-appropriate girlfriend. Kids need that shit. Kids need routines and they need to be bored. As stupid as that sounds, I think it's really fuckin' important.


*Distortion Magazine:* Wouldn't it have been easier to just enroll Blair at a public school in Los Angeles instead of having him move all the way to Montreal?


*The Blade:* No way, man. La-La Land was already turning into a bad place for him and he ain't even eighteen. It was time to shake up his

whole reality, know what I mean? I grew up in Dayton, Ohio, and went to a shitty public school that I fuckin' hated, and I want the same damn thing for him.

*Distortion Magazine:* Why?

*The Blade:* Because it's normal and it's boring . . . (*He laughs for a second, then becomes serious, looking me straight in the eye*) But at least you can still dream, man. L.A. kills dreamers, and Blair's too damn young to not still have his head way up in them clouds . . .

*Distortion Magazine:* Would you say you regret bringing him on tour with you?

*The Blade:* (*shakes his head*) I dunno. I just wanted him to see the world with me, ya know? It's like an education all its own. But thinking back on it, yeah, I probably shouldn't have always brought him on tour with us, because tours are hard work, and they're totally unpredictable, and as cliché as it might sound, sex, drugs, and rock and roll is a very real thing, no matter how old you are, know what I'm sayin'?

*Distortion Magazine*: And do you think Blair's drug use upsets you more because you've been sober for over twenty years now?

*The Blade*: Of course, man. 'Cause I've seen what drugs can do. I've been to the dark side and back, brother. Drugs actually killed me. When I OD'd on tour in 1997, I was clinically dead for over four minutes. They thought I was brain dead! (*He laughs quietly*) I won't lie to you though, drugs were a lot of fuckin' fun, but then one day they weren't anymore. I don't know exactly when the shift happened, but it happened fast enough, ya know? And by that point I was too far gone to know the difference. (*He shakes his head*) Nope, there's no way The

Blade's gonna let his son walk down the same dirt road. No fuckin' way.

*Distortion Magazine:* Which is why I find it interesting that you sent him back to live with his mother, considering you originally gained custody of Blair in 2004 because she was a drug addict.

*The Blade:* (*laughs*) Aww man, yeah, Marilou had some hard times back then, and yeah, I definitely dragged her name through the fuckin' mud and back, but she's been sober herself for almost ten years. And now she's about as boring and normal as you can get. Doesn't even listen to metal anymore, can you believe that? (*He laughs*). People can change, ya know?

*Distortion Magazine*: Has Blair changed then?

*The Blade*: Yeah, I think so. Once the media stopped caring he adjusted pretty quickly. He's passing all his classes and he's made some friends, he even hooked up with a band and they're starting to play gigs around the city . . .

# MARCO

Randy's been going through a bit of a Peepin' Tom phase lately. Not in the pervy sense, where he climbs trees and tries to see girls changing in their bedrooms, nothing like that, he just likes to peek in windows and get a glimpse of people doing regular stuff in their homes. Like a family eating dinner together or an old lady washing dishes in the kitchen or a couple chilling on the couch watching TV, normal stuff like that.

He told me about it one night a couple months ago, back when it was still warm out and we were hanging at Chopin Park drinking a bottle of wine I stole from my mom's stash.

"Can I tell you something weird?" he asked.

"Always," I said.

"OK, well, I don't really know why I've been doing this, but for the last month or so I've been kinda looking in on this house across the street from where the bus drops me off after work."

"What d'you mean, looking in?"

"Like, watching the family that lives there."

I laughed, thinking he was kidding. "So you're stalking some strange family? Do they have a hot daughter or something?"

"No, man. It's nothing like that. I just like watching them. And on nice nights they leave their windows open so I can even listen in on their conversations.

"Black kid hiding in the bushes alert!" I said.

Randy laughed. "Yeah, I'm totally aware of how it might look, and I know it sounds fucked up, but it's not, I swear. They have this giant window that you can see directly into from the street, and they're just an ordinary family with two little girls maybe around eight and ten years old. One night I watched the dad helping the older kid with her homework for like a half an hour. I think it was math, because she was getting really frustrated at first, but after a while you could tell she figured it out because she was smiling, and her dad kept giving her high-fives. Do you remember how awesome it was when you didn't understand something and then finally it just clicked and changed everything completely? And afterwards you couldn't even see it the wrong way anymore because the right way made so much fuckin' sense?"

"Haha, you're wasted," I said.

"I know," he replied, grabbing the bottle from me and taking a swig. "Don't tell anyone about it, though, OK? They'll think it's weird."

Randy says he doesn't really know why he does it, but I think it's because his own home life has been a mess over the last year and a half, ever since his older sister Nicole died from a car crash. It was sudden. She was driving home from her friend's house one night and was hit by a drunk driver speeding through a red. He'd dropped his phone and was reaching for it under the seat. He walked away unharmed. Nicole died at the hospital later that night from internal bleeding. It was really awful.

Nicole was such a cool person. She never treated us differently just because she was in college and we were still in high school, and she used to buy beer for us before Tank could grow facial hair. She babysat me and Jules a bunch of times when we were younger and she'd always let us stay up and watch the shows on cable that my mom wouldn't let us watch, like *Game of Thrones* and *The Walking Dead*. Randy hated it when guys talked about how hot his sister was, but she was really beautiful, and probably the first girl I ever had a crush on back when I was eleven or twelve.

His parents sued the guy who killed her, and then had to re-live the accident every day in court for like a month. In the end, he got charged with impaired driving causing death and was sentenced to five years in prison, but it didn't seem to make Randy's parents feel any better at all.

And now, his mom's all zombie'd out on prescription drugs and his dad never seems to be home anymore. I'm not exactly sure what's going on, but it's a pretty sore topic and Randy doesn't like talking about it at all. But mainly I think he just really misses things being normal like they used to be, and when he peeps in on families in their home, he gets to kind of feel like he's being normal with them or something . . .

So I'm not surprised when I spot the beer in the snow about a block down the alley but no Randy.

"Fuckin' guy's already drank two of our beers!" Tank says, grabbing the cans. "Yo, Randoo! Where you at?" he shouts.

"Wait, shhh," I say. "He's probably in one of these yards," I say.

"What? Why?"

I shrug my shoulders and ask him to toss me a beer. "Hey, I bet I can shotgun my beer faster than you," I say, changing the subject, knowing Tank never backs down from a challenge.

"Oh, you're on, bro," Tank says, pulling his keys from his jacket pocket. He has a little Swiss Army knife on his keychain and the blade is the perfect tool to pop a hole in the can. He stabs his beer near the bottom and passes me the knife and I do the same.

"You ready?" Tank asks.

"Yup," I say, as I stab my can too.

"All right, three, two, one, go!" he says. We both pop open our cans of beer. Tank pours his down his throat like water, and I barely drink half of mine before spitting out a mouthful of foam. I pass Tank my can and he gulps the rest of it and burps triumphantly. Tank and his football bros are all about chugging beer and doing keg stands and playing beer pong and getting as shit-faced as possible. To tell you the truth, I don't really like chugging beer. I get drunk fast enough as it is, so sipping works just fine for me.

"Why do you even try, Marco? You know you can't beat the master!"

"But I know you can master the beat!" I say laughing, already feeling the beer warming my toes.

"That doesn't even make any sense," Tank says, tossing me another can. I crack it open and take a swig.

"I feel warm and toasty already!" I say.

"Such a lightweight," Tank says. "You're worse than Jules."

I'm about to tell him to screw off, but we hear a whistle up ahead, and see Randy walking towards us, talking on the phone.

"OK, hold on one sec," Randy says into the phone, taking it away from his ear.

"Where you been hiding, bro? You missed all the action," Tank says.

"Yeah I know, I saw most of it but then his phone rang," Randy says, showing us the phone he's using is Bianca's Dad's.

"What the hell, you took his phone?" I ask.

"I didn't mean to, but when I saw the cops show up, I was like, nope, my black ass ain't going back there with weed in my pocket and booze on my breath. Fuck that, man."

I hear a girl's voice screaming Randy's name from the phone. It sounds like she's totally freaking out.

"Who are you on the line with, Ran?"

"Oh right," he says, holding the phone out to me. "It's Bianca."

# JULIANNA

The way Marco tells it, all the guys at school weren't very happy when they found out Blair Matthews was the new kid at Trudeau High in September, because just by walking through the front doors he immediately became the most popular boy there.

And this ticked the guys off because popularity at Trudeau is something that is earned and built over the course of your five years there. But it's also really fragile, and many guys and girls have had to fight to keep theirs in check after making some sort of social blunder.

It happened to Marco in Grade 9 after he drank half a bottle of Southern Comfort at a party and then, eww, it was so gross, he got sick on the front lawn and passed out next to his puddle of puke. Well, poor Marco sure paid the price for that, because a couple kids snapped his photo and put it on Instagram and boom he was known as "Lawn Vomit" for the next six months. Even our English teacher Miss Stewart called him L.V. a couple times to get him to shut up when he was acting out in class.

But Marco rallied back and slowly rebuilt the cool quotients he lost because of his unfortunate So-Co incident, and for the next year he was careful not to do anything too foolish that might blow back on him: no drunken rants, no stupid shenanigans, and no sketchy hook-ups. Instead, he started playing guitar, and dressing cooler, and even developing a little tact. I mean, he's still a loudmouth that says rude and ignorant stuff, but he's quick-witted and usually knows when to draw the line. And to top it off, he started dating Bianca Marcuzzi, who's one of the most popular girls at Trudeau High.

Bianca is gorgeous and I hate her.

I pretended to like her when Marco was dating her, but I cannot stand her, and I know she doesn't like me either.

All she cares about is shopping, makeup, clothes, and her cell phone. I swear, there's nothing of substance about this girl at all. In the year that she and Marco were together, I don't think I had one meaningful conversation with her.

I'm not a violent person, but there were a few times I came close to hitting her because she could be so disrespectful to Marco. I wear this big ugly emerald ring that was my grandma's, and more than once I imagined clocking Bianca right in the face and twisting the sharp edge of the emerald into her perfectly photogenic cheekbones.

I hated the way she treated Marco when they were together, and he became sooo whipped. She basically brainwashed him and he's still not over her, even though they've been broken up for months now and she's dating Johnny Temple. Marco is a great guy and he deserves a girl who will treat him just as awesome as he treats her, ya know? And one that he can trust completely. He needs a girl who's capable of having intense conversations with him about books and music and aliens and death and the meaning of life and conspiracies about our totally fucked up world, and one that has the capacity to get excited and terrified about the future with him.

In my eyes, Bianca's about as interesting as a plastic bag. I really don't know what Marco sees in her. Well, except for her adorable smile and her long brown hair and her drop-dead gorgeous body with those perfect boobs and stomach and legs and butt.

God, I hate that bitch. Like seriously, drop dead, Bianca.

Vicky told me that Bianca's recently been talking shit about me at school, saying that it's obvious Blair doesn't really care about me because he hasn't posted a picture of us together on social yet.

Do you think I care about stupid stuff like that? Of course not! Do you think it bothers me that there's a picture of him and Marco together from the Eric's Trip show we all went to last month but not one with me?

God, I hate you Bianca . . .

I grab my phone and check to see if Blair's texted me even though I know he hasn't. So I text Marco:

> Where are you bro? I ditched Blair and wanna hang.

And then I text Vicky:

> Where you at babe?

I put on a black cardigan that I borrowed from Blair and go to the bathroom to pee, and I notice a new zit forming on my cheek. Ugh, looks like it could be a big one. Perfect. FML. My skin has been a total mess this winter. Super dry and mega prone to breakouts. I wash my face, dab some benzoyl peroxide on it and then try to hide it with some concealer. But now it looks even more noticeable. I fight the urge to squeeze it, knowing it's not ready yet and I'll only make it worse. But I'm already feeling pretty crappy about myself so why not make it worse? Why not squeeze it and throw myself a little pimple pity party?

My phone buzzes in my back pocket.

It's a text from Vicky:

> Just woke up from a nap. My parents
> are out and I still have vodka from last
> weekend. Get over herrrrrrre!

I write back:

> Aww yeah! Sounds perfect.
> Be there soon!

She immediately writes back:

> Hurry up bitch

And then:

> xoxo

I don't usually wear much makeup, but I put on some thick eyeliner and dark purple lipstick. It makes me look vicious. Makes me look like someone else. I like it. I think Blair will like it too.

I go to the kitchen. There are some beers in the fridge that my mom's boyfriend Ronnie brought over a couple nights ago. I grab one, open it and take two huge swigs. I have to drink fast because my mom's going to be home any minute now, so I burp, and keep on chugging until it's empty. My stomach tingles with beer bubbles. I grab another bottle and put it in my purse so I can drink it on the way to Vicky's. A road soda, as Tank calls it.

Headlights flash across the living room window. My mom's home. I suddenly don't feel like seeing her at all. She'll say something about my makeup or ask me something that will annoy me, so I grab my jacket and purse and slip on my boots. I wrap my scarf around my neck and sneak out the back door, just as I hear my mom fumbling with her keys at the front.

I zip my jacket, lace up my boots, and run away from the house as fast as I can, kicking through the drifts of snow, imagining Blair is chasing me, trying to catch me and throw me in a snowbank, so he can leap on top of me like a leopard and cover my face and neck in hot kisses.

# MARCO

"Yello?" I say into the phone, my voice cracking like a pre-pubescent nerd's.

"Marco! Marco! Oh my God! What's going on with my dad? What the hell's going on with my dad?! Where is he? Is he all right? Is he all right? *Please* tell me he's OKAY?!"

Even though she's freakin' out, the sound of Bianca's voice in my ear is amazing. Just hearing it turns some emotional switch on inside of me and I forget all about her dad and I only wanna talk about us, just me and Bee, and the way it used to be.

I'm smiling like an idiot, not listening to any of Bianca's frantic questions, because I'm thinking about our first date and how I manned up at the last second and kissed her on top of an abandoned boxcar as a train chugged by and it was so loud and electric and awesome. I'm thinking about how in the weeks leading up to asking her out I thought of nothing but her, my emotions a flame constantly burning in my stomach. I'm thinking about how many hours we've spent on the phone, how unlike so many girls our age Bianca likes to chat instead of text, and how we'd stay on the line talking till two in the morning and do that whole stupid

"No you hang up first" thing. One time we both drank a bottle of wine while Facetiming, and she passed out and I listened to her little drunken snores as if we were sharing the same pillow. I'm thinking about her smile and her lips, and the way they always taste like vanilla-flavoured lip gloss. I'm thinking 'bout . . .

Tank gives me a shove and I almost fall over. "Snap out of it, bro, and handle this like a boss!" he says.

I nod gratefully at him. "Sorry Bianca, we got cut off there for a second," I say.

"What the hell happened Marco? Randy said he's in a coma—"

"Well, Randy's an idiot," I say, shooting him a dirty look. "Your dad's okay. He had a heart attack but he's in stable condition," I tell her.

"A heart attack! Omigod, omigod, omigod! No! No!"

"But he's okay Bee, he's gonna be all right!"

It sounds like she's hyperventilating.

"It was a mild one, Bee! He should be fine, I mean, he *will* be fine! I swear!"

I hear her gulp. "Randy said you gave him CPR? Is it true?"

"Yeah, I mean, we had to, the ambulance was slower than usual because of the snow," I tell her. I remember my hands pumping hard and fast in the centre of his chest, hard and fast in the centre of his chest. I shiver and take a swig of beer. "He's on his way to Hotel-Dieu, so you and your mom should head over there right away!"

"Mom's gone to the chalet," she says. "I'm actually at my dad's place."

"Oh shit, I'm like a block away from you right now. I'm coming to get you and we'll go to the hospital together," I say, feeling like I might have a heart attack myself.

"You will?" she asks, her voice squeaking a little like it did back when she was still shy and nervous around me.

"Of course," I say. "Meet me outside, I'll be there in like five minutes, okay? See you soon." I hit the End Call button.

Tank nods at me. "You da man, Marco!"

I look over at Randy. "Can you spot me a twenty for a cab? I'll pay ya back tonight, I swear. I just don't have any more cash on me."

"All I had was the twenty I gave to Tank," Randy says. "Speaking of which, where's my change and my smokes?" he asks.

Tank comes up to me and gives me a quick hug. "Check your back pocket, bro," he says, and as Tank gives Randy his cigarettes and change, I pull a mysterious twenty from my pocket.

"Abracadabra! Now get the hell outta here! Text us later."

"No service in The Tunnels!" I say.

"Well, we'll be there all night."

And with that, I'm gone. Running through the drifts of snow to Bianca, excited and scared, praying that her dad will be okay and that I can remain calm when I see her face. Suddenly, I'm believing in second chances and fresh starts and new beginnings and clean slates and a bunch of other cliché expressions, as if by helping to save a man's life, I've created some new strength for my own.

# JULIANNA

I run for a few blocks, kicking through snow on the sidewalk, before ducking down an alley to crack open the road soda. There's a hush to the streets as if it's the middle of the night instead of early evening. I take two huge sips of the beer and burp louder than Tank. A car has recently driven through the alley, so I walk in its tracks and drink my beer. I don't want to think about Blair, but I can't help it, I'm obsessed.

Flashback to first day of school in September: As I said, all the guys are angry that Blair is suddenly Trudeau High royalty, so a bunch of them decide he needs an immediate humbling in the form of getting his ass kicked. Most boys at Trudeau are all mouth and no fist, but there's a few tough guys like Jay Marcelloni and Gary Belanger that are always starting fights at lunch and after school. And because Tank's built like a brick wall, he's constantly forced to defend the territory, getting swept into fights even when he doesn't want to.

But after school on the first day when Jay and Gary and their jock buddies brought Blair to the park across the street from school, Tank intervened. He stepped in front of Blair and was like: "Sorry boys, you want him you're gonna have to go through me first."

I wasn't there but I've heard this story like fifty times. So everyone is shouting at Tank to get out of the way and let pretty boy Blair get what's coming to him, but Tank just put his hands on his hips and shook his head.

Nope. Bulldog Face says no. Brickwall Tank says hell to the no.

And it was all because of that Tim Horton's commercial. Tank loved it, and so did his Nonna, who had passed away a few months earlier, so Tank told everyone he'd be damned if Blair was going to get his ass kicked.

"I don't think so, boys. Back it up. Walk away, go catch your buses, go grab an afternoon snack, and get the hell outta here, 'cause Blair Matthews is going home safe and sound for you, my dear sweet, Nonna!" Tank said, looking up at the clear blue sky.

All the guys were shaking their heads confused, but as soon as Marco heard Tank mention his beloved Nonna, he realized why.

"Oh, he ain't kidding, guys!" Marco said to Jay and Gary, who's hands were still clenched in fists at their sides. "Tank's Nonna, may she rest in peace, loved that stupid Mmm, *je t'aime,* Tim Horton's commercial—"

"You're damn right she did!" Tank yelled, in a rare display of public emotion. "And so do I for that matter. Every time I see that commercial (*and now he was speaking directly to Blair*), I get a lump in my throat, and I think of Christmas at Nonna's when I was a kid, eating manicotti and playing cards with her and my brother, and the TV would always be on in the background playing old movies like *Home Alone 1* or *Home Alone 2* and every time that commercial came on my beautiful Nonnina, without fail, would start crying. Every time, bros! But she'd be crying with a little smile on her face, and I miss that sweet loving smile more than words can say. So back the fuck up, boys, 'cause I suddenly feel like starting senior year off in a real ugly way."

And just like that Tank became Blair Matthew's protector.

Since our mom was working late (as usual), Marco and Tank brought Blair to our house. Seeing my celebrity crush in my own house was the last thing I expected on that first day of school.

But having him see *me* dancing around in my bedroom in a halter top and gym shorts, while using a neon pink hi-lighter as a microphone to rap out the lyrics to "Who Knew" by Eminem, is pretty much my definition of completely fucking mortified.

He was walking by my room on the way to the bathroom and my door was half open and he watched me for like a minute before I noticed him. I love Eminem and know every word to "Who Knew", so I had the volume cranked, and I was really going for it, because it feels amazing to rap out a whole verse without making any mistakes.

And just as I was about to hit the refrain, I turned around and saw Blair Matthews leaning against the doorframe with a grin on his face.

I was too surprised to scream, too embarrassed to faint, but I felt my cheeks turning tomato red, saw a snowstorm in my vision, and I dropped the hi-lighter on the ground. Blair strolled into my room with more confidence than all the guys at Trudeau combined, and he scooped up the neon pink marker and continued where I left off, singing Eminem's chorus about getting super famous and affecting his fans.

He grabbed my hand and danced around me rapping out the last verse perfectly. His voice was nasally and he sounded almost exactly like Slim. I'm pretty sure I was swooning like a southern belle who'd just been roofied.

"C'mon, sing it with me!" he shouted, handing me back the hi-lighter, and I somehow managed to keep it together.

Blair was my celebrity crush, he was famous, he was in my bedroom, and he was so goddamn handsome. But he was candid and natural, just a boy, just any other kid who listened to Eminem over and over until the rhymes got etched into his brain. I got my Slim swagger back and sang out the chorus with Blair, showing him a little two-step dance move that me and Vicky always do together. He caught on fast, and we danced and laughed until the song ended.

"Sorry for interrupting you there. Hi, I'm Blair," he said, holding out his hand for me to shake.

I handed him back the hi-lighter. "Um, yeah, I know," I said, becoming shy and stupid now that the music was over.

"Marco mentioned he had a twin sister, but he didn't tell me your name."

"It's Jules, well Julianna, but uh yeah, everybody calls me Jules."

"Well, hi Jules. Pleasure to meet a fellow Eminem fan," he said.

"Isn't everyone?" I replied, blowing my bangs out of my eyes.

"OK, pleasure to meet a very cute fellow Eminem fan," he said, with that same shit-eating grin from the Tim Horton's commercial.

I pretended like I didn't hear it, but OMG I would play that moment over in my head more times than a mathematician could count. My whole body was pretty much gravy at that point, my fingers and toes pudding, but still I managed to keep it together.

"So, how was your first day slumming it at Trudeau?" I asked. "I'm sure you thought it was awful."

"It was definitely kinda weird, like it didn't really feel real to me, but it was okay, I guess. I'm also super glad I met Tank and Marco, because they just stopped me from getting my ass kicked."

It was not the response I had expected from him. It was honest and humble. I assumed he'd say something snobby or pretentious, and definitely not reveal any weakness about himself.

"Oh my God! Really? Who was it?"

"A bunch of giant jock bros that all looked the same, but the two main guys who got in my face were Jay and Gary. You know them?"

"Unfortunately, yeah," I said. "Total meatheads, but they're scared of Tank, so you should be fine."

"It was weird. As soon as it started to happen, I immediately accepted it. This is what's supposed to happen on your first day of public school, I thought, as Jay shoved me and called me a 'spoiled little faggot'. It was like it was already written. The rest of them swarmed around me and were squawking like seagulls and I could literally feel their hatred, and I was thinking I better take the first swing because there's no way I'd get a second one, and then this giant shadow stepped in front of me and sucked all the bad voodoo out of the scene. It was Tank. My new hero!" Blair said in a Texas drawl, while fanning himself.

I laughed. "As Marco likes to say, Tank is a beast—"

"And he's a boss and a beefcake and a brainiac!" Marco said from the doorway. "I see you've met my lesser half," he said to Blair. I shot him the look of death. "Just kidding, Jules is also a beast and a boss and a total babe, ain't she?" Marco said, giving me a wink. He knew all about my crush on Blair. "Hey, come downstairs, I wanna show you our jam space, and Tank wants you to check out his amp."

"OK, cool. It was nice meeting you, Jules," Blair said, giving me that perfect TV smile.

"See ya around," I said.

As soon as they were gone, I shut the door and fell on my bed, my body humming and my heart stuttering it was pounding so hard. I stared at the ceiling in shock for a few minutes before calling Vicky and telling her everything everything everything.

# MARCO

I called a taxi to Bianca's dad's place and I'm surprised to see it's already outside his building when I arrive. As soon as Bianca sees me, she comes running out of the lobby and into my arms. I hug her tight and can feel the warmth of her body even through her big parka. She is a mixture of amazing smells: shampoo and soap, perfume and lotions. She's crying and talking at the same time so I can't understand her, but her embrace is enough to make me the saddest and happiest guy in the world.

It's starting to snow again, fat flakes falling all around us.

"This is our cab," I say, leading her down the sidewalk towards the car. We get in and I tell the driver to take us to Hotel-Dieu as fast as he can. We sit close in the backseat, and I hold Bianca's hands. I look at her face and even with mascara running down her cheeks she looks beautiful.

"I know it'll sound stupid," she says through tears, "but as soon as he left I got this really anxious feeling in my stomach, as if I knew something bad was gonna happen." She hiccups and blows her nose in a kleenex. "And it's my fault Marco, because I've been bitching about that Christmas tree for like a month. I mean, you saw the thing, it was beyond dead and it's February for God's sake. So after dinner he decided he was finally gonna get rid of it, and I was like, 'there's a frickin' blizzard out, Dad, it can wait till tomorrow,' but he made a whole show out of it, throwing it off the balcony into the alley below, which was actually pretty funny. But if it wasn't for me bitching about the tree, he wouldn't have . . ."

"Hey, it's not your fault, it's gonna be okay," I say to her a bunch of times. I reach in my jacket and pull out her dad's cellphone and hand it to her. "This fell out of your dad's pocket. It's how we figured out who he was," I say.

The heat is blasting in the cab, but after a couple minutes I start shaking like crazy, and the more I try to stop the worse it gets.

"You're frozen! How long were you outside for?" Bianca asks.

"I guess it was a while."

"I can't believe you gave my dad CPR, Marco."

"Fuck, me either," I say, and then I see my hands on his chest and spit flying from Tank's mouth as he counted to thirty. I see the paramedics shocking him and his body lurching like a zombie. I shiver. "It's crazy, because if Randy hadn't gone behind the store to check out the graffiti, we would've never even seen him and he'd probably still be there right now," I say, the gravity of the situation finally starting to hit me.

And now it's Bianca who's comforting me instead of the other way around. She rubs her hands on top of mine and asks if the cabbie can turn the heat any higher. She lifts my hands to her mouth and blows on them, her lips touching my fingers, and an image I've been willfully pushing from my mind since the night it happened comes racing back to me. I shiver again but this time it's not from the cold.

Blair and I were at Club Soda, right at the front of the stage waiting for Quicksand, one of our favourite bands to go on. It was an 18 and over show, but Blair was on the guest list and the giant bouncer didn't even check our ID's, he just said "What's good, Blair?", slapped him five, and swept us inside the club.

The concert was on a Wednesday night so I had to sneak out, but that was easy because it was Mom's date night with Ronnie so she was preoccupied. Blair picked me up on the corner of my street in his stepdad's Toyota Prius. In L.A. Blair drove The Blade's 1983 Ford Mustang GT, and so he said he felt like a suburban tool driving around in a goddamn Prius. But for me, any kind of wheels were awesome, and before the show we drove down Saint Catherine Street and blasted tunes from the car stereo and I at least felt like we were hot shit.

Blair gets the VIP treatment pretty much everywhere he goes, but this was the first time we went to a show together, so I was super impressed. People whispered and pointed when they recognized him, bartenders gave him free drinks, girls asked to take selfies with him, and he introduced me as the kick ass bass player in his new band.

"What's the name of your band?" dude with a ponytail or chick in an old Danzig shirt would ask him.

And Blair would pull a coin from the pocket of his jeans and flick it to them. "The Bad Luck Nickel," he'd say as they caught it. And that's all it took to create some buzz for the band. A pocket full of nickels with a black X over the Queen's face. Pure genius if you ask me.

So, I was feeling pretty fucking cool because I was with Blair Matthews at a sold-out show on a school night drinking a free Heineken and about to see one of my favourite bands live. We pushed our way to the front of the stage, and as soon as the lights went out a bunch of people around me, including Blair, lit up joints. Quicksand took the stage and strapped on their guitars without saying a word to the crowd. The drummer clicked his sticks once and the band roared to life, opening with their big hit "Dine Alone". Blair handed me the joint and I took a few hits before passing it back. I watched the bass player and got lost in the heavy groove of the song. I imagined it was me on stage playing bass and Randy behind me beating hell out of the drums. The crowd was getting into it, pushing and shoving a little, but they hadn't started a full-blown mosh pit yet.

As the song ended, the lights came up on the band and the crowd in front of the stage. I looked to my right and saw Bianca sipping a mixed drink and wrapped all cozy and snug in some guy's arms. I did a double take convinced I was just stoned and seeing things, but it was her. And the guy she was with was the guitarist from the opening band, Full Watt Drug. He looked like he was twenty-five years old. He was tall and had a perfectly stylish beard and his arms were covered in tattoos.

Everyone was clapping and cheering, and Bianca turned around to face him and as she did, he accidentally hit her drink and it splashed all over his hands.

And what did Bianca do? She took this handsome bastard's hands in her own and started kissing each of his fingers and sort of like licking the drink off his fingertips, and the whole time she's doing it she's looking him dead-sexy in the eyes. It was a way too intimate moment in a way too public place, and I was probably the only one that even noticed it.

Quicksand kicked into the next song but all I heard was buzz and feedback and cymbal crash. I chugged my beer with the hopes of stopping the ache in my gut. And of course I got angry, and wondered what the hell she was even doing here, because she's underage and doesn't even like this kind of music. I looked over again and she was raising her plastic cup in the air and bobbing her head to the song as if she'd been a fan for years. And then some sweaty dude with no shirt on shoved me and I smashed into Blair, and Blair shoved me back towards the sweaty dude, and when I tried to push him my hands slid off his greasy chest and I fell over right in the middle of the mosh pit.

Random hands dug into my armpits, lifted me up, and pushed me into the crowd of bodies. Arms flailed and legs kicked out around me. It smelt like stale cigarettes and beer and nine different kinds of B.O. and I just kept jumping around and knocking into people as I tried to stay on my feet and not get punched in the face.

"Hey, you wanna go up?" some older guy with a straggly beard asked me after I bumped into him.

"No, I'm good thanks!" I shouted, but then he patted me on the head like I was a small dog.

"Oh, you're going up!" he yelled, as he and some other dude grabbed me by the belt loops of my jeans and tossed me on top of the crowd.

*My phone, my keys, my wallet!* I thought, as I did my best to flip over on my back as fast as possible because I was scared someone would punch me in the balls. But as I surfed on top of the crowd, I was surprised at how gentle everyone was, considering the circumstance. There seemed to be an unwritten code within the pit.

Hands politely grabbed at my legs and butt and back and head and moved me in one direction and then the other, people said "Hey dude!" as I passed by them or patted me on the shoulder or slapped me five as if to say, "You're doing a great job up here, Marco!"

I saw Blair for a second, and he shouted: "Yeah, man!" as he momentarily became part of the collective of limbs that kept me floating above the crowd. I spread my arms and legs like I was making a snow angel and gazed up at the flashing lights and the crowd watching from the balcony. I made eye contact with a cute black girl who was filming the mosh pit on her phone and I blew her a kiss. She caught it and waved back at me. I smiled, imagining how cool I'd look on the video, and then I was falling, headfirst to the floor.

I closed my eyes waiting for the thud, but just before I hit the ground, a bunch of helping hands grabbed at my jeans and T-shirt and hair, and lifted me back up above the crowd, and hurled me feet first towards the stage. I was moving fast and headed straight towards Bianca. I lifted my head and saw she was still at the front of the stage wrapped in the protective embrace of the hunky asshole guitarist from Full Watt Drug. And the hands of the crowd continued to push me in that direction as if on purpose, as if on target, faster and faster, gaining more speed and momentum, until my shoes crashed into the hunky asshole guitarist's head.

I saw a drink splash and heard him shout: "What the fuck?" but then Quicksand kicked into a heavy part of the song, distortion pedals blasting, and the hands pulled me back away from the stage, away from the scene of the crime, and this time they unceremoniously dropped me in the middle of the mosh pit. I landed hard on my shoulder but was up in a flash, narrowly missing an elbow to the chin. I squeezed my way out of the writhing crowd towards the bar, patting my pocket for my phone, and still feeling the contact my Vans made with the hunky asshole's head.

And now here she is, here's Bianca, breathing warmth into my frozen hands, her lips accidentally touching my fingertips, and all the newfound strength I thought I had, is just draining out of me like my brain and heart both have flat tires or something.

"You okay?" Bianca asks.

I close my eyes and hear Tank screaming at me: "Snap out of it bro, and handle this like a boss!"

"Yeah, yeah, I'm fine, Bee," I say, taking a deep breath. "I just can't stop thinking about your dad," I say, which is a lie, because now I just can't stop thinking about how we'd only been broken up for like two weeks, and how way comfy she looked in the tatted-up arms of the hunky asshole guitarist, who's name I found out later is Johnny Temple.

I think the hardest thing for any guy to admit is that he isn't good enough, like, there's always going to be some other dude out there that's better than you at something, whether he's better looking or better at playing guitar or has a car or he's older and has more cash.

And the harsh bottom line is, after a while I was no longer good enough for Bianca. She wanted someone older, richer, stronger, cooler, and the worst goddamn part is she found him before she even broke up with me. That's the shit that fucking scrapes – the fact that she cheated on me when all I wanted to do was make her the happiest girl in the city – that's the shit that fucking burns, yo.

And I mean, yeah, I had a feeling that something wasn't quite right, like, she started acting kinda distant or whatever, and spending more time with her friends than with me, but I just never thought I'd be one of those guys that gets cheated on, ya know?

Because then you just can't help wonder, over and over, what the fuck you did wrong?

"Can you drive any faster?" I ask the cabbie. He shakes his head and mutters in French about how bad the roads are.

And sure, I get it, I know we're still young and we're always looking for the fresh, the unknown, the excitement of the new new new, but it wasn't until I saw Bianca in Johnny Temple's arms at the show that it all became crystal fuckin' clear – she had cheated on me and was already over me, and I was nothing but a high school chump.

I look at her next to me in the backseat and even though she's crying and trying to comfort me and grateful that I helped her dad, I have an urge to hurt her, to make her feel even shittier than she already does.

After the Quicksand show I was able to turn my woe to anger and for a month and a half I basically just got stoned every day and made Randy come over and jam with me after school. Tank was busy with football and Blair hadn't joined the band yet, so it was just me and Randy, the pulse of the band, the bass and drums.

I'd never say this to Randy, but he wasn't really a good drummer until his sister Nicole died. He was sloppy, spastic, would miss changes and play too fast or too slow, but in the months after she died, Randy's drumming changed. Everything about him changed actually. He became less awkward, more mature, and more aware of life's bullshit and harshness. And on the drums, Randy got faster, louder, more technical, and he suddenly never missed a beat. The sticks looked so much more comfortable in his hands, and he started adding all these simple off-time flourishes on the snare and cymbals. Randy caught the groove with an almost mathematical precision.

Now, I know there's really no comparison, but I kind of feel like the same thing happened to me after I saw Bianca with Johnny Temple at the Quicksand show. Maybe it was because of all the weed I was smoking, but as soon as I strapped on my guitar and started playing I would think of nothing but my fingers on the strings and what I had to do to get the sound that I wanted. And all the anger and hurt I was feeling would drain out of me and come out of my guitar instead. It was the only thing that made me feel good. I started using an old distortion pedal of Tank's and me and Randy would jam out in the basement until we were covered in sweat or my fingers started to blister or he busted a drum skin or my mom came home and made us stop.

It was therapy. And it was fucking heavy. But it was trippy and beautiful too.

A lot of the new songs we're working on right now came out of those stoned sessions in the basement.

After the anger faded a bit, I saw Bianca at a Christmas party and we small-talked for like five minutes, and that's all it took for me to feel like I was still in love with her. I'm such a loser. But being with her in the cab right now is the first time we've been alone together since the breakup and I'm happy that I feel angry again, it feels so much more real to me.

So I turn to her and start to say: "I know you fucking cheated on me," but before I can spit it all out, the cab driver slams on the brakes and the car hits a patch of ice and starts to fishtail.

"*Tabarnak!*" the cabbie yells, pumping the brakes and trying to regain control of the car. A horn honks, headlights flash through the windshield, and I pull Bianca close, bracing for impact.

# JULIANNA

As I'm ringing the bell to Vicky's house, I get this weird feeling about Marco. Like something bad just happened. A lot of people might not believe in the crazy connection between twins but let me tell you it's true. It seems to have faded a bit for us over the last few years, but when we were little, me and Marco used to be able to talk to each other in our heads. Like we'd be lying in our beds in separate rooms and have full conversations with each other. If I woke up in the middle of the night from a nightmare, I'd call out to Marco in my mind, and he'd tell me it was just a bad dream and to go back to sleep because I was safe. We used to believe we had superpowers, and one winter we spent an entire month trying to turn light switches or the TV on with our minds.

Marco says it was just our imaginations and how we dealt with our parents always yelling at one another, but I swear I can remember it clearly. I think we're all tapped into a strong psychic energy when we're young, but unfortunately the older we get, and the more we get sucked into routines and jobs and the noise of the world, the more we lose touch with the hum of the universe. And as we get older, it just keeps fading into the background, getting dimmer and dimmer, until we can't really feel it anymore except in those quick moments when you just wake up and are still half in dreamsville.

Like how many times have you have woken up a few seconds before you get a text or your phone rings? And how often do you know who it is without even thinking about it? I really think that if the modern world wasn't so goddamn loud and busy and distracting and didn't force us to think in linear and logic-based ways, we'd be able to hold onto these extrasensory powers we're all born with. Like think of dogs and how they somehow know when their owners are going to come home, waiting at the front door, wagging their tails and whimpering in excitement. I'm convinced animals are definitely connected to the psychic energy of the universe.

I get on this topic sometimes when I'm stoned, and Marco thinks it's hippy-dippy bullshit, but Blair is totally into the possibility of metaphysical connections and things that are way beyond our control.

I think people have the power to do anything. Maybe even fly. But the white noise of the modern world keeps pulling us back to the earth, rooting us there in both body and mind, and effectively cancelling out the energy and mystery of the universe that's waiting for us just above and below the surface!

OK, OK, I hear it now. I do sound pretty out there. But there must be more to our reality than just reality, don't ya think?

Vicky opens the door as I'm checking my phone to see if Marco's replied to my text.

"Whaddup, Julio!" she shouts. "Get in here, girl, it's freezing out!"

Just from her volume level, I can tell Vicky is already buzzing. The stereo's blasting Michael Jackson and she's all red-faced and sweaty from dancing by herself in the living room.

"I've seen you so little this week I almost forgot you have blue hair!" I say. "I think it's my fave colour on you yet!"

Ever since Vicky bleached her hair for Halloween last fall, she's become obsessed with dyeing it. First platinum blonde, then bright pink, and now sky blue.

"Yeah, I'm really diggin' it," she says, whipping her hair around her head. I kick off my boots and follow her into the kitchen. "Damn Jules, you look severe with that lipstick, I looove it, it's sexy and mysterious!"

"Thanks, babe. Hey, have you heard from Marco or Tank?" I ask. Vicky grabs my arms and swings them up and down to the music, pulling me over to the counter where the bottle of vodka is. "Well, have you?"

She shakes her head and sings along to the song. "Make yourself a drink!" she shouts, shaking her booty and slapping it like ten times. "Doesn't my butt look amazing in these jeans? I've gotta pee! I'll be right back!" she says, shimmying down the hallway to the bathroom.

I call Marco, but his phone goes to voicemail, so I make a stiff vodka and orange juice. I'm going to need a few to catch up with Vicky. I still can't shake the feeling that something bad happened, it's created a low-level anxiety that's running through my entire body. Hopefully the vodka will help get rid of it.

I call Tank and he answers after a couple rings.

"Hey Jules, what's up?"

"Where's Marco?" I ask, running to the living room to turn down the music.

"Oh yes, I'm fine, thanks for asking."

"C'mon, where is he, Tank?"

"I guess you haven't heard?"

"Heard what?"

Vicky comes back from the bathroom, and I put the phone on speaker so we can both listen as Tank fills us in on what happened.

Vicky keeps saying, "No way!" and "Holy shit!" but I stand there silently, visualizing Marco and Tank giving Bianca's dad CPR in the snow. It makes me super anxious.

"And the cop said we probably helped save his frickin' life!" Tank says, to which Vicky replies, "No way!" She's totally flirting with him, even though she hooked up with Randy last weekend after the show at Acapulco Delight.

"As far as I know, Marco's with Bianca at the hospital. So I'm not sure when he'll meet up with us, but you ladies should make a couple of tasty road sodas and come join us in The Tunnels. We've got beer and Randy's got his spray paint and stencils if you're feeling artsy."

"I thought you guys were playing tonight?" Vicky asks.

"Show's cancelled," Tank says.

"Oh, that sucks! How come?" she asks me.

"I'll fill you in after," I say. Vicky sips her drink and goes back to the living room and starts dancing again.

"Are you all right, Tank? Giving a guy CPR in an alley? That's intense!" I say.

"Yeah, it was totally crazy! But it all went down so fast it was over before it even started."

"And what about Marco?" I ask, wanting to tell Tank about our twin minds and that I knew something happened.

"You should've seen him Jules, he handled it like a boss!"

"Yeah, and I bet he's already counting the ways he can use this to his advantage with Bianca."

"Hey, let him have his moment, okay?"

"Fine, fine."

"For now, let's just hope Bianca's dad will be okay, and then you can worry all about her shattering Marco's heart again, all right?"

"Her dad will be okay though, right?"

"I mean, I hope so. The doctors will probably have to do a bunch of tests and shit to figure out exactly why it happened. But as long as he doesn't have another one tonight, I think he should be okay. Is it even possible to have two heart attacks in one day?"

"I dunno, Tank."

"Can you imagine? Now that would be a shitty fuckin' day! But hey, we just made it to The Tunnels and I'm fuckin' freezing, so we're gonna go in. We'll see you guys in a bit?"

"Yeah for sure, we're gonna have a drink or two and then head out. I'll text ya when we're leaving," I say.

"No service in The Tunnels."

"Right, I always forget."

"So just show up when you show up, we'll be here all night," Tank says. "Hey, is Blair with you?"

"Nope."

"Perfect. No offence, but we need an old school Blair free night. See ya soon, Jules. Oh, and Randy says to tell Vicky he says hey."

I say bye to Tank, grab my drink and join Vicky in the living room. "Randy says hey," I say.

Vicky shrugs. "Whatever. He pretty much ignored me all week. He sent me one text and all it said was: *Hi Vicky* with some stupid *Star Wars* meme. What a dork! But ya know who just keeps getting hotter and hotter to me? Tanky Poo! Mmm, I think I wanna make out with a big strong hero tonight. I'd let him practice CPR on me alllll night!" she says with a cackle.

Vicky is tiny, she isn't even five feet tall and weighs less than a hundo, but I swear she has one of the loudest laughs you'll ever hear. She blames it on the fact that she's Filipino, but I gotta say, us Italians can be pretty fuggin' *rumoroso* too, huh?

"All Flips are loud as hell, it's in our blood, we can't help it," Vicky told me years ago. "But my mom likes to say 'the loudest is the rightest', so that's probably why we're always screaming at each other."

It's true Vicky's entire family is pretty darn loud, but I'm used to her personal decibel level. I sit down on the couch, and Vicky keeps dancing, shaking her butt right in my face until I smack it.

"Oh yeah, girl! Beat it good!" she screams.

I laugh at her and grab my phone so I can text Marco:

I just heard what happened!
Hope you're all right bro. Let me
know what's going on as soon as
you can.

I know he must be freaking out right now, especially being alone with Bianca.

I've never seen anyone so torn over an ex. He totally hated her for a while and then he got all sad and mopey about her and then he went back to hating her, but lately he seems to be more on the *I still wanna be with her* side, which is pathetic because he knows she cheated on him with Johnny Temple and has turned into quite the Full Watt Drug groupie.

I think she's a total bitch and poser, but hey, who am I too judge? At least I don't switch my musical tastes to suit my boyfriend.

The MJ song Vicky's dancing to ends and she flops next to me on the couch. "Hey, where's Care Blair?" she asks. "I thought he was with you."

I frown. "Yeah, he was, but we kinda got in a fight."

"Oh shoot, what happened?"

"I dunno, I guess it's partly 'cause he's pissed the guys are bailing on their gig tonight."

"Yeah, what gives? How come they're not playing anymore?"

"Some of their gear got damaged last weekend when Blair let everyone up on stage."

"Oh my God, but that was the best part of the show! Everyone was going wild!"

"I know," I say, remembering Blair on stage like a man possessed, his eyelids fluttering and his knuckles white from gripping the mic stand. A strobe light began flashing wildly as the crowd rushed the stage and Blair kept screaming: *Something tells me it's my cross to bear!* and the rest of the guys rocked out as hard as I've ever seen them.

Those final minutes of the show were amazing, everything clicked perfectly, and every single person was swept in the moment, completely lost in the groove of The Bad Luck Nickel.

But then, someone knocked over Tank's amp. After it toppled, it started making this weird feedback that actually sounded pretty cool and it made the stage-crashers go even crazier until some guy fell on top of Randy's drum set.

"Their set was really good, but that last song is a jam! I was looking forward to hearing it again tonight," Vicky says, taking a sip of her drink. I take a sip too. "OK, but like why did you and Blair get in a fight?"

I sigh. "I dunno, we were having a really nice time, and we fooled around and it was super romantic, but then I brought up The Blade's interview and he like totally freaked on me and stormed out."

"Ooh, harsh," Vicky says.

"I feel so shitty, because I wanna believe him, ya know? But he gets so defensive about it, and I mean, why would his dad lie about it? Blair says it's a publicity stunt for Hesher's new album, but I'm calling bullshit. Did you read the link to the interview I sent you?"

Vicky nods.

"So what d'you think?"

"Something sure doesn't add up," she says, leaning over and spilling her drink on the rug. "Oh shit and crap!" she says, laughing wildly. "I dink I'm trunk."

"Damn Vicks, you gotta pace yourself! You drink like Tank but aren't even half his size!" I say with a laugh.

"Don't worry, I've got just the thing that'll keep us in the moment all night," she says with a mischievous grin, soaking up the spill with her sock by stepping on it.

"What're you talking about?" I ask.

"Pass me my backpack," she says. I grab it off the floor and hand it to her. She pulls out a pill bottle and gives it a shake. "*Voilà!*"

"What are they?" I ask, so she tosses me the bottle.

"Edwin's dosing himself off his Ritalin. He's supposed to take three pills a day, but for the last couple weeks he's only been taking one and a half. He hasn't told our parents, because they think he'll go nuts without it, and his therapist says she doesn't want to lower his dose for another couple of months, but he's convinced it's not helping him focus anymore and is making him feel really shitty. So he gave me his stash to sell for him and we're gonna split the profit."

"You're gonna sell pills to people?"

"Ten bucks a pop."

"That's crazy!"

"Why? It'll be easy. I was hoping to sell some at the show tonight. Have you tried it before?"

"Um, you know everything about me, Vicky—"

"Right. Well, it's supposed to make you feel amazing! So chug that vodka and let's sample the merchandise!"

"I don't know, Vick . . ."

"C'mon, I can't do it alone. We can start with a half of one if you want."

I don't want to do it, but I have a feeling from the way the vodka is going down, that I'm gonna turn into a sloppy, emotional mess, and will rant about Blair all night to Vicky and be a total drag and buzz crusher. I did say I was going to forget about him tonight, right?

Like Tank said: it'll be nice to have an old school Blair free night . . .

"OK, let's start with a half," I say.

**EXCERPT FROM *Distortion Magazine*, issue 17, volume 9, Winter 2018**

"A Double-Edged Blade: Hesher's frontman talks teenage rebellion, getting older and wiser, and the band's return to form, with their tenth studio album, *Bow Down To The Bull God*."

*The Blade:* Nah man, I don't give a shit about weed, Blair's been smoking since he was twelve years old. First time I caught him was with Matt Cameron's daughter when we were in Jersey on tour with Soundgarden. She's a year or two older than Blair and he had a crush on her and wanted to impress her, so of course he did whatever she did, stole some beers, smoked some dope, hung out on the beach till dawn.

*Distortion Magazine:* I find it strange that you're such a strong advocate for a clean life-style but don't care that your son was smoking weed at the age of twelve.

*The Blade:* You gotta pick your battles, man. Blair grew up in L.A. smelling weed more often than cigarettes. I figured a little dope wasn't gonna hurt him. I thought of it as summer fun, ya know? Blazing a joint on the beach at night with a cute girl, that's pretty much an essential experience for every young dude out there, know what I'm sayin'? I'm sure you've been there before, right? (*He laughs for a few seconds and then turns serious*). But messing with blow and strippers? I don't fuckin' think so.

*Distortion Magazine*: So *that's* where The Blade draws the line?

*The Blade:* Hey, screw you, dude. You got any kids? Pfft, didn't fuckin' think so. Kids gotta live their own lives, man, you gotta give 'em room to breathe and figure some shit out by their goddamn selves, and if that means smoking a joint or making dumbass choices here and there, so be it. Shit, if I shoved my straight-edge vegan lifestyle on him, he'd probably be in juvie right now. It's a way of life that works for me, okay? But I ain't no smug holier than thou cocksucker, I'll tell ya that. And I'll tell ya one more thing, I have always, *always* tried my goddamn best to keep an eye on what Blair was up to ...

*Distortion Magazine:* All right, all right, my bad. I apologize, let me rephrase that. So then where *do* you draw the line?

*The Blade: (he shakes his head and sighs)* When you can see the trajectory of someone's life veering off all helter fuckin' skelter, you gotta step in. Especially when it's someone you love. So when I saw Blair rip a line off a little mirror like a goddamn pro and then jump up and down on the hotel bed like a ten-year old, it really fucked me up, man. It was the clashing of innocence and experience, and it pissed me off because I felt like it was my fault he'd been pushed over the edge too soon. (*He looks at the ground for a moment, and his large biceps flex involuntarily*). Ya know, the whole situation reminds me of a line from William Blake. He says: "You never know what's enough, unless you know what's more than enough." And let me tell ya, I've been there done it, brother, and that quote speaks volumes for me and Blair's situation.

*Distortion Magazine:* Speaking of William Blake, you've mentioned in other interviews that his work was a big influence on Hesher's new record, *Bow Down To The Bull God.*

*The Blade:* Yeah, it's not the first time we've turned to ol' Blakey for inspiration when we're writing new songs.

*Distortion Magazine:* And do you think what happened with Blair was an influence too?

*The Blade:* Of course. This new record is a mix of all the shit that was going on in all our lives at the time. Look at Graves' guitar work on these tracks, especially on "Human Abstract". Doesn't he sound darker and more pissed off than ever? I think a lot of that has to do with he and Betty splitting up. It's catharsis man, plain and simple. Everything comes out when we're writing new music, the good, the bad, and the fuckin' heavy. (*He laughs*).

# MARCO

As the taxi fishtails into the other lane and the cabbie tries to regain control, I pull Bianca close, holding her tight in my arms. Bianca's eyes are shut in anticipation of the crash, but mine are wide open, and I stare at her and have a flashback to the early days, when we'd make out in the basement for entire weekends, and how when her face was that close to mine, she looked like a completely different person. Her smile seemed brighter, her eyes a richer shade of brown, and the freckles on her cheeks looked like little chocolate chips. Sometimes when I gazed at her from that distance her two eyes would merge into one, and she'd become the hottest cyclops in the world.

It's weird, but people look so different up close. Up close is when shit gets real and intimate and special. Seeing Bianca in the caf at school or from across the room at a party was completely different than when her face was an inch from mine, and her eyes blurred into one, and we spoke to each other in hot whispers and left our mark on each other's necks.

Young cyclops vampires in a dark basement, wanting the night to never end, holding each other so tight it almost hurt. Listening to my dad's old Radiohead records and feeling like there was no other place we'd rather be, our emotions so vivid, it was like laughing and crying at the same time . . .

"Hang on!" I say to her, as the taxi collides with a grey SUV. The SUV crashes into the front passenger door and the window shatters, spilling glass all over the seat. Bianca screams and the cabbie curses as the cars skid to a stop in the middle of the street.

Bianca still has her eyes closed and her teeth clenched as if waiting for more. "Hey, it's okay," I say. "It's over. Are you all right?"

She opens her eyes and seems surprised the damage isn't worse. "Oh my God, Marco, I thought we were gonna get T-boned and die instantly," she says.

"But we survived, Bee!" I say with a laugh, my hands still wrapped around her.

She immediately turns on the cab driver. "Hey, what the fuck were you thinking, huh?" she shouts at him in French. "You almost killed us!"

"It was not my fault, madame!" he says.

"Yeah man, what the hell's wrong with you? You gotta drive more carefully!" I say. I know it wasn't the guy's fault, but Bianca used to love it when I'd smart mouth adults, so I do it almost without even thinking about it. "Hey," I say to her, "the hospital's just up there, like two blocks."

"Let's get the hell outta here then!" she says, kicking her door open with her boot.

"No no, you cannot leave!" the cabbie yells. "I need you as a witness!"

"*Va chier!* Fuck you, asshole!" Bianca says as she gets out of the cab.

"I'm sorry, we gotta go, her dad just had a heart attack," I say quietly, pulling Tank's twenty out of my pocket and giving it to him.

I get out of the cab and slam the door. "Can you believe that guy? What a dick! Like, do they even teach people how to drive where he comes from?" I say.

"I doubt it," Bianca says.

The driver of the SUV is already out of his car and assessing the damage. He starts swearing in French as he notices his front fender has pretty much completely fallen off.

Bianca links her arm with mine and we cross the street as the cabbie gets out of his taxi and begins talking to the owner of the SUV. A car honks impatiently behind them and the driver shouts: "Move your goddamn cars out of the middle of the road!"

"I'm fucking shaking, Marco! That was literally the scariest thing that's ever happened to me! No joke!"

"What about when that guy crashed his scooter into the bus shelter? I think you screamed even louder that time."

"Oh my God! Monsieur Moto! I almost forgot about him! I barely knew you back then. What's with us and glass smashing?"

"I dunno. I guess it's our thing," I say with a little laugh.

What she says reminds me of a new song we're working on, where Blair sings: *It was a night of shattered glass! Another night of shattered glass! It ain't the first and it ain't the last, another night of shattered glass!* and then me and Tank rip into this grungy punk rock riff and Randy's drums sound like a machine gun going off. Blair starts screaming at the top of his lungs and I'm not even sure what he says, all I know is that it makes us super amped. It's like a battle song. It's going to be awesome once we get it down tight.

"But seriously, is it Friday the 13th today?" Bianca asks.

"Shit Bee, it could've been way worse. We're really lucky that no one got hurt. We could've killed an old lady, or a baby, or a pregnant lady about to have a baby. Or imagine if it was a head-on collision and the cabbie smashed through the windshield and the guy in the SUV also smashed through his and then the two of them collided in mid-air and started beating the shit out of each other! That would've been fuckin' nutso!" I say, slapping my hands together, and we both laugh.

Just like when we practice that new song, I'm feeling super hyper.

"But instead, it's just another night of shattered glass!" I sing, kicking through the snow on the sidewalk. "Another night of shattered glass! It ain't the first and it ain't the last, another night of shattered glass!" I don't have the melody exactly right, but it still sounds pretty good. There's something really propulsive about it.

Bianca laughs. "I miss your random songs," she says with a smile. I don't want to tell here this one isn't mine, so I don't say anything. We're almost at the hospital. A giant snow plow drives by us on the road, followed by a salt truck flashing its lights. "I'm glad you're here, Marco," she says, putting her head on my shoulder for a second as we walk up towards the hospital's main entrance.

But I don't get to stay long, because once we get inside and Bianca finds out that her dad is stable but in ICU, a large nurse in faded pink scrubs blocks my way and says: "Immediate family only."

"But I'm . . ." I start to say, but I don't know how to end the sentence.

"He helped save my dad's life!" Bianca says.

"And we're all very grateful, but if he isn't family, he can't go any further. I'm sorry."

I stand there like an idiot for a second and almost want to cry. Bianca looks frightened, like she doesn't want me to leave her there alone.

I think back to that day when we were in the bus shelter. I was on my way to Randy's when the thunderstorm started, and Bianca had been heading home from the public pool around the corner. The day had been hot and humid but out of nowhere the wind picked up, the sky turned this scary green colour, and the storm hit. There was a ton of lightning and it started to hail, so I ducked into the bus shelter for safety. I'd only been in the rain for about a half a block, but I was totally soaked.

I was wringing out the bottom of my shirt when I saw a girl racing down the sidewalk. She had her bag over her head kind of acting like an umbrella, and she was wearing cut-off jean shorts and a white T-shirt over a turquoise bikini top. I forgot all about the storm as she ran towards me. It wasn't until she was in the bus shelter that I realized it was Bianca Marcuzzi, and I'd be a liar if I didn't say how goddamn hot she looked all soaking wet with her hair clinging to her face and the strap of her bikini sliding down one shoulder and her T-shirt stuck to her tanned belly.

But it was her eyes that got me. Those big brown eyes. They were like Bambi's eyes after his mother got shot. She was totally freaking out. When she came into the bus shelter we made eye contact and she looked so scared, but then she recognized me and sighed in relief, happy she was no longer alone.

"Oh my God, Marco! I'm so glad you're here! That hail hurts! Is this like a tornado or something?" she asked.

"I dunno," I said. "I hope not. But did you see the colour of the sky? It's fuckin' trippy! I've never seen a green sky before."

There was a gust of wind, and we heard a scary cracking sound and something falling from the sky. A huge branch from an old maple tree crashed onto the sidewalk exactly where Bianca had just been.

I looked at the branch and then I looked at Bianca and I could tell we were thinking the exact same thing: what if she'd showed up thirty seconds later? Like, what if she stopped to pee before she left the pool instead of trying to make it home before the storm hit? Or what if she forgot her phone and had to run back to the locker room to grab it? Or what if her mom called and held her up for a little bit? Just the tiniest variable has the possibility to create such a huge change. Later, I'd often think the same thing about Bianca and I meeting up in that bus shelter. If it wasn't for that storm, I don't think we would've gotten together.

Tiny variable can equal big fucking change. Right place right time maybe? I think some people call it serendipity.

Bianca's eyes started looking like Bambi's again, so I took a step towards her to try and comfort her. Then there was a flash of lightning and a really loud clap of thunder. It was so close I could feel it in my throat. I flinched and Bianca screamed.

She rushed into my arms and pressed her head into my chest for a second before saying: "I'm sorry, I'm just super scared of storms . . ."

"Lucky for you, I don't feel awkward at all," I said, but I don't think she could hear me over the hail and rain hammering the roof of the shelter. Her hand was grabbing my bicep, and I remember feeling super happy because I had worked out my arms and chest that morning. I tried to nonchalantly flex. She smelt like chlorine and tropical suntan lotion, and her being in my arms was about the best thing I'd ever felt in my life.

And just as she was about to step out of the embrace a crazy thing happened: a guy on a scooter smashed into the bus shelter. He was driving on the sidewalk going probably 25 kilometres an hour, and who knows, maybe he turned his head to look behind him, or maybe he couldn't see the branch from all the rain on his visor, because it wasn't until the last possible second that he tried to dodge it, and then he lost control of his bike and blasted into the bus shelter head on.

The glass buckled for a second and then shattered. The way we tell the story now is that at the exact moment the dude hit the shelter there was a flash of lightning and a deafening crack of thunder, but it was probably just the headlight on his scooter and the sound of it smashing into the glass. He held onto the handlebars but still flipped over the bike and came crashing through the glass, landing at our feet.

But he was up almost as fast as he'd fallen. He started shouting in French about his wife going into labour and how he had to get home asap. I just stood there in shock, holding Bianca in my arms, as he stepped through the broken window of the shelter, got back on his scooter, and tried to drive away like nothing had happened. His bike had a flat and after riding it for about a half a block he left it leaning against a tree and ran off into the summer storm to save his pregnant wife.

*Monsieur Moto! A modern day superhero!*

But man, I gotta give it to the city for not skimping on glass when they replaced all the shelters last year, because I think if it had been even just a little bit thinner Monsieur Moto would've driven straight on through and fuckin' mowed us down. Although when I was telling Randy about it afterwards, I imagined what a legend I would've been if people heard that me and Bianca Marcuzzi were found dead in each other's arms in a bus shelter.

Still, I was obviously much happier about the real result because that superhero on the scooter helped seal the deal for me. Bianca screamed as loud as anything I've ever heard, way louder than in the taxi just now, and she jumped up on me, wrapping her legs around my waist. With her in my arms, I also jumped to the other side of the shelter, my back pressing up against an advertisement for the Jazz Festival. The moment was so insane I didn't even realize that I was grabbing her ass to hold her up and could feel her boobs pressed up against me. I looked at her face so close to mine and she looked completely different. A totally new version of the Bianca Marcuzzi from my English and Math class that barely ever spoke to me. This was the real Bianca, vulnerable and beautiful and shy, and I knew at that moment that I wanted to know everything everything everything about her, and I also somehow knew that we would end up together . . .

But instead of being together right now, we're being split up by some tired old nurse, and I'm having so many conflicted feelings I'm starting to shiver again.

Somewhere deep in my brain I hear Tank whisper: "C'mon bro, you've been a champ this far!"

So instead of crying in front of Bianca like a high school chump, I muster up all of my goddamn guts and in a voice of pure calm I say: "You'll be fine, Bee. Go and see your dad, he needs you right now. And hopefully your mom will get here soon."

She nods in agreement, blinking her big eyes rapidly.

"But please text me later to let me know how he's doing."

"OK, I will. Hey, thanks for being here, Marco," she says. The nurse is still standing behind us, arms crossed, impatient for us to say our goodbyes. "Seriously, thanks for everything."

"No problem," I say, as Bianca gives me a quick hug and a peck on the cheek. "I'll see you later," I say, as she steps out of my embrace, and turns towards the nurse.

I start to leave when Bianca calls my name. I spin around, half expecting her to run back into my arms.

"Yes?"

"Johnny's playing a show near the end of March at The Sala Rossa and they're still looking for an opening band. You think you guys might want to play?"

"Uh, yeah sure! That'd be awesome!" I say too loudly, Johnny's name fired like a gunshot between us in the hospital's otherwise peaceful hallway.

"OK, I'll ask him. Bye Marco, thanks again!" she says, with a little wave, before she turns the corner and is gone.

I frown and start trembling. I feel like I'm gonna pass out. I lean up against the wall for a moment. I clench my teeth and try to let the annoyance I'm feeling take over and destroy my terrible heartache. *Why does it hurt sooo damn much?* There's a water fountain next to me and I take a super long drink, slurping away like a dog until my stomach is full and just as cold as the rest of me.

Surprisingly, the water makes me feel a little better. But what in the fuck? Is she offering us the gig as some sort of compensation for breaking my heart and mind and spirit?

I replay my voice all high-pitched and childish in my head: *Yeah sure! That'd be awesome! Thanks so much! You're so great, Bee! And you and Johnny Temple are just about the hottest couple I've ever fucking seen!*

Bah! I'm such a loser and feel like a complete charity case. Still, I want to play that show. I fish my phone out of my jacket pocket and see a bunch of missed calls and messages from Jules. I know I should call her and let her know I'm okay, but instead I phone Blair as I walk towards the exit.

He answers after a few rings. "What d'you want?" he shouts. I hear a crowd in the background.

"Where are you?"

"At The Coach trying to salvage our reputation. Les Poumons are super pissed that we're blowing off their invite. I made up a bunch of excuses, but I doubt they'll ever ask us to play with them again."

"Well, I just got us a way better gig," I say.

"With who?"

"Full Watt Drug."

"How?" Blair asks.

"Through Bianca."

"Hold on," he says. I hear him running up The Coach's rickety stairs. "Sorry, I had to go outside so I can hear you better. Fuck, I hate this weather. What's the venue?"

"The Sala."

"When?"

"I'm not sure, she said sometime near the end of March."

"And you really wanna play this show, Marco?"

"Yeah, man," I say, as I leave the hospital and head down the snowy street, trying to figure out where the closest metro is.

"D'you think we're even ready to play such a big show?"

"I think we could be. It's still like six weeks away. We're just gonna have to practice every day from now on."

Blair is silent for a second before he says: "OK, I'm in, but I have one request."

"What's that?"

"I wanna play guitar."

"But Tank's our guitarist," I say.

I hear Blair sigh. "I'm not saying we should kick him out, I'm just saying that maybe we could both play."

I don't reply, but I know Tank won't be down with this.

"Look, I'm not trying to step on anyone's toes, all right? And I know Tank's gonna think I want him out of the band or some bullshit, but I don't. He's a perfectly capable guitarist, but all I'm saying is that his power chords aren't gonna cut it if we really want to develop our sound. I know you know what I'm talking about, Marco."

"Yeah, I guess so . . ."

"We can do so much more with two guitars. More melody and texture and volume. Where are you right now?" he asks.

"Walking towards Sherbrooke metro station."

"What the hell you doing down there?"

"Long story, dude. I'll tell ya later."

"You still with Tank?"

"No, he and Randy went to The Tunnels," I say.

"Perfect. You think your mom's home right now?"

"I dunno. There's a good chance she's out with Ronnie. Why?"

"Well even if she's home it doesn't matter, we can play acoustic," he says.

"What are you talking about?"

"Meet me at your house in a half an hour. We'll jam a little and then you can decide what you think."

"About what?"

"About me playing the fucking guitar in the band. Cool?"

Now it's my turn to sigh. "OK, fine. But can you please grab some beer?"

"No problem. I'll see ya soon."

"Ciao," I say, jamming my phone in my pocket as I push open the heavy door to the metro.

Tank ain't gonna like this one bit. He's already annoyed with Blair about his busted amp and more. Although he'll never admit it, I think Tank is a bit jealous of Blair and Jules, and also how Blair's become the new leader of our group of friends just because he is who he is. And him wanting to play guitar is just going to be one more thing for Tank to resent.

I hear a train coming into the station, so I race down the escalator and through the turnstile, rush down the stairs, dodge a group of cute girls all wearing the same Timberland boots, and slip through the doors of the train just as they're closing. I snag a seat and shut my eyes, listening to two older girls next to me talk about how shitty their boyfriends are. I put my earphones in to tune them out and think of Bianca holding me for dear life in the back of the cab. I can still sort of smell her perfume on me, and I bring my scarf up to my nose and sniff it like a drug fiend.

Yup, it's official, I'm a fuckin' loser.

# JULIANNA

We're in the kitchen and I'm sipping my second vodka-OJ as Vicky crushes up one of her brother's Ritalin pills with a spoon. She read that if we want a more intense buzz it's best to snort it. Once she's smashed the pill to powder, she separates it into two lines with her Trudeau High student card.

I've seen this ritual in movies, of cutting and dividing up cocaine into lines, but seeing Vicky do it feels a bit weird.

"You look like you've done this before," I say.

Vicky laughs. "They always make snorting drugs so glamorous on TV, but I feel kinda trashy," she says. "I bet you Care Blair would be able to do this like a real pro!"

"Hey! Old school Blair free night tonight, remember?" I say, but of course I've been thinking about him the whole time. I picture Blair doing coke with the Hesher groupie and wonder what he'd think if he knew I was about to snort my first ever line of drugs. Sure, it ain't cocaine, but it's still gonna mess us up. I take a big slug of my vodka, feeling anxious and excited.

"Ladies first," Vicky says, as she hands me a straw that she's cut in half.

"No way. Come on, we have to do it together," I say.

"OK, fine." She grabs the other half of the straw and sticks it in her cute little nose. "Make sure to plug your other nostril really tight and inhale as hard as you can," she says. "And maybe use the left one, so your nose ring doesn't get in the way. You ready?"

I'm totally not, but I nod yes and she counts to three and we both sniff up our line. It burns my nose a little, but that sensation quickly goes away as it feels like a sea is parting in my head, creating a clear open path that was never there before. The path is full of soft warm light and a million answers. I feel like I know the truth about everything. Life no longer feels complicated or scary. I think about a math problem that I couldn't understand today in Algebra class, and it instantly makes sense. I see a whiteboard in my field of vision and I write out the quadratic formula, plug in the equation, and the answer solves itself. It's so easy, I giggle at its simplicity.

I think about the essay I have to write this weekend on *Oryx and Crake* by Margaret Atwood, and I'm happy to see it's already been written on the Word document in my mind.

I think of my upcoming driving test and pull off a perfect parallel park in one fluid motion. I line up my side mirror, crank the wheel to the right, reverse, and slide into the space before gently spinning the wheel back to the left. It's so graceful, like a parallel park ballet.

I take a deep breath and blow out all the nervous apprehension I've been carrying around in my neck and shoulders. My stress dissipates and my entire body feels loose. The usual noise in my head has gone silent. I swing my arms around and look over at Vicky. She has a small smile on her lips and is looking right through me as if into another dimension.

"Yo, Vick?" I say, waving my hands in her face. She snaps out of her trance and goes to the fridge and pulls out a can of Redbull. She opens it and takes a big swig and then hands it to me as she burps.

"Go ahead," she says, so I take it and chug the rest of it. As I slam the can on the counter, my eyes open wide, and I feel myself becoming part of my body again. I still have complete clarity of thought, but I also start to really feel my feet touching the ground. They have never been more solid, my balance has never been so steady, it's like I can feel roots growing out of the soles of my feet, pushing through the kitchen floor and down into the basement, and tunneling through the foundation, until they reach the cool, dark earth.

Vicky lets out a super loud *whooooop* sound, claps her hands together, and rushes into the living room.

She whips her blue hair around her head, as she grabs her phone and starts searching for a song to play.

I feel my roots growing stronger and thicker and I think about my parents, and it makes perfect sense to me why they split up. I understand that some people aren't meant to be together and that sometimes love fades away. My parents thought that two nutso twin kids could keep them together, even though we weren't planned, and they didn't really love each other.

My dad told me the first thing he ever said to my mom was *"enchanté"*, which is French for 'Nice to meet you', but the literal translation is enchanted, and Dad said that's exactly how he felt when he looked her in the eyes for the first time. I think that shit's so romantic. I was totally enchanted too, the first time I met Blair, when he sauntered into my bedroom and rapped Eminem's rhymes with me.

One night when my mom was tipsy on wine she told me that when she and my dad started dating they were young and horny and infatuated with each other and thought they were invincible, and then my dad knocked her up after only four months of dating.

Me and Blair have basically been together for the same amount of time. *Oh my God, I wonder what I'd do if Blair got me pregnant?* I don't even think I'd care, I think I'd be so happy and thrilled to have his baby. I have this super strong maternal instinct and I know I'd be a great mom.

Thinking about this makes me shiver and I can feel my heart beating really fast and I look down at my hands and see they're closed in tight little fists.

"You ready, Julio?" Vicky shouts, pressing play on her phone.

As if reading my mind, she starts playing "Lose Yourself" by Eminem. As the song begins, the open path in my mind fills up with all the lyrics, and I can feel the roots in the soles of my feet retract. As soon as the guitar starts to strum, my feet come unhinged, and I race into the living room to join Vicky. She grabs my hands, and we start dancing and shouting the words at the top of our lungs.

I jump up on the couch and blast out a whole verse as Vicky swings her hair around and around and around. I leap off the couch and run into the kitchen, my socks sliding down the shiny hardwood. I grab my vodka and finish it. My heart is beating fast and so is my mind, but time feels like it's going in slow motion.

And now I'm back up on the couch, scream-rapping another verse, and Vicky squeals as she spills more drink on the carpet, and I laugh and cheer and pump my fists in the air, and Vicky keeps on dancing dancing dancing.

# MARCO

I get home about a half an hour later and Blair's waiting
for me in the backyard. My mom's car is in the driveway,
but there's no lights on in the house so she must be out
with Ronnie.

"How'd you get here so fast?" I ask.

"Took an Uber," he says, passing me a bottle of beer
from a six-pack that's in the snow by his feet.

"Thanks for grabbing these," I say, twisting off the
cap and taking a big swig.

"You got a light?" Blair asks. I pass him my lighter
and he sparks up a joint. "So, like, what is this bullshit
about you saving some guy's life?" he asks as he exhales.

"It's not bullshit, man," I say, taking the joint from
his outstretched hand. "Me and Tank gave a guy CPR in
the alley behind the dep on Lajeunesse."

"For real?"

"Yeah. Here, check this out," I say, pulling my
phone out of my pocket. "This is when the paramedics
showed up." I press play and hand him my phone. Blair
cringes when they zap him and shudders as he watches
him puke.

"Holy shit, Marco! That video's fuckin' crazy! You
gotta put that online!"

"I would, but guess who the guy is?"

"Who?"

"Bianca's dad!"

"Your Bianca?"

"Yeah. He had a heart attack while he was dragging an old Christmas tree to the dumpster in an alley," I say, handing the joint back to Blair. "And then, I ended up taking a taxi with Bianca to the hospital, and on our way there it smashed into an SUV!"

"Seriously?"

I nod and take another big sip of my beer.

"Did anyone get hurt?"

"No, everyone's okay, we weren't going that fast, but the SUV crashed into the shotgun side and busted out the window."

"No shit! That sounds like a total trip, dude," he says, giving me the joint. "How was it seeing Bianca?"

"She was crying and shit, but it felt good being with her . . . I mean, it was weird, I was super pissed off until we got into the accident, and then I was all nostalgic and like, feeling things for her, until she mentioned Johnny fucking Temple and then I got mad again."

"Well forget about that turd," Blair says, spitting in the snow. "And forget about Bianca too. You should've seen how many chicks were at The Coach tonight, Marco! Gigs will get ya girls, man," he says. "And regardless of the epic night you've had so far, I'm still pissed you guys blew off the show."

"I know, I know," I say. The joint's out, so I hand it back to Blair and chug what's left in my bottle. "But it was pretty much outta my control," I say with a burp.

"Pfft, you could've convinced them."

I look at Blair and sigh.

"Whatever. You want any more of this?" he asks, holding out the roach.

"Nah, I'm good for now."

"Well let's go inside, I'm freezing!"

"Let's do it!" I say, grabbing the six-pack. We go in through the back door, kick off our boots and head downstairs to the basement. The basement has a chill-out area with a TV and stereo, a laundry room off to the corner, and what used to be my dad's workshop has been turned into our jam space. It's pretty bare bones and still has a wall of screwdrivers and crap, but we've tried to make it comfy. Randy strung up some Christmas lights and we have an old lava lamp of my mom's on a shelf in the corner.

The lamp's on and I love walking into the room and seeing all our gear lit up in its green glow. Randy's drums are stacked in a pile by the door because we haven't set them back up since our last show at Acapulco Delight.

"You don't have your mic, eh?" I ask. Blair has an expensive old microphone that was The Blade's that he always brings with him when we jam.

"No, it's at home, but I'll just sing without."

"Can you play guitar and sing at the same time?" I ask.

Blair shoots me a dirty look. "Are you fuckin' kidding me?"

"What? It ain't easy," I say.

"Can you suck a dick and jerk off at the same time?" he asks.

"Barely," I say. "But practice makes perfect. How 'bout you pull out your Hollywood wanger and let's find out?"

Blair laughs. "Maybe later," he says, winking at me, as he plugs in the Christmas lights and grabs Tank's guitar out of its case. It's a Fender Telecaster that Tank bought off of one of his brother's buddies. Blair starts tuning it, while I open another beer even though I'm buzzing pretty hard from drinking the first one so fast.

Funny enough, I've never really heard Blair play guitar before. Sure, a little strumming on an acoustic here and there, and he's given some advice to Tank on chord progressions, but he's usually just focused on the vocals.

Blair reaches behind Tank's amp to turn it on. "It's busted," I say.

"I just wanna see what's wrong with it," he says, as he flicks it on. It's an old Peavey stack that Tank's uncle gave him when we started jamming together. The amp buzzes for a second as it starts up, but then hums quietly. Blair strums a D chord, then a C, and a G. He starts finger-picking a quiet little melody, and then turns up the volume and plays a quick riff.

"Sounds fine to me," Blair says.

"That's so weird, 'cause when Tank tried it a few days ago it wouldn't stop buzzing."

"Well, it seems to have worked itself out. So now Tank can chill the fuck out. Grab your bass and plug in."

I take a swig of beer and grab my guitar out of its case. It's a cheaper model Fender Jazz with crappy pickups, but I love the way it sounds. I rub my hand over the felt inside the guitar case and breathe in its smell. It still smells fresh, like a new car. I find a patch cord, plug into my amp, and make sure I'm in tune with Blair.

"All right," Blair says, "start playing 'Shattered' and just keep playing the opening part over and over." I do a four-count and start the song. "OK, so this is what Tank is currently doing!" Blair shouts, as he strums three power chords for a few measures. "Now imagine," he says as he stops for a second, "if at the same time Tank is playing those chords, I do this over top!"

He starts strumming this complicated melody that's both off time and perfectly on time. It sounds so messed up I screw up and start laughing.

"Do that again!" I say as I replay the bass line. He comes in with the melody and shouts: "Let's go to the refrain this time!"

Blair steps on the distortion pedal and blasts out the same chords as Tank, but plays the barre chords instead, and he starts screaming: "It was a night of shattered glass! Another night of shattered glass! It ain't the first and it ain't the last, it was a night of shattered glass! I'M SHATTERED!"

"One more time!" I yell, as we start again from the beginning.

It sounds good, like really good. I'm stoned and giggling while playing, waiting excitedly for Blair to rip into the refrain of the song again and begin yelling the chorus. This time when he starts I join him, concentrating really hard not to mess up the bass line as I shout along.

Blair looks up at me with a grin and nods. "Yeah, buddy! That's the shit right there! That sounded sweet! OK, let's try to make it all the way to the end! And then I wanna show you what I'd add to 'Delusional' . . ."

"Hold on for one second," I say, as I grab my phone out of my pocket, set it on the workbench behind us and press record. I need to capture this moment because I already know it's the beginning of the next phase in The Bad Luck Nickel's evolution.

This time Blair starts, and I count out a few measures before I join him. I can already hear Randy's drumbeat playing in my head – a three count on the hi-hats with a double snare pop every other bar. I look at Blair glowing green like the Northern Lights because of the gleam from the lava lamp. *Aurora Borealis would be a sweet name for a song*, I think to myself with a stoned grin. Blair looks like a real pro, standing there and jamming out on Tank's guitar. He's already an impressive frontman, but he looks even cooler now with a guitar strapped over his shoulder and his dark hair hanging in front of his face.

Blair's a fucking crazy good guitarist! I smile all excited-like as I remember that he's actually The Blade's son! It's not like I didn't know before but watching Blair play guitar it's clear to me he's most definitely a chip off the old Blade.

Yup, Tank ain't gonna like this one bit, but we're onto something super dope here . . .

# JULIANNA

We leave Vicky's house and start racing each other to The Tunnels. But not before we loaded up some empty water bottles with vodka and OJ. And not before we danced to like five more songs. And not before we crushed up another pill and snorted it.

We're running in the middle of the street, slipping and sliding and screaming at the top of our lungs. It's still snowing but doesn't feel cold at all.

"You think you're faster than Usain Bolt, but you ain't shit!" Vicky shouts, grabbing at my jacket and pulling me to the ground. She lands on top of me with a thud and my head smacks off the snowy road, but I don't really feel a thing. I laugh and watch my breath swirl around Vicky's blue hair like a satanic halo.

"Get off me, bitch," I say, pretty sure I could kick her and send her sailing across the street.

"Make me."

"Don't tempt, Vick! I've got superhuman strength right now!"

"Prove it!" she screams, so I grab her by the arms, flip her off me, and pounce on her, straddling her stomach. Vicky yelps in surprise and roars in laughter.

"Jesus Christ! That was like jiu-jitsu or judo or some shit! When the hell'd you learn jiu-jitsu, Jules?"

"I dunno, but I feel like I know everything right now!"

"Oh yeah, what's 14 times 21?"

"294!" I say without even thinking.

"What's the capital of Peru?"

"Lima!" I shout.

"Where's the male G-spot?"

"In his butthole!" I scream.

And then we fall into hysterics. I roll off of Vicky and lie next to her and we shriek and howl and hyperventilate until there's tears in both our eyes.

Vicky just keeps saying: "I can't even . . . I can't . . ." in between her squeals. I feel like I'd be completely happy spending the rest of the night lying right here in the street, but then a horn honks and headlights flash over us. We gaze into the lights, two wild animals caught in their glare.

"Oh shit! It's the cops! Get up, get up, get up!" I say to Vicky, jumping up and grabbing her arms to help lift her off the street. "Omigod, omigod, omigod, omigod," I mumble, shivering in fear. We stumble backwards into a pile of snow by the curb, and I grab on to Vicky to stop from falling over.

"That ain't the cops," Vicky says.

What I thought were police lights on the roof of the car is actually just a storage rack for bikes or skis. I let out a huge sigh of relief, as the car begins to slowly drive by us. The driver rolls down his window and calls out in French that we have to be more careful, what the hell were we doing lying in the road in the dark?

"*On regarde la neige,*" Vicky says all poetically.

"*Mais dans la rue? C'est tellement dangereux!*" the guy says.

"*Peut-être,* but the snow is sooo beautiful!"

"*Tabaouette, vous êtes des grosses caves, vraiment des fucking idiots!*"

"Why thank you, sir. Have yourself a lovely evening and please drive safe," Vicky deadpans in a British accent, as she puts her arm in mine and quickly pulls me onto the sidewalk. We walk in slow motion until the car disappears up the street, but then Vicky bursts out: "Jesus Christ, Jules! You almost made me pee myself! *Get up, get up! It's the fucking po-po!* Holy shit, you had me freaking out for a second there—"

"Sorry babe, but I totally thought it was a cop car. Woof! Omigod, my heart is still pounding. I thought we were busted for sure! And like, why the hell were we lying in the middle of the street?"

"Because we're smashed!" Vicky says with a laugh. "It made perfect sense to me at the time, though."

"Haha, yeah me too. I was feeling so comfy and relaxed."

"Can you imagine what we looked like? Two total heat-scores, sprawled out in the road, drunk and stoned out of our minds, screaming about G-spots!"

I giggle with Vicky and skip down the sidewalk. I'm feeling really good right now, so I decide to forget about how stupid we just were.

*Backspace, backspace, backspace, annnnd delete.* Perfect.

"I feel really good right now, Vick! Like super confident and pretty calm overall, even though my heartbeat is still pumped up a few notches. How 'bout you?"

"I'm great, but I hope Randy or Tank has a joint to smoke with us, 'cause that'd be the icing on my big baked cake."

"I think it's road soda time," I say, pulling out a bottle from my jacket. I pass it to Vicky and she takes a sip and then so do I.

I feel the vodka in my throat and fingers and toes, and I picture a satellite high in the sky, watching us through the storm like a Peeping Tom from space as we lay in the road. Spying on us even now, as I tip my head back and take a second slug of the vodka. I gaze up and am convinced I can see the satellite's green light blinking at me through the snow and the clouds and the stars and all the fucked up mysteries of the universe.

I pass the bottle back to Vicky and as I'm wiping my chin on the sleeve of my jacket, two guys, one big, one small, come walking up to us on the sidewalk. They're both wearing Canada Goose parkas with the hoods up, so it isn't until they're a few feet away that I recognize them. It's Yannis and his annoying friend, Andre. They go to Saint F-X, the French high school down the block from Trudeau, and are total shit disturbers.

Vicky dated Yannis for a while back in junior high, and everyone thinks he's super handsome, but I've known him for so long I see way passed his good looks. Sure, he's tall, dresses well, has dark curly hair, light brown eyes and a nice smile, but he doesn't care about anyone but himself, and he can be a real dick sometimes.

He lived across the street from us until his parents split up a couple years back, and he and Marco used to hang out all the time. But over the last year or so they've had a major falling out, because Yannis dated Bianca before Marco (ya know, bros before hos and all that), and for some reason he's convinced that Marco and Tank ratted him out to the cops about stealing

Trish Lauzon's car at a party, even though they left way before Yannis swiped the keys from her purse and took it for a joyride. He ended up getting community service because it was his second offense, and he blames Marco and Tank for it.

The other guy, Andre, is a bit of a loose cannon. He's never admitted to it, but everyone is pretty sure he lit his neighbour's garage on fire when he was twelve. Bit of a pyro that one. He acts really impulsively and has this blank look in his eyes that's kinda creepy. He also has this nasty blond crustache that he's been growing for like a year, that he should really just shave off. Every day it's something stupid and stupider with these two, so seeing them on the street is a major buzz kill.

"*Salut, les filles.* Where you headed?" Yannis asks.

"Nowhere really. Just wandering," I say.

"Hey," Vicky says to Yannis. "I heard you got suspended for pulling the fire alarm today. Is it true?"

"No, I didn't get suspended, 'cause they haven't caught me yet."

"But you did it, right?"

"*Ben oui,*" he says with a proud grin. He pulls his hands out of his pockets and his left is splattered in dark ink.

"I always thought the thing about the ink was an urban legend," Vicky says.

"Yeah me too," Yannis says with a wild laugh. "But it looks pretty real now, doesn't it?" He shoves his hand in Vicky's face.

"Get your filthy hand outta my face," she says, smacking it away, and Yannis laughs even louder.

"Why'd ya do it?" I ask.

He shrugs his shoulders. "My girl had a big math test that she didn't study for, so I got it postponed for her. Guess you could say I did it for love!" he says, grinning.

"Then how come you're with this clown, instead of her?" Vicky asks, giving Andre a dirty look as he lights a cigarette. Andre used to pick on her brother Edwin because he talks with a lisp, so Vicky is not a fan.

"Cops are looking for me. Can't go home or to her place. Gotta get this ink cleaned off first."

"And how you gonna do that?"

"Dre's a mad scientist, ya know? He's got some ideas on how to get it all cleaned up."

"Yeah, I don't think pissing on it is gonna help," Vicky says. She looks at me and we both crack up. Vicky laughs so hard she accidentally snorts and we crack up even more.

Last summer, Andre got super drunk at a house party and pissed in the corner of the living room in front of a bunch of people and it's been hauntin' his dumb ass ever since.

Andre ignores the comment and our giggles. "Hey, you girls look *tellement* fucked up, what are you trippin' on?" he asks. He takes a step towards me, puts his hands on my shoulders, and looks deep into my eyes.

I shove him. "Don't touch me, dude."

"Yeah, get the fuck away from her, you little French worm!" Vicky shouts.

"Hey, hey, hey, no need to get racist now. 'Specially you, Vicky. What's your last name anyway, Won-ton or Chicken Chow Mein?" Andre asks.

"I'm Filipino not Chinese, you dumb shit."

"Pfft. Same diff. *C'est pareil.*"

"Um . . .no it's not."

"Whatever who cares? *Maudite crisse de folle.*"

"*Va chier,* you fuckin' psycho."

Andre spits in the snow near Vicky's feet. "Any dog's missing in your neighbourhood, Yan? Check Vicky's freezer. It's her favourite food."

"Oh, go fuck your cousin again!" I yell at him.

"*Ta gueule,* ya dumb pizza-faced wop! Where's your rock star boyfriend tonight? Probably out banging another stripper, huh?" Andre says with a high-pitched cackle.

I make this weird growling sound and charge at him. I smack his cigarette out of his hand, grab the hood of his parka, pull it down over his face, and knee him hard in the balls.

*"Ooof,"* I hear him groan, as he slumps to the ground at my feet. I fight the urge to boot him in the head.

Vicky and Yannis explode in laughter.

"Holy shit, Jules! That was rad! I think you really do know jiu-jitsu!" Vicky screams, as she runs over and gives me a high-five. The whole thing seemed so easy – I saw it all happening two steps in advance. I feel like Keanu Reeves in the first *Matrix* movie when he realizes he knows kung-fu.

"Hahaha! Oh snap, Dre! This tiny chick just whooped your sorry ass! Damn! Whatever the fuck you girls are on, I want some," he says, leering at us and rubbing his hands together.

"You got any cash?" Vicky asks, instantly turning into a serious businesswoman.

"No, but Old Blue Balls over there does," Yannis says, still laughing at Andre.

"I've got Ritalin. 15 bucks a pill."

"How strong are they?"

"Twenty milligrams. One each will have you flying."

"Sold!" Yannis says, walking over to Andre lying in the snow. He reaches into Andre's jacket pocket and pulls out a wad of cash, mostly five-dollar bills. Andre sells shitty pre-rolled joints to the junior high kids that hang out at the arena. "Will you give me four for fifty?" Yannis asks.

"Ummm, I dunno," Vicky says.

"C'mon! Your girl broke his fucking balls. Give us a deal, for old time's sake!"

Vicky winks at me and says: "OK, fine." Yannis counts out the money and she taps four pills into his inked hand. "It's best to crush them up and snort them," she advises. "They'll hit you faster."

Yannis tosses two pills in his mouth. "No worries, I'll just chew 'em. Tastes like ass, but works just as good," he says, as he pockets the other pills and walks over to Andre to help him up out of the snow. He's still holding his crotch and cussing me out in French. "C'mon Dre, get up, man. You'll be fine as soon as you take your meds. *Merci bien, les filles!* See ya later!" Yannis says.

Vicky links arms with me and whispers: "Let's fuckin' hope not," and we start walking away.

"Oh and make sure to tell your dickhead brother to go fuck himself!" Yannis yells. "And let him know I'm tappin' Bianca again on the regular too!"

*Yeah, I'll get right on that for ya,* I say to myself, as I wave good-bye without turning back. "God, I hate those guys," I whisper to Vicky. "Hey, I thought you were selling the pills for ten bucks each?"

"Five-dollar ex-boyfriend tax," Vicky says with a laugh. "Oh my God, Jules, I wish I would've got a video of you taking Andre down. You were like a fucking sexy ninja! Edwin's gonna die when he hears about it! Overcharged him and kicked his ass! Love it!"

"Let's turn around and I'll do it all over again!"

"Have you ever kicked someone in the nuts before?"

"I don't think so. Maybe Marco when we were little, but I can't remember—"

"Man, I've wanted to kick Andre in the balls for probably like six years now. How'd it feel?"

"Way better than popping a finger in his butthole, that's for sure . . ."

Vicky tilts her head to the sky and laughs so loud I'm pretty sure people in the alternate versions of our reality can hear it as clearly as I can.

"Oh my God, I fuckin' love you, Julio!" she says, hugging me and taking a swig of her road soda. "I think we might be the drunkest girls in the city right now!"

It's weird, I can tell I'm drunk, but the Ritalin is definitely taking the lead. I really like how it makes me feel super focused and like I'm two steps ahead of the rest of the world. I don't want the sensation to go away anytime soon.

"Can we have one more little sniff before we get to The Tunnels?"

"I didn't crush up anymore before we left, but we can totally do that once we get there."

*I want more now!* I think to myself a little savagely. I take a big sip of my vodka and feel my phone buzz in my pocket. *Oh my God, BLAIR!* I scream in my head, fumbling for my phone like an idiot, realizing I've barely thought about him at all for the last hour. My heart is pounding super fast, but when I look at the screen it's a text from Marco saying he'll meet us at The Tunnels soon.

"Who dat?" Vicky asks.

"Marco. He says he's gonna meet us."

"You think he's with Bitchy-Poo?"

"You mean Bianca? Didn't you just hear? She's meeting up with Yannis."

"Ha. Yeah, he wishes."

"Her Dad just had a heart attack. I'm sure she's still at the hospital."

"You never know with Miss Bitchy-Poo. If she shows up with Marco, you better pull out your sexy ninja moves again and smack that skank upside her head."

"Gladly," I say, punching the air as I make stereotypical karate sounds.

"Are you chilly? I think I'm starting to feel chilly."

"A true ninja feels neither cold nor pain."

"Well, I ain't no ninja, so can we motor to our destination, *s'il vous* fucking *plaît?*"

*Sooner we're there, sooner I can have another sniff*, I think, so I start running and Vicky follows.

"Tonight's like the most exercise I've had in months!" Vicky yells, but I ignore her, because I'm already locked into the rhythm of my feet and my breath, feeling like I've just figured out the mystery of running – it's all about the breath – in through the nose and out through the mouth, measured and slow. It's so simple! Just the running, the breath, the running and the breath. I watch my huffs and puffs, and picture them swirling above my head like satanic halos, and then I feel my left foot give out under me as I hit some ice, and I nosedive into a pile of snow. Vicky howls in laughter from somewhere behind me and I roll over, wipe snow off my face, howl back at her, and look up at the satellite that's blink blink blinking at me and watching our every move.

# MARCO

Blair and I hit a major groove. We play "Shattered" and "Delusional" a few times, and it's seriously like I'm playing them for the first time. With Blair on guitar the songs are absolutely next level.

Blair asks me to start something up and I play a song I've been working on for a while now that I haven't even shown Randy yet. It's in drop D tuning, so we re-tune our guitars and I play it twice all the way through. Blair stands there, straight-backed, eyes closed, like he's meditating, and when I start it up the third time, he joins in as if we've been playing the song together for ten years.

He does some cool fingerpicking, and it sounds like the notes he hits are about a half a beat before mine, but it creates this really driving rhythm that we get locked into. We bob our heads and shoulders to the groove, and it is so fucking good! I close my eyes and can feel this weird energy swirling around in the air between us as Blair keeps hitting this one note that really resonates. He's using Tank's delay pedal, and it sounds super moody and a little wistful.

We go into the change and Blair stomps on the distortion pedal and so do I and we're just chugging away, amps cranked to ten, strumming as fast as we're able to until the lights flick on and my mom's standing in the doorway, all 4 feet 8 of her, screaming for us to stop.

Her voice is so goddamn loud, I can hear it over the amps.

"How many times I gotta tell youse guys no jamming after nine o'clock? I could hear ya in the car from down the street for Chrissake!"

I'm so pumped about what me and Blair were just doing, I ignore her and start up the bass line again, but Blair unstraps Tank's guitar and flicks off the amp.

"Sorry Mrs. Catalano," Blair says. "We were just trying out some new songs."

"Which sounded fucking amazing!" I say. "Dude, I don't know what note you kept playing there at the beginning, but it was hitting me right in the fucking balls!"

"Your mouth, Marco!" my mom says, shaking her head at me. "Where's Julianna?"

"I dunno," I say, still focused on Blair. "And that riff you were playing was so heavy! It sounded like early Smashing Pumpkins! Can you imagine how awesome it'll be with Randy going nutso on the drums? Let us play for ten more minutes, Ma."

"No. You're done for the night. I've had a long day, and I don't wanna listen to any more of your racket.

Besides, Ronnie's here, and we're gonna watch a movie."
She looks over at Blair. "D'you know where Julianna is?"

"She's probably with Vicky," he tells her.

"Did you eat the pasta I left in the fridge, Marco?"

"Negative," I say.

"Aren't ya hungry?"

"Negative."

"What's the matter with you? You been drinking?"

"Nooo!" I say way too quickly, realizing the six-pack is in plain sight on the floor next to the drums, and there's an empty bottle at my feet. All my mom has to do is look down and she'll see it. I'm so psyched about the music we were playing I feel like I'm on a completely different planet. "What do you care, anyway?" I say, being a dick just to be a dick, and because I know I'm about to get busted and probably grounded.

My mom's about to rip into me, but Blair swoops in like the dark angel he is and manages to create two diversions and diffuse my Mom's displeasure at the same time.

"Don't listen to him, Mrs. Cee," he says, walking over to block her view of the beer. "He's in a bad mood because he bumped into Bianca (*he says her name in a whisper*), and you know how he gets when he sees her. So we came here to jam a little and let him clear his head. But don't worry, he's fine. I do think he's a bit hangry though and could actually use some of that pasta you left for him in the fridge. I like your sweater by the way, is it new?"

"Oh thanks, Blair. It *is* new! Ronnie got it for me a couple weeks ago."

"I love the colour, the green really makes your eyes pop, ya know what I mean?" he says, directing her out of the room and up the stairs as if he has her on remote control or something. He winks at me as he follows her up the stairs.

"What a boss!" I say, swooping up the beer bottle at my feet and hiding the six-pack behind the hot water heater. I think of Bianca's dad lying in the snow and me and Tank giving him CPR and it all feels like a dream.

*Hard and fast in the centre of the chest, hard and fast in the centre of the chest.*

I want to tell my mom what happened in the alley with Bianca's Dad, 'cause it's a crazy story, but I know that as soon as I get upstairs and am actually looking at her, the urge will go away. I used to tell my mom every single thing that happened to me, but over the last year or so I stopped telling her stuff, started keeping my thoughts to myself. It's like I put up this little wall to block her out. I didn't even tell her that Bianca broke up with me until like a month after it happened, and I think it was actually Jules who was the one that told her.

It's weird, I'll talk to my mom in my mind, but when it comes to doing it face to face these days, I'd rather hold back.

I grab my cell phone off the workbench, hoping maybe Bianca wrote me, but there's just one new text from Jules:

> Me and V going to tunnels, meet
> there later?

I text back:

> Be there soooon.

Then I text Bianca:

> Hey Bee, how's everything going?

I stare down at the phone for like sixty seconds waiting for the ( . . .) to pop up on the screen, but it doesn't happen. So I put my guitar back in its case, unplug the lava lamp and Christmas lights and head upstairs. My mom's already got two plates on the table and the pasta warming on the stove.

"Sit! Sit! You boys hafta eat!" she says. I figure it's probably a smart idea to get some food in my stomach if I'm gonna keep drinking, so I take a seat and say hey to Ronnie.

"How's it going, Marconi?" he asks.

I shrug my shoulders. "It's Friday," I say. I can tell he and my mom are a bit buzzed themselves because her cheeks are rosy, and Ronnie's got this chilled out look on his face that he gets after a couple pops. Almost every Friday they go to this little restaurant nearby called Graziella's for dinner and cocktails.

"Why don't you open up the bottle of wine and let it breathe a bit," my mom says to Ronnie, as she passes him the corkscrew.

"OK, but if I open it and it's not breathing, should I give it mouth to mouth?"

My mom giggles too loudly. "Whatever floats your boat, Ron," she says with a smile.

"Hey Silvana, guess what the first thing on my bucket list is?" Ronnie asks.

"I dunno, what's the first thing on your bucket list, Ron?"

"To fill it to the brim with wine!"

My Mom laughs even louder, which I know will just encourage a glowed-up Ronnie to keep going. He's beyond corny sometimes and tries too hard to get me and Jules to like him, but he's all right I guess. I mean, he's waaaay fuckin' better than most of the deadbeats my mom seems to be attracted to, he's just a bit of a dork.

"Hey Blair, what d'ya call a fake noodle?" he asks.

"I don't know, Ronnie, what?"

"An impasta! Hey-yo!"

I groan and my mom grins at Ronnie from the stove.

"All right, settle down there, Ronnie! I think you're over the legal limit of hilarity," I tell him.

"Hold on, hold on. I got one more. You ready?"

I roll my eyes at him but nod.

"OK, OK, so I'm going to a concert next week and it only costs 45 cents. Guess who's playing?"

"Who?" I ask.

"50 Cent and Nickelback. And I still feel like I'm being overcharged!"

I can't help but laugh. So does Blair. "OK, I'll give ya that one, Ronnie. It's so bad it's actually good."

"Did ya get me a ticket too, ya cheapskate?" my mom asks, and then she starts singing "In Da Club" by 50 Cent, all high-pitched about Bacardi and birthdays.

She and Ronnie start dancing with each other around the kitchen, and it makes me wanna puke. "Oh my God! I will pay you both fiddy cents to please just stop!"

They shimmy over to the stove and Ronnie grabs the bottle of wine along the way. He starts pouring two glasses.

"Can we have some?" I ask my mom.

"Nope."

"C'mon, we need something to wash this impasta down with."

Ronnie looks at my mom. "A little splash ain't gonna hurt 'em."

"OK, fine," she says.

Ronnie pours us two small glasses and brings them over to us with a wink.

"Big ups, Ronnie," I say.

I feel my phone hum in my pocket and I quickly grab it, hoping it's Bianca, but when I look at the screen there's no new notifications. Just a phantom vibration. I've been getting these all the time lately. My Mom scoops a bunch of pasta onto our plates and the two of them disappear into the living room as me and Blair wolf back the noodles like the animals we are.

"Hey, can you send me the videos you took?" Blair asks, looking at my phone on the table.

"Sure, but I don't know how good the sound quality is," I say.

"It doesn't matter, I just want to hear what I was playing in "Shattered" again, so I don't forget it."

I unlock my phone and start playing the video. We nod our heads and smile at each other.

"Shit man, it sounds really good. I wanna jam some more," I say with my mouth full.

"We will. Tomorrow," Blair says, wiping his chin with a napkin. He grabs my phone and presses play again. "So, am I in or what?" he asks.

I laugh. "Fuckin' right you are," I say, and we clink our wine glasses together and chug them back.

A half hour later, Blair and I are passing a joint back and forth as we head down the snowy alley that leads to The Tunnels. Bianca still hasn't texted me back, but I've decided to stop obsessing over her, so I take a big haul on the joint and hold it in for as long as I can. Bass lines are playing in my head and that feeling of cosmic energy swirling between us when we were practicing is still there.

"I don't know if I'm high from the weed or still stoked from us jamming," I say through a puff of smoke.

"Probably both," Blair says. "The two complement each other perfectly. I always feel like I've never actually heard a song until I've listened to it stoned, ya know? And playing music when I'm high is even better."

"It's so true," I say, passing him the joint. I slip on some ice hidden underneath the fresh snow and the beer bottles clink in my backpack. There are no tire tracks in the alley so we're walking up against the building hoping to mask our footprints and not be heat-score and leave a trail right to the door of The Tunnels.

Randy likes to call the entrance to The Tunnels "The Bat Cave" because it's in plain sight. You could easily walk by it a hundred times, because it looks like a rusty old emergency exit that only opens from the inside, but the latch is busted so all you have to do is carefully wedge your fingers in the crack at the top of the door and pull it outwards.

It was Tank who originally heard about the tunnels, because his Nonno worked for the STM, or if you wanna sound fancy, the *Societé de Transport de Montréal,* for over thirty years. Tank's Nonno has a ton of crazy stories about homeless guys living underground during the winter, and about this group of nutso athletes that used to race the trains, and about how often people try to kill themselves by jumping on the tracks. I guess it was such a big problem in the 80's there used to be a deal that if a subway driver was unlucky enough to have three people jump in front of their train, they were granted early retirement. Just imagining it gives me the shivers. I don't think I could handle it happening once, let alone three times!

Tank's Nonno never hit anyone, but he has one story where he was pulling into Snowdon station near the end of his shift when he saw a guy with no clothes on jump down onto the tracks. His train was at the far end of the station, so he knew he'd be able to stop it before it came close to hitting him, but then the naked guy lay down on the tracks, put his hands on the third rail, and electrocuted himself. Tank's Nonno says he still has nightmares about it fifteen years later.

But what's even crazier is that there's an Emergency Response team, whose job it is to clean up the "mess" as quickly as possible, so the subway service isn't disrupted for too long.

"They literally get paid to clean up guts and gore as fast as they can! What kind of sick fucker would want that job?" Tank always asks.

And then Randy deadpans: "I'd do it."

Tank likes to tell his Nonno's STM stories often. They're great, because they can really spark up your imagination. You can't help but imagine the woman next to you leaping onto the tracks just as the train's chugging into the station and then *EL SMACKO!* And you can't help but wonder how you'd react if something like that happened. I think a big reason why it's so fascinating and scary is because it totally could happen.

But the tunnels that we hang out in are abandoned ones that the trains don't drive through. Around ten years ago, the STM expanded the metro north into Laval and in the process, they made a hell of an underground mess. There's a whole maze of tunnels down there, as if the workers were digging blindly for a few years until someone finally looked at the blueprints and was like oh shit, we fucked up. But Tank says the mazes make sense because they needed a lot of room for their equipment, and they probably even had makeshift offices down there too.

Our tunnels run parallel with the new tracks, so we hear the trains rumbling by us every five minutes or so, but we can't see them. It was really freaky at first because it almost sounds like the trains are coming right towards you, but it's just your ears playing tricks, because noise reverberates like crazy in the tunnel. It'd be an amazing spot to record an album.

As Blair and I arrive at The Bat Cave, I notice the door isn't closed properly, and there's a bunch of half-buried footprints leading up to the entrance from the other direction.

"What the hell?" I ask, looking at the boot prints in the snow. No one ever leaves the door open.

"Maybe Tank and Randy left to go get more beer or something," Blair says.

"Even if they did, they'd never leave without closing the door all the way."

Tank is nutso about keeping The Tunnels a secret. *First rule of The Tunnels is we don't talk about the goddamn tunnels,* he likes to say. He'd never forget to shut the door no matter how wasted he is.

Blair pulls open The Bat Cave door and we step inside. The hallway is lit by a motion sensor lightbulb that clicks on as we walk in. I see a trail of wet boot prints leading down the hallway to the door that heads downstairs to The Tunnels. We call this one "The Blue Door" because Randy painted the handle bright blue.

"Maybe Jules and Vicky brought people with them," Blair says, as we walk down the hall.

*They better not have*, I think to myself. I suddenly feel very territorial. *This place is our secret hangout. It'll be ruined if other people find out about it.*

The hallway acts as an emergency exit for some of the offices and businesses of the strip mall. The STM used to have an office here back when they were expanding, but they've long since moved out. In fact, half of the stores are empty, there's an Italian bakery, a hair salon, a bubble tea shop, and a Value Village thrift store, but not much else. So after nine o'clock the place is deserted. Tank had to steal a set of old work keys from his Nonno to get us passed The Blue Door and down into The Tunnels, so it's a goddamn hidden gem when it comes to party spots and I'm definitely not ready to share it yet.

I pull open The Blue Door and Blair taps the flashlight on his phone so we can see our way down the stairs. There's the red glow of an exit sign at the top of the steps but it's still pretty dark down there. An old elevator shaft, which must've been used to move all the heavy equipment stands empty next to the stairwell.

I hear music playing from Randy's portable speaker. The bass echoes towards us from the tunnel.

"Well, everything sounds normal," Blair says.

I nod in agreement, and then Jules screams.

# JULIANNA

Tank is rubbing his forehead and looking down at Andre, who's curled in a ball by his feet, when Yannis comes up from behind him and sucker punches him in the side of the head.

"Tank look out!" I try to yell, but all that comes out is this weird puppy dog yelp.

Yannis' fist makes a quiet thud as it connects with Tank's temple and sounds nothing like you hear in the movies. But it catches Tank off guard, and he staggers, falling to one knee, and Yannis follows through with a boot to his cheek. It's hard to see much with just the flashlight on my cell phone, but Tank's head snaps back awkwardly as Yannis' boot makes contact.

Yannis laughs like a maniac as Tank goes down. "Looks like you ain't the only ninja in town now, huh?" he shouts, looking at me with crazy eyes. He jumps on Tank, pinning him to the ground with his knees.

"Get off him!" I scream, looking over at Vicky for a second. She's crouched on the ground next to Randy, who's spitting blood and maybe a tooth into the palm of his hand.

"Up and at 'em, Dre! Don't miss your chance to kick Tank in his dumb head," Yannis says. "Y'ain't so tough now eh, ya fuckin' rat!" he says to Tank, giving him a jab to the ribs. "I hafta fucking clean shit off the side of the highway 'cause of you!"

I'm freaking out, mainly because I've never seen Tank go down before. But also, because I've never seen anyone's head spring back like a bobblehead before . . .

Everything had felt like it was going in slow motion, until it started going really fast. Vick and I had made it inside The Bat Cave door, and I immediately bugged her to crush up a pill before we went down the stairs and into The Tunnels. She was game so we stuck a pill in an old Ziploc bag and smooshed it against the wall and took turns snorting it with the half of a straw I'd put in my pocket.

The teeny little tug of anxiety I was starting to feel melted away and I kissed Vicky on both cheeks and told her I loved her.

Vicky pulled open The Blue Door and as we started to go downstairs someone knocked on The Bat Cave door from outside.

"How'd they open it?" I heard a voice say in French.

I looked at Vicky and her eyes were super wide. "It's fucking Andre and Yannis," she whispered.

"Oh shit," I said.

*The first rule of The Tunnels is we don't talk about the goddamn tunnels. And the second rule of The Tunnels is we don't ever let anyone follow us to the goddamn tunnels.*

Sorry Tank, looks like my ninja abilities don't extend to the sixth sense, or even the fifth for that matter, because I had no clue Andre and Yannis followed us. And me and Vicky definitely weren't thinking about the second rule of The Tunnels, 'cause we were running down the alley kicking up fresh snow, and leaving breadcrumb trails all the way to The Bat Cave door.

Yep, we fucked up.

"Yo, Julianna, open up!" Yannis shouted as he pounded his fist on the door.

"Let's go, let's go," I said, giving Vicky a little nudge towards the stairs. I was thinking that if we could get down there and find Tank fast enough, maybe he'd be able to lock The Blue Door before Andre and Yannis figured out how to open up The Bat Cave.

We ran down the stairs and followed the sound of the music towards the left tunnel. There's a few different tunnels down here but the left one's the least scary and has electrical outlets that work, so it's the one we chill in. We'd brought in a couple lamps and old chairs and Randy had stolen a portable spotlight from his dad's construction gear so he could shine a light on the walls and practice his graffiti. He'd been spray painting a giant

Bad Luck Nickel logo in the left tunnel for a couple weeks now and it looked awesome. We'd also dragged an old love seat down there that someone had left outside the Value Village a while back. Tank and Randy were lounging on it when we came rushing in.

I somehow managed to tell them what happened, and Tank jumped off the couch and rushed out of the tunnel towards the stairs.

"Stay here!" he shouted, but we all followed him.

"We cannot let those assholes get in here!" Randy said. "Did you say they're jacked out on speed?" he asked.

"Yeah."

"Fuck, d'you remember that time Yannis and Marco took all those caffeine pills at the Trudeau dance in Grade 9? Yannis went completely nutso. He started a mosh pit during some shitty dubstep song and hit Jason Morley so hard he gave him a concussion."

All I remember from that night is getting sloppy drunk on less than a half bottle of wine, and Vicky making me leave the dance early because one of the teacher chaperones noticed I was Amy Winehouse'd.

"Sadly, I don't remember much from that night," I said to Randy.

"Yeah well, dude can't handle his pumpkin spiced lattes, I'll tell ya that."

The stairwell lit up as Tank pushed opened The Blue Door.

"Why're you guys following me?" he asked in a harsh whisper from the top of the stairs.

"Can you lock it?" I asked, running up the stairs.

He put his finger in front of his mouth to shush me. "No. There's no lock on the inside," he whispered, as we joined him in the hallway. "Only way to lock it is from out here. Are those your boot prints?" he asked me and Vicky. We checked them out but couldn't really tell for sure. It was all just a blur of melting snow.

Randy went and put his ear against The Bat Cave door. "Should I open it?" he asked softly. Tank joined him by the door, and we all stood there like we were mannequins. I could hear the buzz of the fluorescent light above our heads. Tank counted to three on his fingers and then shoved open The Bat Cave door. A puff of cold air tickled my face. Randy peeked his head out.

"There's no one here," he said, as he and Tank both stepped outside to look around.

"Holy shit. It looks like you two were running around in circles out there," Tank said to me and Vicky.

"Ya, we pretty much were," Vicky said. "We completely forgot about the second rule, sorry."

"Well, lucky for us those two losers are too dumb to even figure out how to open a door," Randy said with a laugh.

"Oh yeah, YA THINK SO!?" Yannis' voice boomed from behind us, from the bottom of the stairs. We all spun around in surprise. Shit. He and Andre were already in the tunnels. "Come say it to my fucking face, bitch!" he screamed.

This is when things began to speed up.

Tank pushed by me and Vicky and ran back down the stairs. "Yo, Yannis! Where you at?" he shouted.

We rushed down the stairs after Tank and clicked on our flashlights, illuminating all the dark corners where someone could hide. Realizing that Andre and Yannis had actually been hiding in the shadows when we walked by made me shiver. They must have just made it down the stairs and into the tunnels before we came back with Tank and Randy. Vicky flashed her light into the elevator shaft, and we saw someone in there.

"Hey! Hey! Hey!" I shouted, unable to make any other words come out of my mouth. Randy came rushing back, but we realized it was just a Canada Goose jacket hanging from a pole.

"Shit, I totally thought it was Yannis," Vicky said, and then we heard his wild cackle echo from somewhere ahead of us.

"The guy's a fuckin' nutbar," Randy muttered, as we turned around and followed Tank back to the left tunnel. Yannis wasn't in there, but Andre was, staring up at The Bad Luck Nickel logo on the wall. He had a can of black spray paint in his hand.

"Shit boys, this is a sweet spot you got down here," Andre said. "How'd you find it?"

"Where's Yannis?" Tank asked, but Andre ignored him. Tank's hands curled into fists and his eyes darted back and forth from Andre to the entrance.

"Nice work, Randy, *pas pire*," Andre said, still gazing at the band logo. "I like this one too," he said, pointing at Randy's personal tag, which spelt out King Krang framed in a golden crown. "I saw it in the alley behind the arena, didn't know it was you though," he said as he started shaking the spray can in his hand.

I sensed trouble. I mean, the whole situation was already trouble, but I had a feeling things were going to turn ugly fast, so I thought I'd try and distract Andre.

"Hey, did you take those speeds, Dre?" I asked.

"Don't fuckin' talk to me, Pizza Face," he said.

"I'm just curious if they kicked in yet?"

He didn't reply, just stared at me. The usual blank look in his eyes had changed with the Ritalin. Now he looked smug, as if he could see just past me, a couple steps ahead into the future. It was way creepier than his normal gaze. He frowned at me and chuckled quietly.

"You think you're funny don't you?" he asked me.

"I'll tell you what's funny," Vicky said, coming to stand next to me. "Jules beating your sorry ass!" She laughed loudly and Andre's face twitched. "Oh man, you guys should've seen it! Jules put the smackdown on him—"

"*Ferme ta yeule!*" he shouted. "You all think you're such hot shit, but you're a bunch of pathetic losers," he said. "Always have been, always will be. And your band is fucking garbage by the way," he said looking at Randy and Tank. "The only reason anyone cares at all is because of that fag Blair Matthews, you know that, right? And you're not the only chick he's banging, Pizza Face, I hope you know that too."

I shook my head at him angrily and told him to shut up, but he just laughed at me.

"Where's Yannis, Dre? You guys need to leave now," Tank said.

"We ain't going anywhere, bro," Andre replied, shaking the can again. "Your band logo is cool, but I think I can make it better."

"Hey man, please don't fuck with that," Randy said.

"Ya know who I'd love to fuck with, Randy? Your

sexy ass sister, Nicole. Damn, I love them mixed race girls. But oh wait, I can't . . . she's dead."

I think everyone went into shock for a few seconds after Andre said this. But he looked Randy right in the eyes, grinned at him like a psychopath, and then pressed down on the nozzle of the can and started spraying over the logo on the wall.

A train began to rumble past, shaking the tunnel. The sound made Andre pause for a second, and Randy flashed by us, screaming in a high-pitch wail. Andre turned the can on him like it was pepper spray, but Randy grabbed him and wrestled him to the ground. The train was making a ton of noise as it whirled by us on the other side of the wall, but I could still hear Randy screaming and crying and saying, "Fucking Asshole!" over and over as he jammed his knee into Andre's neck and punched him in the head, once, twice. It felt like the entire tunnel was shaking all around us. Randy grabbed the hood of Andre's parka, pulled it over his face and started to smother him with it like a pillow. Andre flailed wildly underneath him, but it just seemed to make Randy stronger.

Andre still had the can of spray paint in his hand. He swung it blindly and cracked Randy in the mouth. Randy fell backwards, hit the spotlight, the bulb smashed, and everything went dark.

Vicky and I tapped on our flashlights and watched as Andre jumped up, shouting for Yannis' help. He tried to run but Tank grabbed him by his jacket, pulled him towards him and head-butted him hard in the face. Andre crumpled at Tank's feet, and then Yannis appeared out of the shadows like a serial killer in a horror movie . . .

Which brings us zooming back to the present moment. Tank splayed out on the ground with Yannis on top of him. Andre collapsed in a heap next to them. And Randy spitting blood and crying and calling both Yannis and Andre assholes.

But wait . . . what the heck? Now Randy's up and running towards Yannis.

"Let's do this, boys!" Randy shouts, as I see two more serial killers emerge out of the shadows.

Vicky screams when she spots them and so do I, convinced they're more of Yannis' goons, but then I see Blair, *my* Blair, putting Yannis in a headlock.

"Hold him down!" Blair yells, looking as if he knows exactly what he's doing. Randy and Marco grab Yannis' arms and he starts thrashing like a grizzly bear in a trap, but Blair locks one arm tight round his neck. He links his other arm behind Yannis' head and leans into him, applying a ton of pressure around his neck.

Blair squeezes and within seconds Yannis' body relaxes and he's passed out cold.

"Quick, help me pull him off," Blair says, as he and Marco grab Yannis by his armpits and drag him off Tank.

I am literally in shock over what's transpired in the last two minutes.

"Oh my God, Jules! You and Care Blair are *both* sexy ninjas!" Vicky says, as we continue to shine our flashlights on the scene.

"Hurry, he ain't gonna be out for long. Is there something we can tie his hands with?" Blair asks.

Randy runs over to the smashed spotlight and unplugs the extension cord out of the socket on the wall and brings it to Blair. Marco continues to hold Yannis up by his armpits, while Blair wraps his arms behind his back and ties them with the extension cord. Once Blair's done, they lean him up against the wall.

"Untie his boots and take 'em off," Blair says to Marco. "That way he won't be able to run when he wakes up."

Randy kneels over Tank, flashing his cell phone on his face, while gently nudging him. Tank groans quietly. "Can someone plug in one of the other lamps so we can see?" Randy asks.

"I'm on it," Vicky says, grabbing the big stand-up lamp by the love seat and plugging it in to the wall. She turns it on, and the whole thing looks like a battle scene, a nutso *tableau vivant* from Drama class.

"What the hell happened? Is Tank okay?" Marco asks.

"Yannis' all goofed up on speed and he sucker punched him in the head," Randy says.

"What should we do with this one?" Blair asks, pointing at Andre. He's still on the ground, moaning, holding his face in his hands. I'm pretty sure I hear him say he thinks his nose is broken. Good, I hope it's fucking shattered in three places.

"If he tries to get up I'll stomp on his stupid face," I say viciously. Blair looks at me and our eyes lock for the first time since he appeared out of the gloom like a dark angel. He seems surprised, turned on even, by the tone of my voice.

"Who are you?" I mouth to him, still amazed by his expert level ninja chokehold. He shrugs and gives me his famous smirk and I start to smile back, but then Yannis wakes up, gasping for air like he's just surfaced out of super deep water.

# MARCO

I'm pulling one of Yannis' boots off when he explodes back to life, gulping like it's his first and last breath. It's not quite as dramatic as Bianca's dad's resurrection but it still makes me jump.

Yannis' eyes lock with mine. "Where'd *you* come from? Why're you taking my boots off?" he yells. He tries to move his arms, realizes they're tied behind his back, and starts to flip out. "UNTIE ME, RIGHT NOW! I will fucking *KILL* you, Marco!" He kicks at me and clips my chin with his socked foot.

Yannis has that same gleam in his eyes he used to get when he'd chug a can of Coke as a kid. Once he gets sugar or caffeine in his system, he changes, and becomes all moody and aggressive. I didn't understand it until my mom asked me if I ever noticed Yannis seeming a little different after we went to the dep and spent our allowance on chocolate bars, gummy worms, and slushies. That's when she explained that she thought he had an intolerance to sugar, which at the time, I thought was the worst possible thing a kid could ever have.

But yeah, he'd be quick to pick fights and intimidate people whenever he was all sucrosed up. And the same vibe transfers over when he's drunk too. He's fine after a few beers but once he's had that one too many, he shifts, and becomes an antagonizer, poking and prodding at whoever he's with, deliberately trying to piss them off and make them feel like shit. We don't hang out anymore, but I've noticed he's become super paranoid and suspicious of pretty much everyone lately. He also likes to spread rumors about people and lie for no reason at all.

Yannis kicks at me again and growls as he tries to raise his bound arms over his head. When we were kids, he used to freak out whenever someone held him down by his arms and legs. He's super claustrophobic and doesn't like to feel trapped. So when he tries to get up, I push him down and sit on his legs. He bucks like a bull underneath me and almost tosses me off, but Jules and Blair come over and help hold him down.

"Thanks guys," I say, and then Yannis hocks a loogie at me. It misses my face but gets all over my jacket. "Uggh, dude!" I scream. "You gotta chill out!"

"I will MURDER you, Marco! And both of you bitches too!" he says, gnashing his teeth at Jules and Blair.

"Listen Yan, I don't know what's been going on with you lately, but you seem fucked up to me, man.

I know we're not friends anymore, but you know I'd never fucking rat on you to the police. That's not me, man. Or Tank. We weren't even there, so I have no idea why you keep riding our asses about it. And as for Bianca, c'mon bro, you dated her for like three months in Grade 9. That was some kiddie shit. You gotta let it go."

"I banged her yesterday!" Yannis spits. "And we're gonna smash again tonight!"

I think of Bianca crying in my arms when our taxi fishtailed into oncoming traffic, and I can't help but laugh at Yannis.

"I ain't fuckin' kidding!" he shouts.

"All right, I've had enough of this," Jules says, calmly pulling her phone from her jacket pocket. "Listen to me, Yannis. Marco and Tank didn't snitch on you that night, but I will happily rat you out to the fuckin' cops right now!" she says.

"Go ahead!" Yannis shouts.

Stupidly, I nearly blurt out Tank's line: *No service in The Tunnels!*

"You think I'm joking?" Jules asks. She dials 911 on her keypad and shows it to him. "Here's the deal. You and Andre are going to leave right now, or we will ditch you down here and let the cops find you. You'll get busted for trespassing and having weed on you, not to mention, the whole pulling the fire alarm thing."

Yannis is about to say something, but Jules puts up her hand.

"OR . . . we'll let you leave right now, and you can go to Andre's and try to get that ink off your hand like you should've done in the first place."

Yannis' face is a flipbook of contrasting emotions. He's super angry, but I can tell he also senses defeat.

I hear a cough from Tank as he sits up and rub his head. "Shit! What happened?" he says, glancing around at the scene. He spots Yannis and sneers at him. "Oh, you son of a bitch!" he yells, starting to get up.

"Whoa, whoa, whoa!" Randy says, holding him down. "It's under control, just chill for a second!"

"Last chance, Yannis," Jules says in a voice that sounds like it's run out of patience. Yannis keeps his eye on Tank for a few seconds, making sure he doesn't get up and rush him. "Do we have a deal?" she asks, hovering her thumb over the Call Button, and putting the phone in his face. Yannis clenches his teeth together and groans in response.

"All right fine, your loss. Tie his legs up too," Jules says, pressing the Call Button and putting the phone to her ear. "It's rinnnging!" she sings.

"OK, OK, OK fine! Fuck! We'll go!" Yannis says.

"Smart move," Jules says. She clicks the phone off and stuffs it in her pocket.

*Damn Jules, your bluff game is strong!*

"Hey yo, Dre? *Ça va*, man? Can you get up?" Yannis shouts.

I didn't even know who the other guy was until now. I should've guessed it was Andre, but everything had happened so fast. Andre mumbles something to Yannis in French that I can't understand. I look over at Blair next to me and have a flash of him laying a pro chokehold on Yannis, and then another of him rocking out on Tank's guitar, awash in the green glow of the lava lamp. What a boss.

Andre slowly raises himself to a sitting position and tilts his head back. His nose is a dark, bloody, mess. "I fink it's brogan," he mumbles, carefully touching it. Shit, what'd Tank do to him?

"You'll be all right, Dre. C'mon, *on y va,* let's go!" Yannis says.

Tank sees Andre's face and laughs. "Oops. Did I do that? I'd love to tell ya I'm sorry bro, but I ain't. Hopefully, it'll teach you to keep your mouth shut the next time you wanna talk shit about someone who's passed away. Insensitive fuckin' prick."

"And you!" Tank says, turning to Yannis, while craning his neck to the left and right. "You should release all that pent up craziness you got on the football field, instead of sucker punching people in the head. What a bitch ass move, bro. I know, I know, you'll say you were just standing up for your boy, but I ain't sure he's really worth standing up for, know what I mean?" Tank gets up and stretches, acting as if he wasn't just knocked out unconscious five minutes ago. He leans down, grabs Andre by his shoulders and helps him get up. "There ya go, Big Mouth, you're all good," he says, patting him on the back like they're buds. What a boss.

Jules, Blair and I slowly release our grip on Yannis. He stands up and I toss him his boot.

"Can you untie me please!"

"Nope," Blair says.

Yannis looks around at all of us, shaking his head while he glances at Andre's bloody face. He jams his foot into his boot. "Broke his balls and his nose," he says to Jules. "This is one fucked up night," he says bitterly, spitting on the ground.

"OK, goodbye!" Jules says.

"We're goin', we're goin', *tabarnak de calisse.*"

He and Andre slowly make their way out of the tunnel.

"Can you and Vick hang back and quickly grab all our stuff?" Tank asks Randy. "The rest of us will make sure these assholes actually leave."

"No probs," Randy says. A train starts to roll by, creating a wall of sound. It's rhythmic and loud and seems to be coming from every direction at once. We leave the left tunnel, our cellphone flashlights brightening the corners as we follow Dre and Yannis towards the exit. Andre grabs Yannis' jacket out of the elevator shaft and they head up the stairs.

"If I were you guys, I'd suggest you just forget about this place. You were never here. You feel me?" Tank says. They shove open The Blue Door, walk into the hallway and slam it shut. About twenty seconds later, we hear The Bat Cave door slam too.

Jules lets out a sigh of relief, but Tank runs up the stairs to make sure they've left. I go with him. The extension cord is lying in a tangle on the wet ground. Tank pushes open The Bat Cave door and I'm happy to see that they're running through the snow, already almost halfway down the alley, but I have a feeling this ain't over by a long shot.

Jules and Blair join us in the hallway. "So like, what the heck, babe?" she's saying to Blair. "Are you a secret ninja or something? Do you have a black belt in karate? Kung Fu? Jiu-Jitsu?"

"Purple belt in Judo, actually," he says.

"I can't believe it! How come you never told us? And what about the first day of school, when all the jocks almost kicked your ass?"

"The Tank Bank came along and saved me before I had to do anything."

"But you made it seem like you were helpless," Jules says.

"That's 'cause there was like five guys surrounding me."

"Well, you sure helped save his ass tonight," I say. "That chokehold was dope, dude!" Blair just shrugs it off and puts his arm around Jules' waist. "And damn, Jules, your poker face was insane! Yannis bought that shit one hundo percent. I've never seen you so unfazed and chill in my entire life. That was a boss level bluff, sis."

"Thanks Marco. I'm in the zone tonight," Jules replies. "But if anyone's a boss it's Tanky Poo. I think you must have superhuman strength," she says to him.

"Nah, just used to getting tackled is all."

"But when Yannis kicked you, your head snapped back like a spring!"

"Boy-yoy-*yoinng!*" Randy sound effects from the stairs. He and Vicky also join us in the hallway.

"Wait, I thought he punched you in the head?" I ask Tank.

"He double whammied me," he says, rubbing his neck. "And what about you, Ran? How's your mouth?"

Randy smiles and there's a big chip in his front tooth. "Ta-da!"

"Oh shit!" I say.

"Do I look like old school Danny Brown?" he asks.

I laugh. "A little bit. How come you're not totally freaking out?"

"I dunno. I feel kind of numb right now."

"Do you have the piece of tooth?"

"Eww," Vicky says, patting her jeans. "Yeah, I got it tucked away in my condom pocket," she says with a chuckle, looking thoughtfully at Randy.

"Holy crap, this night has been frickin' gonzo! You guys gotta give me the play by play!"

"And then you and Tank have to tell us about your super CPR moves!" Jules says.

Tank pushes opens The Bat Cave door and looks down the alley again, making sure Andre and Yannis are still gone.

Blair pulls out a joint. "Who's got a lighter I can borrow?" he asks.

"Check your back pocket, bro," Tank replies.

Blair sticks his hand in the back pocket of his jeans and pulls out a pack of matches. "When in sweet hell did you even put these in there, Tanker?" Blair asks with a laugh.

"Alakazam, my dude!" Tank says.

Blair lights up the joint, and I pull the beers out of my backpack and pass them around. Vicky and Jules take road sodas out of their jackets and sip them as they recount their initial run in with Yannis and Dre, and then Tank and Randy fill in the rest of the blanks.

"Hallway party!" Vicky yells, raising her road soda in the air.

"Man, I wish I would've seen you knee Andre in the balls!" I say to Jules.

"And I wish I would've seen Tank headbutt him!" Blair adds.

"Tank's forehead is fucking weaponized!" Randy says with a laugh, exposing his chipped tooth.

"I will feel kinda bad though, if I actually did bust his nose . . ."

My phone starts buzzing like crazy in my pocket. Sometimes it takes a few minutes for it to reconnect with the server after I've been in a dead zone for a while, and now it's come back to digital life. *Finally, Bianca!* I shout in my head, my pulse spiking. I step away from the group and pull out my phone. There's a bunch of notifications on the screen about a post Blair tagged me in on Instagram and yes, *finalement*, a couple texts from Bianca! I tap on her message:

> WTF Marco?? Why would you post
> that video of my dad? It's bad enough
> he almost died and you put it online?
>
> Fuck you immature asshole
>
> And you wonder why I broke up with
> you??? You guys can forget about
> show with FWD . . .

I read Bianca's texts five times in a row, and my pulse spikes up eleven notches. I look over at Blair as he puffs a huge cloud of weed smoke in the air. My neck and shoulders feel tense as hell as I open Instagram and see the video of the paramedics doing CPR on Bianca's Dad as Blair and I play "Shattered" over top of it. As soon as they zap him, it cuts to the original video of me and Blair jamming in the basement.

I sidle up to Blair. "What the *hell*, man? You posted the video of Bianca's Dad?"

"Have to keep the buzz building, man. Especially since we ditched the show tonight. Oh nice! Looks like it's blowing up too!" he says, grabbing my phone, and scrolling through the comments.

"Dude! *Why* would you do that?"

My left eyelid starts fluttering. Blair doesn't reply just keeps scrolling and liking comments. I sigh. "And when the hell did you even have time?"

"I did it when you were talking to your mom before we left. It took like twenty seconds—"

"Bianca is super pissed, Blair! Her dad literally just almost died. She's never going to talk to me again! And she said to forget about the show with Full Watt Drug!"

Blair smiles at me. It's like he doesn't give a shit at all. He looks back down at my phone and likes a few more comments before handing it back to me. "I'm sorry Marco, but that video is too good to not exploit. No one will ever even know it's her dad."

"Except for her, man. Delete that shit now . . ."

*Hard and fast in the centre of the chest. Hard and fast in the centre of the chest.*

I want to scream and tell Blair how incredibly fucking uncool he's being.

He puts a hand on my shoulder. "Don't worry, all right? I'll talk to Johnny and get shit sorted. And if she's still upset about everything, we can take it down. I promise."

I suddenly feel super tired and cold and just wanna go home to bed. It feels like there's a rock in my gut.

"We good?" he asks, and I zombie nod. Blair goes back to the group and wraps his arms around Jules, and she kisses him on the cheek. I could totally use a big hug from Jules right about now. Tank's in the middle of telling them about our CPR moves, so I rejoin the gang in our weird celebration, even though I just want to go home.

"And this crazy bastard recorded the whole thing! Show 'em, Marco!" Tank says.

I side-eye Blair, but he ignores me.

"C'mon, man!" Tank says, so I hand him my phone and they all huddle around and watch the video. They cringe and shudder and laugh and scream and Tank fights back a dry heave.

We finish up our beers and Tank walks over to The Blue Door and pulls out his Nonno's keys. "You sure you grabbed everything, Randy?" he asks.

Randy nods, so Tank locks it up.

"Well, since there's a ton of heat on this place now, I've just come up with the third rule of The Tunnels," Tank says. "You wanna know what it is?"

"Sure."

"The third rule of The Tunnels is lights out till spring, my friends!"

# PART II

# MARCO

"Hey, easy on the beers, Ran! I thought we agreed no more than two before the show."

"I know, I know, but I'm nervous. There's a lot of people out there," Randy says, cracking open his third beer and taking a swig.

"You're gonna kick ass, man!" Blair tells him, as he peeks out at the crowd from the chillout area backstage at The Sala Rossa. "Here have a hit of this," he says, holding out his weed vape but Randy shakes his head. "After the show you can get as drunk as you want, but until then we need you to be on the money!"

"I'm rock steady!" Randy says, holding out his hand. It's shaking like crazy. He laughs anxiously, showing off his newly capped front tooth.

"As soon as we start playing, you'll be fine," I say, grabbing the vape pen from Blair. I hold out my hand and see it's shaking a bit too, so I take a big haul on the vape.

"It's good to be nervous. Adrenaline is the best drug before a show," Blair says.

The Sound Guy comes backstage, and I stash the pen in my pocket. "Y'all ready?" he asks, running a hand through his long hair.

"Ten minutes?" Tank asks, tuning his guitar for the sixth time.

"Make it five. The place is packed. Let's get this party started," Sound Guy says. He walks over to Tank, tells him he's pretty sure his guitar is tuned, and grabs it from him so he can plug it in on stage.

I take one more hoot of the weed and think back to us jamming in the basement every day for the last month. We'd meet behind the gym after school where all the smokers hang, and usually blaze up a joint while walking to my place through the frozen football field, and practice until my mom got home from work at 5:30. And once we got to my place, it was straight to work. No video games, no snacks, no phones – just jamming, and trying to get our set as tight as possible. Which meant playing our songs over and over and over. We agreed we didn't want to leave anything to chance when playing live, no bullshit improvising, no surprises, and no fuckin' mistakes.

So we'd play each song at least three times in a row before moving on to the next one. I swear, I've never worked so hard for anything in my life. And once we all finally got over ourselves (well, mainly me and Tank), and let our instruments and the music start speaking for us, everything instantly clicked, and we wrote some awesome new songs. But that took some time.

At first, Tank was the Big Wall of Resistance. This started pretty much the day after we stopped going to The Tunnels, when he saw the video Blair posted on Instagram. The fact it had clips of Bianca's dad getting CPR'd didn't seem to faze him at all. Instead, he was pissed because Blair had been using his guitar, and that we were playing without him, and that I was singing along, and that it got so many views and sounded really good.

"So what? Now you're the lead guitarist too?" Tank asked, getting up in Blair's face. "You know, The Bad Luck Nickel was around way before you showed up. And to be honest, it was a hell of a lot more fun back then . . ."

But Blair was totally ready for all of Tank's lines of defense. He never gave him any attitude or made him feel cheapened or of less value to the band's sound. And he slowly sold him on the idea that they were both lead guitarists, working with each other and against each other to create a Big Wall of Sound instead of a Big Wall of Resistance. And I mean, once Tank saw Blair play, he couldn't deny what a wicked guitarist he is, which I'm sure also frustrated him, because Tank doesn't like to be second best at anything, it's just not in his genetic makeup.

So then Blair's next move: he brought over an expensive multi-effects pedal, gave it to Tank, and told him to have at it.

"One thing I really like about the way you play guitar is all the trippy buzzing and beeping sounds you always make," Blair said, as he showed Tank how to work the controls. "And this should help kick 'em up a notch." He turned a few knobs and clicked a button on the pedal. "Here, let's try it at this setting with the Big Muff pedal for the heavy parts and you can mess around with it yourself later."

We played "Aurora Borealis", the track I showed Blair the first night we jammed together, and it sounded next level. Tank filled out the groove with a warbling little guitar lick that added a really dark edge. I looked at him during the change after we all stomped on our distortion pedals and he was smiling that big Tank grin, and I think he finally realized at that moment that with two guitars he had so much more freedom, he didn't have to play power chords all the time, and he could be way more creative and atmospheric.

"Yeah man! That's the shit!" Blair said, pointing at Tank. "That sounded heavy. OK, let's try it again! Ready? And a one, two, three, four!"

But for me, I'd say it all really started to click once Bianca and her new friend Isabel started coming to watch us practice. After Blair posted the video of her dad, Bianca wouldn't talk to me at school or reply to my texts at all. It made me feel so goddamn terrible.

That night was one of the craziest of my entire life, and I hated that it had this shadow of crap hovering over it. And I hated that Blair didn't seem to care about my feelings at all.

He spoke to Johnny Temple and got the gig locked down for us, but I honestly didn't give a shit about the show if Bianca was still going to be mad at me. And whenever I told Blair to delete the post he'd just sort of chuckle and make an excuse that it was getting way too many views to take down. It really pissed me off, and after a week I told him I refused to practice until he told her the truth.

"Sorry man, I don't care anymore, the jam space is closed until you talk to her."

Blair made some sort of off-handed comment that being a whiny bitch was no way to get a girl back.

And true, maybe I was being a bit of a sap, but I was secretly dreaming that once Bee saw me on a big stage like The Sala Rossa, she'd want me back. She'd see me the same way she first saw Johnny Temple and realize she'd made a mistake, that we should still be together, and heck to the yes my dude, I'd be ready to forgive her and take her right back into my surprisingly toned arms, forever and ever, amen.

Well, I apparently annoyed Blair enough for him to finally talk to her, because he texted me on Sunday night to say Bianca forgave me and wanted me to invite her to come watch us practice during the week. Then he added that I could kindly put my big boy pants back on, fuck right off, and get ready to practice my ass off every day until the show.

Man, he can really be a dick sometimes. But his text was the mental boost I needed, and on Monday I spotted Bianca by her locker before homeroom, and she surprised me by giving me a smile and basically inviting herself over that night.

"So, we're okay?" I asked, sheepishly.

"Yeah, I should've known it wasn't you who posted it. But I gotta say, I do find it a bit weird that you recorded it in the first place—"

"I know, I know, I just got swept up in the moment, it was super intense, but the vid was never meant to be seen by anyone."

"I know, Blair told me everything, so don't worry. But um . . . he's a bit arrogant, eh?"

"I mean, he's had a very hard life, being rich and famous can be really tough, ya know?" I said with a laugh.

"More than you'd think," Bianca said quietly, as the five-minutes until class chimes rang through the P.A. system. "So, do you, um, think it'd be cool if me and my friend Isabel swung by your place after school today to watch you guys jam? You'll like her, she's super chill, and she really wants to meet Blair, she kind of has a baby crush on him. But don't worry, it's harmless, she has a boyfriend. Plus, we both want to hear full versions of the songs Blair keeps posting on Instagram. They sound dope, Marco!"

"OK, yeah sure, come on over whenever. We usually practice until like 5:30," I said, trying to sound nonchalant.

"All right, see ya later, Marco."

Bianca and Isabel showed up as soon as we got home and joined us in the basement. It felt weird to see Bianca in my house again, but I ain't gonna lie, it also felt really fucking good. I could feel the perma-smile on my face, I could feel pent-up anxiety leaving my body with every note I played on my bass guitar.

We had the lights off and just the old Christmas lights twinkling on the wall behind Randy and his drums, and the girls were silhouettes nodding their heads in the festive glow.

Isabel is a few years older than us and was born in Venezuela. She loves punk rock and post-hardcore, but she's also a big-time jock. She plays basketball for McGill and was actually in an Adidas commercial that aired in South America a few years back. She's also had a crush on Blair since she moved to Canada a few years ago and saw his Tim Horton's Christmas commercial.

Do I even have to mention that she's absolutely gorgeous? She's tall and her skin is this rich caramel colour, and her eyes and hair are so dark brown they're almost black. I think the best word I can use to describe her look is smoldering, even if she usually does just wear oversized sweatshirts and leggings and has her hair tied back in a messy ponytail. But I think another reason why she's so attractive is because she's super earnest and genuine and doesn't have that North American apathy and meh-ness that most girls at Trudeau seem to have. Plus, her accent is really sexy. Her and Bianca make quite the goddamn smoke show together, so having the two of them chillin' in the basement and watching us jam, made all of us want to bring our absolute A games and play a tighter more kickass set than Full Watt Drug.

Tank was immediately smitten with Isabel, thinking they were a perfect match for each other.

"We're both half jock and half rock! It's perfect!" Tank explained.

And I think he turned the whole thing into a sort of competition with Blair in his mind, even if Isabel simply had a fangirl crush on Blair and was currently dating Adamo, the 21-year-old drummer in Full Watt Drug. Tank would talk with her about sports and training and was suddenly extremely interested in Women's Basketball. Isabel had practice like every other day, so they'd only show up in the basement once or twice a week, but it was enough to turn Tank ablaze with competitiveness – against Blair, against Adamo, and even against himself. After jamming, he'd take the effects pedal home and fiddle around with it for hours, trying to get his tone and distortion just right. He began practicing his guitar with the same discipline he put in during football season.

"Every day I get a little better, and a little more confident," he explained. "Hey, d'you wanna come watch Isabel's match on Friday night? I can't go alone, bro."

"You know she has a boyfriend, right?"

"I never see the guy around, so as far as I'm concerned, she's fair game," Tank said.

"Of course you never see him around, he's on tour!"

"Whatever. She digs me."

There was no reasoning with him. He was in playoff mode and totally crazy about her. Full Watt Drug had left on a month-long tour of the east coast and wouldn't be back until a few days before our show at The Sala, so I couldn't help but find it rather interesting that Bianca reappeared in my life as soon as Johnny Temple disappeared from hers, but Jules found the whole thing completely suspect. And man oh man, if Jules disliked Bianca before, she absolutely despises her now, thinking it such a bitch move to bring a six-foot tall Venezuelan model over to flirt with Blair in between songs with her sexy Spanish accent. If Jules and Vicky were downstairs watching us practice and Bianca and Isabel showed up, they would immediately leave, bristling like angry cats, rolling their eyes, and retreating upstairs without even saying hi.

"Don't you think it's odd that she's suddenly coming around again? And showing up with Penelope 'I wanna fuck Blair' Cruz? This is some seriously spiteful shit going on right here, Marco. I know you are desperate to believe she still has feelings for you, but I'm sorry, she's up to something, I can feel it," Jules said. And she wasn't done there. "Like, if she had just shown up once, even twice, I'd think okay, whatever, now she can act all cool and tell her friends she got to hear a sneak preview of your new songs, but she's showing up all the time! I don't get it. Is she just bored because Johnny Temple's on tour? Whatever the hell it is, she's stringing you along, Marco . . . again, you're just too blind to notice."

I was so stoked to have Bianca around again, even if was an after school "group hang", that I didn't listen to Jules. She's super protective of me, just like I am with her, but I told her she was being paranoid, and that the whole thing with Isabel was completely harmless and Blair wasn't interested. Which is true. But I also didn't listen to Jules because I couldn't properly explain to her how the crazy night with Bianca's dad has brought me and her closer together, nor could I tell her that we'd almost kissed one night two weeks ago. But it was obviously on the tip of my tongue at all times since it happened, so I told Tank during halftime at one of Isabel's basketball games.

"Soon enough both of those lovely ladies will have defected from FWD straight to The Nick!" Tank predicted with a creepy laugh. "My Nick! If you know what I'm sayin'? Heyo!"

I couldn't help but creepy laugh with him.

Because we practiced our songs over and over, the girls got to know them pretty fast, so they'd sing along and jump out of their chairs and headbang during the heavy parts in the gleam of the green lava lamp.

There's something about playing music in a dark room that makes it feel so special to me. Even in class, when the teacher turns the lights off to show us a video or a boring powerpoint it somehow makes it just a little more interesting than normal school life under those harsh UV lights. And when we're locked in the groove and all our instruments sound like they've become one and that magical energy is surging between us and I don't have a single thought in my head, it feels like we're tapping into something much deeper than we could ever possibly comprehend. It's trippy and amazing.

So when the girls danced around in the shadowy basement to songs we wrote that actually sounded pretty good, it created this intense sensation in my heart and gut that we were actually *doing* something, ya know?

And I think for me, I'm happiest when I'm hammerin' away on my guitar, feeling the rhythm of the bass in my feet and chest, with Randy keeping perfect time next to me, and Blair and Tank building their dark clouds of melody all around us . . .

I'm snapped back to the present when Johnny Temple and Christophe the lead guitar player come backstage. Bianca is also with them, looking incredible in tight black jeans and a sleeveless white T-shirt with a black bra underneath. Her cheeks are rosy, as if she's just come in from the cold.

"You boys ready?" Johnny asks. "Ya brought quite the crowd. I'm impressed."

Blair slaps five with Johnny and says something in reply but I'm staring straight at Bianca, waiting for her to acknowledge me. *Like why is she not looking at me?* I didn't feel stoned before, but now I feel so faded I can't breathe. She looks up at Johnny and smiles, then looks at Blair and laughs, her crooked teeth so white they're glowing. Blair hands Johnny his vape pen and he takes a hit and hands it to Bianca. She takes a puff too and Johnny puts his arm around her waist. He runs a hand through his perfectly coiffed hair and gives me and Randy a sidelong glance. Isabel comes running backstage and I almost don't recognize her because she has makeup on and her hair's down. She's wearing a leather jacket and what looks like only a long white dress shirt underneath. She's with her boyfriend Adamo, FWD's drummer, who's almost as big as Tank, and has a similar sounding nickname: The Turk. I've never seen him up close before and am surprised at how much he looks like Ringo Starr, if Ringo was super hairy and born in Istanbul.

"I'm so excited!" Isabel says, giving us all kisses on the cheek. She smells like what I imagine expensive perfume smells like. "I just wanted to wish you *mucha suerte!* We will celebrate after!"

"Show time, boys!" Johnny says, and they're all heading back out and still Bianca hasn't looked my way! At the last moment, she turns and gives me a thumbs up.

"Fuck," I say in an exhale.

"You all right?" Randy asks, patting me on the back.

"I just got super stoned and super nervous," I say. I look around stupidly for my bass but remember it's already on the stage, plugged in and ready to go.

"Damn, Isabel looked fine, eh?" Tank asks.

"They both did. And I'm sure there's plenty more hot chicks in the crowd too," Blair says. "All right, guys.

Let's do this! It's just another rehearsal in the basement, okay?"

I nod. I'm so stoned I can't feel my feet. Tank hands me his bottle of water and I chug what's left in it.

"Take a breath, bro," he says.

"I'm trying!" I whisper.

Randy taps everyone on the shoulders with his drumsticks as if we're being knighted, and I just keep nodding my head.

"The Bad Luck Fuckin' Nickel!" Blair or Randy yells. We walk onto the stage and all I see are the bright lights.

# BLAIR

Man, the only reason I contacted Bianca in the first place is because Marco kept bugging me to. She wouldn't reply to his texts after I posted the video of her dad getting zapped by the EMT's and Marco was seriously losing his frickin' mind about it.

So, I told him I'd take care of things with Johnny Temple and I did. Marco wanted to play the gig with Full Watt Drug, Marco wanted to take The Bad Luck Nickel to the next level, and I was here to make those dreams a reality for everyone.

But nope, that wasn't good enough, he also *needed* Bianca to stop being pissed off at him, and he was getting really annoying about it, so about a week after that crazy night in the tunnels, I called her up and told her I was the one who posted the video.

"Yeah, I figured it couldn't have been Marco."

"Why not?"

"He'd never doing anything to upset me, especially not something as cold as that shit. Oh, and he totally ratted you out in the four hundred texts he's sent me this week."

"Fuckin' guy. Well, I'm sorry Bianca, but that video is amazing, and no one even knows it's your dad."

"Except me, you big smart ass."

"Oof, true enough—"

"You're just lucky he's okay."

"He's out of the hospital now, right?"

"Yeah, he's been home for a few days."

"Well, even though you probably think I'm a total dick, I'm glad to hear it."

"You better be, ya fuckin' dick," she said with a little chuckle.

"Oof! This girl is harrrsh," I said with my own chuckle. "OK, so like seriously, what can I do to make it up to you?"

"I dunno. What are you doing tonight?"

"No plans really. Why?"

"Full Watt's opening for some band from Toronto at Foufounes, and me and my friend Isabel are gonna go. Come with, buy us some drinks, and maybe jusssst maybe I'll be over your tactless posting of the video by then . . ."

I didn't really know Bianca at this point. She wasn't in any of my classes, and I basically only knew her as being Marco's ex. I do remember seeing her on the first day of school and thinking she was fine as hell, though. And there was something really alluring about her 'I don't give a fuck' attitude as we talked on the phone –

she was reminding me of girls from back home, and I'd been feeling pretty homesick lately. I couldn't tell if she was randomly flirting with me, but I suddenly wanted to start immediately flirting back, so I told her I'd meet her.

I liked the sound of her voice, it was soft but also kind of raspy, and she's got that Montreal-Italian accent that makes her sound like she could be from New Jersey.

"OK, so I'll tell Johnny to put you on the guest list then."

"It's all good, I know the promoter at Foufs."

"Well, look at you! I forgot Mr. Big Shot's on permanent guest list in this city," she said with a laugh. "Well come find us, we'll be the two hot chicks at the bar. Ciao, bye!"

When I got to the club around 9:30 it was still empty, and Full Watt hadn't started playing yet.

Bianca was at the bar by herself drinking a pint of beer. She spotted me as I came in, and our eyes locked. She gave me a little grin before taking a sip of her pint, and it was like a hit of dopamine. And I remember thinking, *Jesus Christ, this girl is insanely sexy, and holy shit, I think she wants me.*

"Hey you," Bianca said, as I walked up to the bar.

*Yup, she wants me.*

From her tone of voice, I was sure of it. And it was surprising because it literally came out of absolutely fuckin' nowhere. Like I said, all's I was trying to do was a favor for my boy, so he'd stop bitchin' and whinin' and we could start practicing for our gig, but as I got a whiff of her amazing perfume I thought, *Why the fuck not? I'll totally chat Bianca up tonight, and give her the ol' Blair Matthews charm*, because suddenly everything about her was turning me on.

"Hi Bianca," I said with a smile, making sure to make eye contact again. Her lashes were thick and nicely done up with mascara. "Cool hoodie, it looks super comfy," I said, just to give her an easy compliment.

"Aw, thanks, isn't it so cute? It's my teddy bear fleece. Got all dressed to go out and it's fuh-reezing in here."

"Yeah, I gotta say, my first Montreal winter is starting to feel like it's never gonna end. I'm so over it. Where's your friend Isabel?"

"Looks like she's even more fashionably late than you."

"And what about Johnny?"

"Oh, ya know, getting obnoxiously drunk backstage," she said with a dismissive tone that I appreciated. Because fuck that guy. She patted the bar stool next to her and motioned for me to sit down.

"So can I buy you that drink?"

"Oh, I already started you a tab with the bartender," Bianca said with a laugh. "But sure, you can definitely order us another round . . ."

Hanging out just me and Bianca at the bar was great. It was kind of nutso (as Marco and Jules would say), because we just totally 100% absolutely connected. It felt so natural to chat and joke around with her. It honestly felt like we'd known each other for years. There was a carefree ease between us, not to mention a wicked strong attraction. I seriously couldn't believe it. I think I was like giddy or some shit because I have seriously never ever hit it off with someone so fucking easily and truly before. We were cracking jokes back and forth, and at one point she gently put her hand on mine while we were laughing, and I felt like I was going to piss my pants. My heart was mad tingling. My brain went numb.

Like I said, it was crazy. I didn't even have to hit on her because it was all just happening naturally . . .

Now take it easy everyone, calm the fuck down, all right? I'm totally attracted to Jules too. She's so cute and sweet and has that killer smile and killer brain, but shit, Bianca is just like *woah*. I dunno, man. The fact that this person was literally sooo close to me the whole time, like not even a half of a half a degree of separation is insane! And if I had just continued to tell Marco to fuck off and not called her, I most likely would've never had the chance to get to know her. That is seriously fucked up. But even though I was instantly infatuated, Blair Matthews always keeps his cool.

And meeting Bianca at Foufounes ended up being a massive game changer for me, that's for damn sure, because she became my confidante that night, which was the universe's way of letting me know I totally 100% absolutely needed her to be in my life.

Isabel showed up just as Full Watt started playing, and damn, she was also super attractive. Exactly what you think of when you hear the word "model" – tall, skinny but still has some curves, really nice smile, she could easily be in a Hesher video as the hot rocker chick. And I could tell she digged me too, but it didn't matter how hot and Latina she was, because I was already full-on Team Bianca, she was absolutely fucking magnetic.

The bar was barely half full, but Full Watt Drug still put on a hell of a show, they were loud and raw and super tight. Seeing them play lit a fire under my ass to want to play an even better set when we opened for them at the end of March.

After they were done, Johnny and Isabel's boyfriend, Adamo, came over to say hey, and told us to come backstage for drinks. Bianca told Johnny we'd join them as soon as I settled my tab at the bar, but as he walked away, she turned to me and said she had to go home.

"I know it's super lame, but I have a curfew and need to be home by midnight. So, you go ahead, schmooze with the band, and I'll see ya again soon."

In my head, I remember screaming, *No no no, you cannot leave yet!*

"How you gonna get home?"

"Metro."

"You'll never make it in time."

"Then a cab I guess, or an Uber."

"Nah forget that, I'm ready to go, I can't drink more than one and drive, right? So lemme give you a lift."

The lovely lady did not protest too much (she was totally 100% absolutely feeling the vibes between us), and we left without even saying goodbye to anyone. Which, when I thought about later, was pretty fucking telling on the state of Bianca's relationship with Johnny Temple, because he was leaving on tour the next morning and she didn't even say bye.

Oof! So harrrsh! I fuckin' love it.

We walked to the car, and I had to stop myself from putting my arm around her. It was snowing out a little bit and cold as balls.

"Fuck this season, man!"

"Well, you gotta dress warmer, ya goof," Bianca said. "You can't wear Converse. At the very least, you need boots and a good jacket."

"Shit, I figure I've made it to February, winter'll be over soon, right?"

Bianca tilted her head to the sky and laughed loudly. "If only!" she said. "You got a long, cold ass way to go, Blair Matthews."

And I nearly blurted, *Well, maybe we can keep each other warm then*, but instead, I nonchalantly linked my arm with hers as we stepped off the curb and crossed the street to my car. She didn't pull away. It was the first time Bianca had said my name out loud and hearing it in her raspy lilt was melody to my practically frost-bit ears.

We got in the car, and yes, obviously I opened her door first. As the car was warming up, Bianca asked if she could hear the full version of "Shattered", so I plugged my phone in and queued the song up to play once we started moving. But as soon as I turned onto Saint Laurent, I got a phone call. I was sure it would be Jules wondering why the hell I hadn't replied to any of her texts, but it was my dad. He never remembers there's a time difference and always calls super late.

I figured he was just calling to say hi, and I thought Bianca would think it's pretty cool to hear me talking to The Blade, so I answered with him on speaker phone.

"Hey, what's up, Dad? You forget what time it is here?"

His usual Zen energy had gone all frantic frazzle.

"Oh shit Blair, I'm so glad I got a hold of you. Listen, we've got a serious problem with your old *friend*, man. Has she tried to call you?"

"Uh no, she hasn't, but um, can you hold on? I got you on speaker phone, let me—"

"She never got the fuckin' abortion, Blair!"

"Wait, what?"

I heard Bianca quietly gasp and I almost rear-ended the car in front of me. We looked at each other and I could see her quickly putting the puzzle pieces together. She'd no doubt heard every rumor and story going around about me and most likely read the interview in *Distortion*.

I wanted to hang up on my dad, but I couldn't seem to let go of the wheel, my hands were gripping it too tight, so it was too fucking late, Bianca was coming along for this ride.

"What the heck do you mean? I thought that was done with months ago?"

"Same here, but now this bitch looks like she's about ready to pop out a kid any minute now!"

"Don't call her a bitch, Dad—"

"Oh *sorry*, my bad! RAINBOW! The charming young lady with the stupid ass name who says she's about to have your baby, and plans on ruining your fuckin' life! Is that better, Blair?"

"Holy shit. OK, hold on, I'm driving. I need to pull over before I crash the fucking car," I said.

"All right, I'm going to text you the picture she sent me . . ."

I turned down a side street and quickly parked the car against the curb. My phone dinged in the cup holder between me and Bianca. I picked it up and clicked on the text from my dad and didn't even bother trying to hide it.

"Did you get it?" he asked.

"Jesus Christ," I mumbled.

There she was. Rainbow. Super fucking pregnant, but still looking super fucking hot in just a black bra with her baby bump and all those tattoos running up and down her arms.

"Did you get it?" he asked again.

"Yeah," I said in a whisper, glancing at Bianca.

"Haven't spoken to her in six months, and today out of nowhere she sends me that pic with a text that said: *Oops still pregnant!* So I was like, pfft, you gotta be shittin' me. I seriously thought it was a joke, or maybe like some role she got in a movie or something, so I called her up and she went off on me. Did you park the car?"

"Yeah," I muttered.

"OK good, because it gets bad, Blair. She's got a whole line of bullshit cooked up to try and fuck with us."

"What d'you mean?"

He exhaled loudly into the phone and was quiet for a second before he said: "She's trying to say you sexually assaulted her, and that I bribed her to get the abortion, and then conveniently shipped you off to Montreal to keep the whole thing quiet."

"Wait, what?"

"I know right? Like c'mon! What a bunch of bull! If anybody sexually assaulted anyone it was her, she's almost ten years older than you, for fuck's sake! And when I walked in that hotel room it sure as shit didn't feel like a room where someone had just been raped. I mean, she was on top of you when I—"

"Um, yeah, I remember, Dad!" I said, quickly cutting him off. "I don't understand. Why the hell is she doing this?" I asked, close to tears by this point. My whole body was frozen.

"I think she's broke and still on drugs and one of her strung-out friends convinced her this was somehow a smart move. I don't know if she wants to blackmail me or if she's trying to capitalize on this as a way to get some media exposure and help launch her bullshit acting career, I really have no idea, Blair . . . but the optics sure ain't good. I would've never thought in a million years she wouldn't have gone through with the abortion." He let out another loud sigh. "Ah fuck, hold on, my lawyer's calling on the other line, I gotta take this. But listen, if Rainbow tries to call or text you do not fucking answer, d'you hear me?"

"Don't worry, I won't."

"And don't say anything to your mom yet, OK? She'll lose her mind over this. I'll call you in the morning. Drive safe, bub."

As soon as my dad hung up, I started shaking like crazy, trying to fight off the tears. I balled my hands into fists and squeezed them as hard as I could, trying not to scream and start punching the steering wheel until my knuckles were broken and bloody and raw.

And for sure I would have, if Bianca didn't take my hands in her own and gently hold them.

"A baby?" I whispered, afraid to make eye contact with Bianca. She rubbed my hands, and I glanced at her in the dim light of the car. She gave me a look that seemed to say she was all in, that I could trust her, that I could tell her everything, anything, and that she'd support me no matter what, like we could go through all sorts of shit and muck together and come out bright as diamonds on the other side.

A few days later, Bianca would say she thinks we're twin flames, two halves of the same soul, a link even stronger than soul mates. And I mean, how else can you explain our intense immediate connection?

It was the first moment since being in Montreal where I felt I could drop whatever act it was I was putting on. Jules tried to break down my walls a bunch of times, but I would just throw up new ones to block her. I can't really say why it felt so easy to let go with Bianca, and finally just be some high-school kid named Blair, rather than Blair Matthews the bad boy, the child actor, son of The Blade, et cetera, et cetera, but it was effortless, like falling asleep after pulling an all-nighter, or like doing savasana in yoga . . . and just letting it all go in one big ass breath.

"I uh, I can't believe it . . . I mean, yeah Rainbow was pregnant, but she said she was going to get an abortion before I even moved here, and we all agreed it was a good fucking plan, but now she's somehow still pregnant? I'm like totally tripping out here, Bianca, I'm sorry you had to hear all this. I don't know what to say . . . I'm so embarrassed."

"Don't be."

"Like what am I going to do? I can't be a fucking parent—"

"Is it possible the baby isn't yours?"

"That's what my Dad kept saying beforehand, he said there was no way he was going to take her word for it, but she told me that night that I was the first person she'd been with in a long time . . . that she'd been in a really toxic and abusive relationship, and I think the only reason she felt comfortable with me because I was younger, and like more innocent, or not a threat to her or something."

"So do you believe her?"

"I did at the time, and yeah, I really don't think she was lying, but I'm just like super confused why she didn't get the abortion. And why is she accusing me of doing something bad to her? Man, that's not cool at all. I would never," I said, fighting back a sob. Bianca grabbed my hands again. "I mean, I'm sure she's pissed that my dad called her a stripper in the *Distortion* article but, still, that seems like she's going way way too far."

Bianca's phone started to ring in her purse. "It's my mom," she said, not even bothering to unzip it and grab her phone.

"Oh shit," I said, looking at the clock on the dashboard. It was 12:01. "You're late."

"It's okay, my mom's just a psychopath."

"Well, let's get you home fast."

"Are you okay to drive?"

"I think so, yeah. Just being able to talk to someone about this is a huge weight off my shoulders. I'm sorry, you had to hear all this crazy shit, but I'm also like, so thankful you are here with me."

I got back onto Saint-Laurent and drove Bianca home as fast as possible, but we didn't roll up to her house until 12:35.

"So, um, I'm staying at my dad's place next weekend, and don't have to be home by midnight, do you um, maybe want to hang out again?"

"Yes," I replied instantly. "I'd like that."

"Me too," she said with a big smile. It felt like we absolutely had to kiss, but as we started inching closer, her phone started to ring again. "Oh my God!" Bianca said, grabbing her phone out of her purse and clicking it off. Then the porch lights started to flick off and on, on and off. "This woman is insane! I'm sorry, I gotta go. But you're one hell of an interesting guy, Blair Matthews."

She winked at me and quickly got out of the car and ran up the sidewalk to her house.

She called me before I even made it home, and we talked until 4 in the morning, and not a single day went by after that without us being together.

# JULIANNA

Vicky and I are in the crowd at the front of the stage sipping vodka sodas. Blair put us on the VIP List, so we didn't need fake ID's to get in, we just said our names to this scary bald dude with a neck tattoo, and he gave us two free drink tickets and whisked us inside.

After checking our coats, we hit the bar, cashed in all four tickets, and pushed our way through the crowd with a drink in each hand. I was impressed with how little I spilt along the way. Vicky and I were already buzzing, because we drank a few of Ronnie's beers at my house while we were getting ready. It had turned into a fashion show dance party, because Vicky brought over a bunch of clothes, and we created different outfits for each other to try on. We wanted to look hot but badass, and definitely not like we're still in high school. We listened to The Cure's Greatest Hits as we tried on different ensembles, each one a little more revealing than the last.

I put on a lot of makeup, dark eyeliner and lipstick, and I had painted my nails dark purple last night. Vicky was wearing light-blue coloured contacts to match her hair and blood red lipstick. She made me try on a push-up bra of hers, a little halter top, and a super short skirt with fishnets. I didn't like the me I saw in the mirror until Vicky pulled out a container of pre-crushed Ritalin pills and tapped out two lines on my dresser. Afterwards, I saw myself anew. I looked confident and beautiful, almost a woman. It was the first time I ever looked at myself and truly thought, *shit babe, you look sexy!* I stepped into a pair of leather boots, added a little jean jacket and the look was complete.

"Damn girl, your tits look amazing! Almost as good as mine!" Vicky said, as she shook her boobs at me and laughed loudly. She was wearing a turquoise bra that she wanted people to see, so she grabbed a pair of scissors and started cutting up an old Sonic Youth shirt she scored at a vintage store in the Mile End. She snipped off the sleeves and the bottom of the shirt so she could show off her cute stomach. I gave her a jean mini skirt of mine to try on over some sheer black stockings and it fit her perfectly.

"It's Friday, and I'm in love, Julio!" Vicky sang, sipping her beer and dancing around my room. I posed with her for a selfie and checked myself out in the mirror one last time before we headed out to catch the metro. I tilted my head, pouted my lips, and couldn't believe how much I looked like my mom back when she was a teenager. I walked over to my record player and turned off The Cure. It was one of the albums my dad mailed me and Marco after he and Mom split up. For a while, I think he thought he could vicariously stay in our lives through music. As if listening to his favourite bands was somehow equal to him tucking me into my bed at night or cheering for Marco at his soccer game or actually being in our goddamn lives.

*Oooh, I've got some ugly pent-ups coming out right now.*

For that first year after he left, he sent us a couple records each month with notes as to why they were so special to him. The Cure, Pink Floyd, Michael Jackson, Nick Drake, Smashing Pumpkins, Radiohead, Eminem, Björk, Outkast, Aphex Twin, all different styles of music, even Hesher's second album, *Reverse Black Hole*, all on vinyl. Which was cool and all, but so fuckin' lazy and cheap, and at the end of the day, just so hollow, ya know? The music stopped coming in the mail after he had another daughter with another woman and pretty much pressed backspace on us, hoping to delete his trial-and-error family.

Yeah, sure, he still calls every month or so and sends us cash on our birthday and he even took us to Italy with his new family two summers ago, and I like to say I've made peace with everything, but honestly, I'm still so angry with him for ditching us when we all needed him the most. I get it, you and Mom were a toxic fucking nightmare, fine, split up, get a divorce, get a fuckin' annulment for all I care, but don't bail on the two people that idolize you more than anything in the world. That shit is cowardly and straight-up unforgivable. Like, be a grown ass man for God's sake and take responsibility for your actions!

Vicky taps me on the shoulder and snaps me out of my sulk.

"Huh?" I say, feeling like another sniff is in order before the show starts.

"Look, those guys are totally checking us out," she says, sipping her drink and smiling at two guys up against the stage to the right of us. One is a light-skinned black guy with short dreads and a plaid shirt, and the other is a tall white guy with a buzz cut, thick-framed glasses, and a tattoo of a treble clef behind his ear. They're both really cute, but I only have eyes for Blair, even if he has been sort of ignoring me lately. He's been pretty much obsessed with this gig for the last month, and I love his passion and ambition, but I like it more when he shows me a bit of that passion too.

"What about Randy?" I ask. Vicky and Randy've been exclusive ever since that crazy night in The Tunnels.

"I've barely seen him. He's all about The Bad Luck Fuckin' Nickel lately," she says, rolling her blue eyes.

"Like, when was the last time you and Blair had some of that 'quality time' together?"

I laugh. "A couple nights ago, but it's been few and far between, that's for sure."

"So then, there ain't nothin' wrong with getting a little attention from Dreads and Buzz Cut over there, especially when we be looking so fine," she says, flipping her hair at the guys and laughing.

I think back to me and Blair's last bit of 'quality time' together and start to feel less sulky. It was a few nights ago and was really hot. We were at his house studying for a biology test worth like twenty percent of our grade, but as soon as his mom went upstairs to take a shower, I literally pounced on him like a mountain lion, lifting his shirt above his head and covering his raven tattoo in kisses. We had smoked a joint earlier and I was still a little bit stoned and when I'm stoned my sense of touch is super heightened and intense.

So instead of memorizing the different functions of the cerebellum, hypothalamus, and medulla oblongata, I pulled Blair out of his chair and dragged him from the kitchen to the comfy couch in the living room. I think he liked the fact I took charge, and the thrill of his mom possibly catching us. And I swear, I wouldn't have stopped even if she'd come down the stairs, because I was gone, completely lost in the moment, his skin on mine making me wild and feverish and blissed . . .

Things between us went back to normal after the crazy night in The Tunnels, and for the next week or so after, before the band started practicing every day, it almost felt like we were starting all over again. Blair was so sweet with me, and he opened up about his childhood, especially since I kept telling him how much his judo sleeper-hold on Yannis turned me on.

I found out that Blair had never went to an actual school before coming to Trudeau. Instead, teachers came to his house, and even went on tour with him and Hesher when he was younger. He learnt all the fundamental subjects like math and science and grammar, but the courses his new-age L.A. teachers focused on definitely aren't part of Trudeau High's curriculum.

Blair took classes like yoga, art and digital photography, guitar, horticulture, and judo. He also had to read at least one novel a month, keep a vlog about current events, and do something called Morning Pages, which is three pages of stream-of-consciousness writing in a journal every morning as soon as he woke up. Plus, he had a finance class, and acting classes to help him prep for all the TV commercials he was in.

Blair told me he actually hated acting and only did the commercials to make The Blade happy. They were obviously fun at first, but the older he got, the more ugly and fake the industry began to seem to him. He started to notice it once he did the Tim Horton's commercial and got pseudo-famous and was dubbed a "bad boy heartthrob" online. After that, he said his phone never stopped ringing, and he did interviews and photo shoots for teen mags and blogs, and an ad campaign for Red Bull, and some web-only commercials for Levi's that played on YouTube, and then all these other "almost famous" people started coming around as if he suddenly mattered, and Blair said it all felt so phony and egotistical, he decided he needed a break from the whole scene. So he fired his agent without telling his Dad.

"At that point, I just wanted to smoke weed and play guitar," he said. "Or drive The Blade's Mustang up Route 1 and take photos, because I'd just got my license. Or pitch a tent in the woods and read books and hide out and pretend I was Jack Kerouac for a while. But of course, I didn't do any of that, and instead I started doing tons of drugs and acting like a total asshole."

"I'm sure you weren't an asshole," I assured him.

"Oh believe me, I was."

Okay sometimes, *shhhh*, in my most privatest of thoughts, like the ones that are so deep down in there I don't even let myself have them, except when I'm juuuust about to drift off to sleep, sometimes in those fuzzy moments, I might also kinda think that Blair may be a bit of an asshole too, and I wonder if the reason why he's been so sweet to me lately is partly because I haven't brought up The Blade's interview again . . .

"Shoot, I have to pee," Vicky says, pressing on her abdomen. She gazes at me with her fake blue eyes, and I think she looks gorgeous.

"Are you sure you can't hold it? The show's gonna start soon, and I don't wanna lose our spot."

"Do you have to go too?"

"No, I'm good."

"Well, can you stay here and hold our place?" Vicky asks, and then she frowns as she looks over at the left side of the stage. "Hey, how come we don't have backstage access like Lil Miss Bitchy Poo over there?" Vicky says, pointing at Bianca, who's slinking behind the stage with Johnny Temple and some other guy.

"I dunno. Blair said it's because it's Full Watt's show, but I feel like he doesn't really want us back there."

"Fuckin' rock stars," Vicky says. "I heard that Johnny Temple had sex with a bunch of girls when he was on tour."

"From who?"

"My cousin in Boston."

"Do you even have a cousin in Boston?"

"Yeah, her name's Flora. She goes to Yale."

"Isn't Yale in Connecticut?" I ask. I only know this because I recently read *The Bell Jar* by Sylvia Plath, and one of the guys the main character Esther dates, goes to Yale.

"Shit! I mean Harvard. She's going to law school there. She saw Full Watt Drug play at some pub in town and she told me Johnny left with some dumb blonde undergrad chick."

"Are you shittin' me?"

"Maybe. But it sounds like a pretty good rumor to start spreading, doesn't it?" Vicky smiles at me and laughs loudly. "Oh hey look, there's a bathroom right over there. See it? I'm gonna go fast fast. Save our spots, okay?"

"Fine, but hurry!"

Usually, I would say: *Hell to the no, you ain't leaving me alone!* but I want to have a quick sniff, and I don't want Vicky to see it.

*Shhhh*, I have my own little stash that I bought off her brother, and she doesn't know about it, okay? Vicky kisses me on the cheek and pushes her way through the crowd towards the bathroom by the side of the stage.

I look around and see Dreads and Buzz Cut leering at me, so I ignore them. It seems like every person in the crowd has at least one visible tattoo or piercing, but still, everyone seems kinda bland and boring. They're all laughing, sipping beer in red plastic cups, looking at their phones, and taking selfies as they wait for the show to start.

I imagine something terrible happening, like a huge electrical fire, or some crazy dude coming in with a gun and shooting the place up. I remember all the stairs it took to get up here and I start to freak out, gazing around for the closest emergency exit. I grab my phone out of my pocket and start to text Blair a mushy note so I'll distract myself and stop panicking, but then I see Isabel also making her way backstage. She's wearing high heels and looks about seven feet tall as she gracefully disappears behind the wall. I imagine her running up to Blair and kissing him and telling him all the things I want to be telling him right now. *Such bullshit!* I stare at my phone and wonder if it looks like I have a double chin when I look down at it, so I put it away, grab one of my drinks off the stage and take a sip, trying to figure out how I can nonchalantly sniff my Rit.

All the gear on stage looks ugly to me. Cords snake everywhere along the floor and are taped down with hunks of duct tape. The drums look cold and metallic and say FWD in a lame font on the bass drum. The overhead lights are off and the amps flash tiny red lights directly into my eyes.

I have my stash in an empty lip balm container. I pull it out of the inside pocket of my jean jacket and carefully twist off the lid. I've been growing my nails lately, so I can scoop a bit onto my baby fingernail and sniff it that way. I crouch down into a squat right up against the stage, use my hair and jean jacket as a shield, scoop a big pile onto my nail and fire it back. *Oooh!* I spin the lid back on the container, slip it in my pocket, wipe my nose, and quickly stand up. I grab my vodka and take a tiny sip. I tilt my head, pout my lips, and grin at the two guys. I look back at the gear on the stage and now it looks like it does at home in the basement, red light reflecting off Tank and Marco's guitars instead of green. It's suddenly beautiful. I spin around to check out the crowd behind me and everyone looks unique and exciting and attractive. I smile at a girl with pink hair and black lipstick and tell her I love her hair and she says she digs my boots.

They've been playing old school hip-hop since we got here, which seems a weird choice for the crowd at a rock show, but everyone seems to know the lyrics. I see Vicky dancing her way through the growing mob of people and mouthing the words to the song.

"Oh my God, I love Wu-Tang!" Vicky says, as she makes it back to the front of the stage. "And I just figured out the perfect way to move through a crowd is to dance through it! Just slide and step, just dance and groove! It's brilliant!" Vicky shouts, grabbing one of her drinks off the stage. She rubs at her nose and sniffs. Looks like she may have had a bit of the Rit herself.

I'm about to ask her, but the hip-hop ends and the lights begin to fade up. The audience cheers as the guys walk out onto the stage. Randy, Blair, Marco, then Tank. Marco looks super tense. His shoulders are raised and stiff, and he's walking like he's got a drumstick up his butt, but everyone else seems fine. Blair confidently strolls to the front of the stage. He looks great. He's wearing a black V-neck tee, black jeans, and red Converse.

He grabs the mic. "Hi. How's everyone doing tonight?"

The crowd claps, whistles, screams.

"We love you, BLAIR!" a group of girls yell behind me.

"Thanks so much for coming out tonight! We're The Bad Luck Nickel!" Blair says. He reaches into his pocket, pulls out a handful of nickels with black X's on them, and tosses them into the crowd. There's a bit of a scuffle as people fight for the coins, and the yelly chicks push their way to the front. I hold on to my vodkas for dear life, not wanting to lose a precious drop, and me and Vicky are forced back from the stage. The yelly chicks have usurped our spots!

I want to be angry, like, that's *my* fuckin' boyfriend up there, you dumbass blonde bitches! But I catch a view of Marco standing on the stage like a zombie that's just been shot in the head. Tank and Blair are strapping on their guitars, but Marco is just kind of wavering back and forth on his heels, with a stunned look in his eyes.

"Oh shit, look at Marco," I say to Vicky.

"What's the matter with him?"

"I dunno."

"He looks like a deer in headlights."

"He's probably just nervous and stoned, but we gotta snap him out of it fast!"

Marco used to get really bad stage fright when he was a kid, and I remember that exact same look on his face when we were ten years old. He was playing one of the three wise men during a Christmas pageant at school, and he totally zombied out, staring directly into the spotlight for almost a full minute, until he was pulled off the stage by my friend Aimee, who was dressed like an elf or an angel or a reindeer or baby Jesus, I can't remember.

"All right, Vick, on the count of three, let's scream, we love you, Marco! Kay?"

She nods and we count to three and both shout: "WE LOVE YOU, MARCO!!"

I've never been more proud of Vicky's loudness in all of my life, because I actually see Marco snap out of his trance. He shakes his head as if waking from a shitty dream he's been stuck in for sixteen years. He looks at the crowd and smiles, straps on his guitar, fiddles around with a few knobs on his amp, and nods to Blair.

"This one's called 'Three Minutes Hate'," Blair says.

Randy taps his sticks together four times and the show begins.

# MARCO

My heart is going so nutso I can't think straight. I try to swallow but I've got the worst cottonmouth ever. It's super hot on stage and I'm blinded by the spotlights. I'm trying to breathe in through the nose and out through the mouth, but I can't even seem to do that right.

Blair starts talking to the crowd and I'm trying to motion to Randy that I can't do it, I can't play. *I'm circling the drain, bro! The gig is cancelled. I'm dead. We're done. I'm gone.*

The crowd screams loudly and out of the corner of my eye I see Tank strapping on his guitar. He looks like a giant on stage, a seriously imposing presence in his army green T-shirt and all black Expos cap, that he's pulled down low to shield his eyes. He thinks it'll make him look more mysterious.

I'm starting to feel tingly. My fingers are like lobster claws. I feel clammy and sweaty. *Why the fuck did I hit that weed pen so many times? I'm such an idiot. That shit is too strong. Too good. I hate it!*

The lights are so harsh they're making me nauseous. I'm gonna fuckin' puke all over the stage and then kill myself...

Outside of all the murk in my brain, I hear: *We LOVE you, Marco!*

I shiver. *Oh my God! Bianca and Isabel just screamed my name! I cannot fuckin' believe it!* And the memory of being outside of Bianca's dad's apartment building and almost kissing her, hits me like a punch in the face!

Her dad had invited me and Tank over for dinner to thank us for helping him, but Tank bailed on purpose, so it was just me and Bee. And as soon as I walked into his apartment it was like I stepped into a Bizarro version of reality, one in which Bianca still looked at me the way she used to. Her eyes hazy with affection. She acted like we were a couple, touching my arm from across the table, and calling me babe, as we joked around with her dad, who swears like a trucker and is a bit of a racist, but besides that seems like a good man, he's just old school ignorant. He let us drink red wine and served some amazing espresso panna cotta for dessert that he bought for Bianca at the Italian patisserie on Jean Talon.

Bianca's dad said he was seeing the world through a whole new pair of eyes now, and he vowed to take better care of his health, not just for Bianca but for himself too. The whole evening was so comfortable and relaxed, and I could tell her dad was super grateful to me and Tank.

"Ya know, you kids really stepped up to the plate that night," he said, refilling my wine glass. "You got balls and I respect that. Some of these punk kids I see out there on the metro or on the street, they'da probably just fuckin' kept walking, but not you, Marco! So cheers to you, bud!"

And then when Bianca walked me out, I went in for the kiss, and I could tell she wanted it, but she turned her head at the last second and I gave her an awkward smooch on the ear.

"That's not a good idea."

"Oh, I think it is!" I whispered, but she took a step back, her cheeks flushed.

"You're a good guy, Marco, and I'm sorry if I hurt you," she said, while pulling at the arms of her sweater. "Listen, um, I gotta get back upstairs, I'm freezing, but thanks for coming. My Dad thinks you're super hilarious. I'll see you tomorrow, okay? Isabel and I will come watch you guys practice after school."

*I get it, it's complicated, you're still with that douche Johnny, but tonight I will win you back, Bianca!*

The ugly weed cloud that's been terrorizing my mind is quickly dissipating, like fog burning off into the atmosphere. I can feel my panicky and paranoid funk shifting into something more chill. My heart is still popping away, but it doesn't feel like I'm going to die anymore.

*It's just another rehearsal in the basement,* I hear Blair say.

I exhale deeply, gaze out into the crowd and smile. I take what feels like my first real breath in minutes. I feel so emotional I want to cry. *This is all for you, Bianca! This is all because of you!* It totally makes sense now why she was ignoring me backstage, it's 'cause she still has feelings for me and doesn't want Johnny Temple to catch our vibe!

I grab my guitar, turn the treble up a touch, nod to Blair that I'm ready, and Randy counts us in for our intro song "Three Minutes Hate".

We start the set with a bang, immediately creating a wall of sound, locking into a heavy minute-long riff without any lyrics. Tank and Blair start jumping around, encouraging the crowd to get into it, but I'm still catching my stage legs and don't want to screw up, so I stand by the microphone and bob my head to the beat. We're playing a bit faster than usual but it still sounds really fucking good. We hit the change, a four-bar melodic interlude, where Blair and I scream: *"War is Peace! Freedom is Slavery! Ignorance is Strength!"* and then Randy pops the snare once and we kick in to overdrive and unleash everything we have in us for another two minutes, rocking out hard. The lights above us flash and my vision strobes, broken into bright fragments. Tank and Blair look like they're thrashing around, and Randy's arms are swinging like he's an octopus . . . and then one, two, *stop* on a dime.

Song done.

It really is only about three minutes long.

"Thank you," Blair says, as the lights go up and the crowd starts screaming like animals.

"Fuckin' A!" I hear someone yell.

"Goddamn, this is a good looking crowd!" Blair shouts after a bunch of girls howl his name.

The spotlights above us turn green. It feels like being at home in the basement with our lava lamp. *Okay, okay, I'm feeling better now, I'm ready to lock into our set and kill it.*

"Y'all warmed up?" Blair asks the audience. "If not, grab a friend and start dancing. This next song is called 'Aurora Borealis.'"

A smoke machine puffs on in the far corner of the stage and Blair looks back at me for a second. I start this one, playing the intro before the rest of the guys join in. My fingers move along the frets and I feel my mind drifting to that happy "non-place", where all thoughts and fears are void and gone, and I'm just a dude playing a guitar, the rumble of the bass gently humming in my feet and chest.

# JULIANNA

The guys begin their set with "Three Minutes Hate" and the crowd near the front of the stage instantly turns into a mosh pit. Vicky and I are about to get swept into it when Dreads and Buzz Cut jump in front of us and start shoving people away. We still have drinks in both hands and are trying not to spill them, but we also don't want to get pushed too far back from the stage.

They hit the quieter part of the song, and the pit momentarily subsides. I look at Vicky and quickly chug one of my vodkas and then the other. Vicky follows suit and we toss our plastic cups on the ground, just in time to shout the lyrics: *"War is Peace! Freedom is Slavery! Ignorance is Strength!"*

The song kicks back in fast and heavy and we push Dreads and Buzz Cut into the pit and jump in behind them. I scream as I slam against Dreads and grab his bicep. It's surprisingly firm. He gently shoves me towards Buzz Cut, who catches me by the shoulders and flings me at Vicky. We smash into each other and jump around, laughing hysterically. Vicky's so small she's getting tossed around like a child, but she's loving it. I notice that Dreads and Buzz Cut are watching out for us, keeping the biggest bodies away when they get too close. Vicky knocks into some chubby dude who already has his shirt off, and she falls to the floor, but Buzz Cut swiftly scoops her up, wrapping his arm around her waist.

The song ends and everyone in the crowd goes nutso! Clapping, whooping, cheering, screaming!

"Oh my God, that was fun!" Vicky says. I hug her and we grin at our mosh pit cuties. "Thanks, guys!" she says. "I'm Flora and this is Sylvie," she tells them, winking at me.

Dreads and Buzz Cut tell us their names, but I can't hear them over the yelly chicks who are once again declaring their love for my boyfriend. Dreads and Buzz are much older up close, probably in their mid-twenties. Can they tell we're only sixteen?

"Hey, how'd you guys know the words to the song?" Buzz Cut asks.

"The bassist is her younger brother," Vicky says.

"Oh yeah? That's cool. These guys are still only in high school, eh?" Buzz Cut asks me.

I nod and smile.

"Well, that first song was tight," Dreads says. "The guitars sounded great."

I wonder how many people noticed that the lyrics for "Three Minutes Hate" come from the book *1984* and I wonder if they even care. Blair said he was going to say something about Big Brother and the Thought

Police and make a connection with the novel and our current fucked up dystopian society, but the crowd is making so much noise, he just tells them they're hot, and Marco starts up the bass line for "Aurora". I can already see sweat dripping down Blair's face.

"You gonna protect us?" Vicky asks our mosh pit cuties with a playful grin. Dreads and Buzz cross their arms in front of them and nod their heads to Marco's bass.

"We got you," Dreads says. Randy comes in with the beat and the biggest dudes in the pit make scary faces and air drum, waiting for the guitars to start.

I think this song is their most complex and math-rocky, and I love how all their instruments seem to fit like pieces of a puzzle. When Blair and Tank join in, their guitars create this off-time rhythm that me and Vicky call The Waltz, because it sounds a bit old timey and makes you want to dance. The crowd is getting into it, swaying back and forth as Blair shouts: *"I've seen the best minds of my generation destroyed!"* and then Randy hits the crash cymbal and they blast into the heavy part and the mosh pit explodes with action.

There's a lot more people in the pit now, and it doesn't look as friendly and fun as it did during the first song. Buzz Cut shakes his head and mouths the words: "Fuck that noise!" and he grabs my arm at the elbow, and we all push our way to the left of the stage and away from the mosh pit.

"Too many freaks in there! I'd rather enjoy the show than get punched in the face!" Buzz shouts in my ear.

I nod and smile at him, watching the green lights reflect off his glasses. It's too loud to say anything back, so I sidle up to Vicky and watch Blair do his thing on stage. I pull out my phone and snap a couple photos of him. His eyes are closed, and I can tell he's in the zone. They all look like they're in the zone now, as Marco and Randy keep up the beat, and Tank and Blair create a bunch of feedback and distortion. They're sounding even better than they do in the basement. Their energy is infectious, and the crowd is totally loving it.

Buzz Cut pulls a flask from the waist of his jeans, sips it, and hands it to me. "Whisky!" he hollers. I take a nip and pass it to Vicky with a shudder. It warms my chest and then my entire body. Vicky slugs it and passes it on to Dreads.

I want to talk to Vicky but it's too noisy for her to hear me, so I start a conversation with her in my head.

"Hey, I hope these guys don't think we're leading them on, Vick."

"Don't worry about it, Julio. It's just concert etiquette. What happens on the dance floor stays on the dance floor."

"Are you sure? Didn't you once tell me that the best flirting happens on a dance floor?"

"Sure, but it doesn't have to be serious. We're just having fun! And so are they! And hopefully they'll buy us drinks afterwards."

"They look a lot older than us."

"Ahh, they're harmless hipsters. Probably graphic designers or bartenders, and I bet they both have girlfriends too."

"They're super fit and cute, eh?"

"Damn straight. Ya know, we could make out with them a little if you want—"

"No way, Vick! Look at our dudes up there! Every chick in this place is fawning over them!"

I turn to check out the audience and see thirty cell phones raised in the air recording everything, and now there's two people crowd surfing above the mosh pit, and the yelly chicks are all gazing up at Blair with "fuck-me" eyes and puckering their bright red lips at him.

The flask comes around again and I take another little swig and cringe. I've never drank whisky before. It tastes like moldy bread and Lysol. But I do like the sensation of warmth and lightness it's creating in my entire being. It feels like I could just close my eyes and float away. The smoke machine has made a thick fog on the stage and with the flashing green lights it actually kinda looks like the Aurora Borealis. I drift off to the music, bobbing my head up and down to the beat. The crowd seems to be moving as one, lost in the groove of the band. Blair looks like he's on a different plane of existence, a human extension of the music. The guys play "Delusional" next and "Glazed" and then "This Eclipse" and I am feeling perfectly drunk from the whisky and vodka, when Vicky pinches my arm hard and points to the mosh pit, her fake blue eyes trembling.

I don't know what she's pointing at, because all I see is a mass of bodies jumping around as one, but then I see a tall guy with dark curly hair, rudely shoving people as he makes his way through the crowd.

It's Yannis.

A lot of kids at school were upset that the show wasn't All Ages, but Blair thought it was perfect. He wanted people to miss out on it to create even more hype for their next gig at Le Ritz in April. And because the show was 18 and over, we didn't think we'd have to worry about Yannis or Andre showing up and causing shit, but we should've known better.

They'd started trolling The Bad Luck Nickel's Instagram page with a fake account a few weeks ago, leaving dumb comments like: This band licks ballz and Blair Matthews sucks his dad's blade. I thought it would piss Blair off, but he didn't seem to care at all, and said he's used to people saying shitty things about him on the internet, and whether positive or negative it's still buzz for the band.

Then Yannis started to harass Marco via text. Writing things like:

> I fucked Bianca last night. So did Blair.
> Want pics? LOL

And:

> A nose for a nose, muthafucka. Watch
> yer backs bitches,,,

even though we found out that Tank didn't actually break Andre's nose. And then Yannis kept asking Marco to give him the key to The Blue Door.

> I want the key.
> I WANT the key.

Gimme the fucking key asshole.
Donne-moi la clé tabarnak.

But Marco kept replying:

Don't know what you're talking about
dude.

So then he sent Marco a picture of a power drill and we were like wtf, are they going to try and drill through the lock on The Blue Door?

"It'll never work! It's a deadbolt," Tank said.

And then a day or two later, Yannis sent a photo not of The Blue Door but instead of The Bat Cave Door, all bent up and barely hanging from its hinges into the snowy alley and covered in an ugly swirl of Andre's graffiti. And he wrote:

Looks like its time for a brand new
door with a brand new lock lol lol lol

Once they realized they couldn't get through The Blue Door, they made sure no one would be able to get back down there, which was an even nastier plan. We were all pretty bummed about it, because The Tunnels is the coolest hangout spot ever, and Blair and I had some super sexy make-out sessions down there . . .

I take a deep breath and gaze at Blair up on stage looking like a total star, his eyes closed, hair stuck to his forehead, and veins popping out of his forearms. Yannis is moving closer to the front, and I quickly scan the crowd, knowing Andre must be around somewhere, but if he is he's too short to see. Yannis looks determined, his eyes dead set on the stage, as he pushes people out of his way. I catch a glimpse of a plastic bottle of Coke or something in his hand.

"What the hell's he doing here?" I shout to Vicky, who's still pinching my arm.

The song ends and the audience whoops and cheers.

"What should we do?" I ask.

Vicky stands on her tiptoes and yells something in Dreads' ear, and then points at Yannis.

Dreads suddenly looks really upset. "Are you fuckin' serious? That guy there?" Dreads asks Vicky, also pointing at Yannis.

Vicky nods and cry blinks at him. "Please make him leave!" she says.

Dreads goes up to Buzz Cut and starts yelling in his ear and motioning towards Yannis.

"What'd you say to him?" I ask Vicky.

"This next song's called 'Shattered'!" Blair says from the stage.

The crowd applauds and I see Yannis unscrew the cap on the bottle he's holding and take a sip. It's Diet Coke. Randy taps his sticks twice and the song begins. Dreads puts his hand on Vicky's shoulder and shouts: "Stay here!" and he and Buzz Cut push their way through the crowd towards Yannis.

"What'd you say!?" I yell.

"I told him Yannis tried to rape me."

"Whaaaa? Are you for real!?"

Vicky shrugs. It's too loud to talk. "I had to say something!" she mouths. I can feel Randy's bass drum pounding hard in my chest. I peer through the crowd trying to keep an eye on Yannis. Dreads and Buzz are nearly halfway there. It's tough to see in between all the people but it looks like Yannis is holding a bunch of small white rocks or marbles in the hand not holding the Diet Coke.

"*It was a night of shattered glass! Another night of shattered glass!*" Blair and Marco sing.

*What the heck, is he gonna throw rocks at them?* I can no longer see his face, but through the mass of bodies I can still see his hands, and holy shit, wait a second, those aren't rocks, they're Mentos! Oh my God, he's gonna drop the Mentos in the Diet Coke and create a soda explosion!

We did this as an experiment in Grade 10 Chemistry class. I can't remember the science behind it, but it has something to do with a carbon dioxide reaction and bubbles and I don't know what else. All I know is it creates an insanely huge eruption. I try to get Vicky to see what I see and shout: "Diet Coke and Mentos!" but she can't understand me over the music.

*"It ain't the first and it ain't the last, another night of shattered glass!"* Blair screams into the microphone.

Dreads and Buzz Cut are two steps from Yannis, and just as he's dropping the Mentos into the bottle, Dreads karate chops it out of his hands and Buzz Cut grabs him. Still, the Diet Coke shoots up into the air above the mosh pit like an atomic bomb. The crowd gasps in surprise, and out of the corner of my eye I see a second geyser erupt close to us from the left of the stage and then a third one gushing ten feet high in the air from the right. These two are in perfect sync and aimed directly at Blair.

He's rocking out on his guitar and his eyes are still closed, and I watch in horror as the geyser from the right blasts him directly in the face.

*Ker-plash!*

Thank God the stream from the left doesn't quite reach him, but it splashes on the stage by his feet and all over his pedal board.

Blair's eyes dart open and I see fear and rage and disbelief flit across his face. The guys have stopped playing, and Blair rips the patch cord out of his guitar. The audience has gone silent, frozen. A collective open-mouthed hush. I quickly glance to the left of me and see a short dude in a hoodie trying to push his way out of the crowd towards the bar. It's gotta be Andre. I look up at Blair, his hair and face dripping with foamy Diet Coke. He runs a hand through his hair, flicks soda froth from his hand, takes one super deep meditative breath, and then gazes out at the hushed crowd, and smiles his shit-eating Tim Hortons holiday grin. It seems like he wants to say something, but instead he starts clapping his hands above his head. He looks back at Marco and Tank who are standing in shock behind him, and they start to clap with him.

Blair sings: "*It was a night of soda splash! It was a night of soda splash! It was the first and I hope the last, a crazy night of soda splash!* C'mon, everyone! Sing it with me!"

And the audience obeys. Clapping their hands with the band and singing along at the top of their lungs as if they've known the song for years. "*It was a night of soda splash! It was a night of soda splash!*" Marco and Randy start up the beat again in the background, as I watch two bouncers drag Yannis and Dreads through the emergency exit. I can't see very clearly but it looks like Yannis is grinning like the Joker. Another security guard has his arms around Buzz Cut and shoves him out the exit too.

Tank starts playing a little melody above the singing, as Blair shouts: "All right y'all, one more time!"

Everyone continues to chant the words, and they cheer and whistle and clap, as Blair stands at the edge of the stage and stares at the crowd in bold defiance.

And I, just like everyone else in the room, am in absolute fucking awe of him.

# BLAIR

Shit man, if Bianca hadn't been up at the front of the stage when I got Diet Coke'd, I don't think I would've been able to keep it together. I mean, seriously, like what in the actual fuck? Diet Coke and Mentos? Jesus Christ. But thankfully I caught her gaze, and just the briefest moment of eye contact with her, allowed me to remain calm and finish the show on top.

There was worry and fear in her big brown eyes, but also a flicker of confidence that I could pull through this goddamn nightmare of a situation. Bianca had helped me through so much over the last month, this was just one more bullshit hurdle of people trying to bring me down, and I sure as fuck wasn't going to let anyone ruin this night.

So I ran my hand through the soda in my hair and flicked it on the stage as if it was my own sweat, took a cleansing breath, and I smiled at Bianca. She winked at me and grinned back, and I started clapping my hands above my head, and suddenly the revised lyrics just rushed out of me as if they'd been there the whole time. And like, as soon as I sang them into the mic, even *I* was impressed with myself, they were honestly too fucking good. The crowd immediately started singing along with me, and I stood at the lip of the stage, looked out at the crowd, but mostly just hyper focused in on Bianca, as if she was the only person in the world.

Bianca was the one who'd told me to not listen to my dad, and to get ahead of things and call Rainbow immediately to find out what the hell was going on and why she was laying this awful accusation on me.

So the day after she and I met at Foufs and stayed up talking on the phone all night, I went to her house, schmoozed it up with her mom a bit, apologized profusely for getting her home late, and fed her some bullshit line about still being very hesitant about driving in the snow, and I was able to charm her just enough for her to like me, and it probably didn't hurt that she was a Hesher fan from way back when.

She wouldn't let me and Bianca go up to her room alone, but there was a cozy TV room tucked in the far corner of the house which at least gave us a bit of privacy, and so we called Rainbow up and Bianca was like my Cyrano de Bergerac, helping me to not say the wrong thing to piss Rainbow off, because I was totally raging about the whole thing.

"So listen, you need to be as chill as possible, all right? I know you're super upset, but you absolutely have to make her feel comfortable and not threatened in any way whatsoever, because if you do, boom, that's it,

Blair, she posts the pic on her social or goes to the media and tells her lies. Yes, she's accusing you of something terrible, but you gotta keep your emotions in check. I know we basically just met, but do you trust me?"

"Yeah, I do actually."

"OK, then just tell her everything I say to you, all right?"

The whole conversation was almost like a dream. I was the mouthpiece repeating back everything Bianca said, but she was whispering so softly in my ear, the sensation of her warm minty breath had me off on an ASMR cloud – I was tingling from my scalp all the way down the small of my back. It allowed me to remain perfectly detached as I spoke with Rainbow for the first time in half a year.

After telling Rainbow that my dad had sent me her belly bump pic, Bianca had me asking her questions about her body, the pregnancy, how she was feeling, how many weeks along she was, if she knew the gender, if she planned on breastfeeding, all these things I basically would have never thought or even knew to ask. Just giving Rainbow some room to talk and feel comfortable, and then she whispered in my ear to ask Rainbow if she was certain the baby was mine.

"You are the only person I've slept with in the last year, Blair, so yes, you are the father."

This raw certainty threw me off for a second, and my entire body went all tense, but Bianca gently breathed: "It's OK, Blair" and then she kissed my earlobe, well, her bottom lip brushed up against it, but ya know, basically the same thing, and it was weirdly even more meaningful because it was subtle and accidental but felt so goddamn natural.

Bottom line, it helped me immediately chill the fuck out, and made me excited for a guaranteed make-out session later.

"OK, ya know, I just wanted to double check to be sure, but I totally believe you," Bianca whispered, and I echoed.

"Good. Because I would never lie to you Blair."

Man, after she said this I looked at Bianca, and clenched my fists, like *Oh yeah? You wouldn't lie. Then what the fuck's all this about me sexually assaulting you?* But Bianca took my hands in her own, looked me square in the eyes and whispered, "Calm the fuck down, bro" and then told me to say: "Well, I'm really glad to hear that, Rainbow. So um, do you think it'd be all right for me to ask you a few questions then?"

"Yeah, sure. Shoot."

"OK well um, the last time I saw you, you seemed dead set on getting an abortion. So I was wondering how come you didn't go through with it?"

*And why the fuck you didn't tell me . . .*

Rainbow sighed and cleared her throat. "To be honest, it was pretty much a night before sort of decision. I had the procedure all set up at Planned Parenthood, and the whole week leading up to it, I didn't do any blow at all. I was still taking Xanax and drinking a bunch, but once I found out I was pregnant I didn't do a single line of coke, and I started to ask myself why? Like, if I was just gonna get rid of the baby, what'd it matter? And then I started thinking that maybe I actually *didn't* want to get rid of the baby, because it'd like, force me to get clean, force me to change my habits before they got worse, ya know? Because I was at a point where I could only see them getting worse. Also – and this one is purely selfish – if I did have the baby I'd be connected with a famous family forever. So like, I'd have that much more of a chance to be taken seriously as an actress. And I mean, it wasn't about you even being a part of this, it was just the connection. Obviously, I planned on telling you, but you were gone to Canada, and then I got a small role on Murder Ink for a three-episode arc and time just went by so fast and suddenly I was fat and the baby was moving around and shit was getting real and I was getting scared . . ."

"OK, wow, that's a lot to process, but I'm glad I know . . ." I paused for a few seconds before repeating the rest of what Bianca whispered. "So like, when my dad called he said something that I didn't really understand. He said you were accusing me of raping you that night? Is that true?"

I started to hold my breath, figuring it would take Rainbow a second to reply, but she launched right into it.

"Look, your father called me a stripper in *Distortion* and then a cokehead in his *Needle Drop* interview. No, he didn't use my name, but the internet immediately figured it out. So I told him I was going to sue him for defamation and also spin it right back on him and his family, because how dare he?"

"Oh so then you'll defame my name just to get back at my Dad? What the fuck is wrong with your head, girl?"

Bianca had her thumb jammed on the mute button before I'd even opened my mouth. She shook her head at me with a severe look on her face. "Don't you fuck this up, Blair. Let's make it through this call *s'il vous* fucking *plaît*—"

"Yello? You still there?" Rainbow asked, and Bianca clicked the phone off mute.

"Yeah, yeah, I'm here, sorry, service is a bit choppy. But you're absolutely right, when I read the *Distortion* article, I wondered why the heck he said that about you," I echoed through gritted teeth.

"It just shows me how little he actually cares about people, he's as fake as everyone else, and so far up his own ass he doesn't even think twice before calling someone a whore, like seriously, fuck him. I'm trying to start an acting career and have a family. Yes, I followed bands around on tour, but I ain't no dumb groupie and I ain't no fucking slut."

"Yeah, I agree, Rainbow—"

"So how d'you think it's gonna look when everyone finds out the druggy prostitute is pregnant with Blair Matthews' baby?"

"What do you want from him then?" Bianca whispered. I was barely able to whisper it back to Rainbow.

"I want him to officially redact his statement, and apologize to me on all his social media, otherwise I'm coming for him, and I'm sorry, but at this point, I'll be coming at him through you."

Bianca could tell I was going to lose it for real this time, and she quickly hung up.

But shit man, that initial conversation paved the way for more conversations, and towards stopping Rainbow from being a psycho and posting bullshit lies about me on the internet, and it was all because of Bianca.

I'm telling you, she's absolutely amazing.

Incredible.

Brilliant.

Beautiful.

Magnetic.

Enchanting.

Just fucking so so hot, man. Mind, body, soul.

# MARCO

"I coulda been fuckin' electrocuted!" Blair shouts. He's pacing the length of the backstage and biting his thumbnail. "And my pedals got drenched! Who did it? It was those assholes from The Tunnels, wasn't it?"

Tank shakes his head. "I dunno, Blair."

But we know. It had to be Yannis and Andre.

I didn't see it until the last second, and as it was happening I had no idea what I was even seeing flying through the air. It wasn't until it splashed all over him that I realized it was liquid. In the moment, I think I thought it was some kind of weird smoke machine effect or something.

"Some of those pedals are my dad's and are impossible to replace! We need to find those fuckin' pricks and make them pay! They think they can fuck with me?" Blair yells, punching his fist into the palm of his hand.

Johnny Temple comes rushing backstage with a huge smile on his face. "That was un-fuckin-believable, Blair!" he says. "How the hell'd you keep your cool, man?"

Blair shrugs his shoulders at Johnny. "I dunno, but I am fuckin' livid right now!" he says. He grabs a beer off the table, twists off the cap, and takes a big swig. "I guess I must've been channeling my dad. He never lets anything get to him on stage. I've seen him get spit on, hit in the head with a steel-toe boot, and once some chick threw a dirty tampon at him. It hit him right in the face, but he just powered through and kept on playing . . ."

"The show must go on, eh? Well dude, you're a fuckin' legend!" Johnny says with a laugh. "Hey, you got that weed pen on ya?" he asks. Blair reaches into his pocket and hands it to him. Johnny takes a big hit and blows a cloud of vapour in the air. "Mentos and Diet Coke! Who woulda thunk it? It's fuckin' mental!"

Randy is standing next to me, and he passes me his phone. There's already a video on Twitter and it's tagged #sodasplash, #cumshot and #reallybadlucknickel. I press play and watch a grainy vid of Blair getting hit by the stream of Diet Coke. The video's on a three-second loop and shows him getting splattered over and over.

"Good Lord, the interwebs are fast!" I say quietly, handing him back his phone.

"And you know, there's gonna be plenty more where that came from," he says.

I pull my phone from my back pocket and see there's two messages from Yannis:

One outta three aint bad

LMAO

I show them to Randy and he frowns. A bunch of people have huddled around the backstage entrance. I see Isabel among them, a head taller than the rest, but I can't tell if she's with Bianca. The other members of Full Watt Drug, Christophe, Adamo the Turk, and Martin, push through the crowd in the doorway, and join us in the chill out area.

"Awesome show, guys! You sounded great!" Christophe says.

Blair shakes his head. "We didn't even get to finish our fuckin' set."

"It doesn't matter, man. The crowd loved it! You should feel good, regardless of the crazy bullshit that happened at the end there," Christophe tells him.

"Do you know who did it?" Johnny asks, blowing another vape cloud in the air above his head.

"Pretty sure, yep. And they're gonna get their asses beat," Blair says angrily.

Martin, the bass player comes up to me and Randy. "Hey, you guys sounded great. You remind me of Cloud Nothings, if they were more shoegazey," he says.

I have no idea what that means, but I say: "Thanks a lot, man," and shake his hand. I let out a sigh, because after I stopped freaking out, I felt amazing up there, and was pretty sure we sounded good and that people actually liked it . . . well, until Yannis' Diet Coke cum shot went soaring through the air.

Tank and Adamo fist bump and I can tell Tank is sizing him up, wondering maybe what it would be like to smash his forehead into Adamo's Ringo Starr nose. But The Turk is a friendly dude, and he pats Tank on the back and tells him he played a great gig. I wonder if he'd still be as chummy if he knew Tank was in love and lust with his girlfriend.

"Yo! It's gonna take some time to clean up the stage, so I say we start celebrating now!" Johnny Temple says. He pulls a big bottle of Jameson and a stack of red plastic cups out from underneath the table. "Come on in, everyone!" he shouts. The crowd milling about in the doorway bursts into the room and Johnny hands each person a cup and pours them a mouthful of whisky.

Bianca's with Isabel and they head straight towards Blair without even glancing at me and Randy. *Like what the hell, Bee? You can't even half-glance my way?* Okay sure, to be fair, Blair did just get blasted in the face with a Diet Coke explosion . . . so I guess he deserves the immediate attention, but like, you can't even gimme a little mini wink as you walk by?

"Oh my God, you were *maravilloso!*" Isabel says, giving Blair a hug. "You were like a real rock star up there! *Muy bueno!*"

"Thanks Isabel," he says, looking at Bianca who hugs him too.

"Eww, you're all sticky," she says.

"Did you see who did it?" Blair asks her.

Someone yells my name from the doorway, taking my attention away from Bianca and Blair.

It's Jules and Vicky. "Heyo Johnny, that's my sister, can you let her in, please?"

"Absolutely!" he says, after he checks them out from head to toe. Jules and Vicky are dressed up for the occasion and look good. Johnny hands them both a plastic cup and pours them some Jameson. "Welcome, welcome, girls! What's your names?" he asks, grinning at them like a total perv. I have an urge to take off my shoe and whip it at his head.

Even though the girls look good, they also look frazzled. They ignore Johnny, rush over to us, and both start talking super fast about Yannis and Mentos and mosh pits and dreadlocks.

"Whoa, whoa, whoa, slow down . . ."

"Where's Blair?" Jules asks, her eyes darting wildly around the room.

"Are you all right, Jules?"

"Yeah, I'm fine, Marco. I just wanna see Blair."

"Well, follow the crowd of hot chicks," I say, glancing at Bianca and Isabel.

"Speaking of hot chicks, you girls are smokin' tonight!" Randy says.

"Thanks, Ran," Vicky says, giving him a hug and a kiss.

Jules is too distracted and doesn't even register the compliment. "I'll be back," she says, heading over towards Blair.

"Is she all right?" I ask Vicky.

"Yeah, yeah, she's fine. She just needs to see her lil Care Blair."

"OK, so what were you two goin' off about then?" Randy asks.

"Omigod, it's so crazy," Vicky exclaims, taking a deep breath before she launches into her rant. "Okay, so like don't be mad, Randy, all right? But we were flirting with these cute guys in the crowd who were protecting us during the mosh pit, mainly because I just wanted them to buy us drinks afterwards, and then I saw Yannis and I started to freak out and I don't know why the hell I said this, but I told the guys that Yannis tried to rape me and so they rushed over to drag his ass outta the bar, and it was perfect fucking timing because one of them knocked the Diet Coke out of his hand just as he was aiming it at Blair!" She takes a quick breath and slugs back the Jameson in her cup. "Bleh! And now I'm like way too embarrassed to ever possibly see them again, and I'm sure that they're looking for us, so me and Jules are gonna have to hide out for the rest of the show—"

Me and Randy are both about to be like, WTF?! but Johnny Temple interrupts to make an announcement.

"Yo, can I have everyone's attention?" he shouts. "Raise your cups in the air for two quick toasts, please!" Thirty red plastic cups go up in the air, as Johnny jumps on a chair. He loses his balance and starts to slip, but Adamo steadies him. "All right, all right!" Johnny yells. "First of all, three cheers to *mes gars* in Full Watt Drug for surviving our first tour together. It was a crazy amazing experience, but lemme tell ya, we're sooo fuckin' glad to be home right now! And second of all, cheers to my new favourite band The Bad Luck Nickel! Blair, you're a serious fuckin' rock star, man, and you guys kicked ass tonight. Ain't no way we're gonna be able to top that finale of yours, so I say we all just get hammered so no one can tell how drunk I am when we play our set! *Santé tout le monde!* And thanks for coming out!"

Everyone whoops and cheers. Me and Randy fire back our whisky and Vicky pretends like she hasn't already drank hers.

"What the fuck, Vick?" Randy says.

"I know, it's totally insane!" she says. "Is there a bathroom in here?"

"Yeah, it's over there," I say.

"I gotta pee, I'll be right back."

Vicky spins on her heel and leaves us, walking by Blair who's still surrounded by a crowd of girls, one of whom is Jules. Vicky grabs her and they head off to the bathroom together.

"Why would Vicky say that?"

Randy shrugs. "I literally never know what is going to come out of her mouth from one moment to the next. She's a total mystery!"

"They seem pretty drunk," I say.

"Drunker than us that's for damn sure," Randy says. "But I say, let's join 'em, bro. Let's celebrate."

As if hearing Randy, Johnny Temple swoops by and splashes more whisky into our plastic cups. "Rock and roll, boys!" he slurs, his hair less perfect than usual, and the smell of B.O. following him, as he saunters around the room in too-tight jeans, sipping at the bottle of whisky like it's a beer.

"He's wasted," Randy says.

"And smells like he hasn't showered in a week," I say. Johnny sidles up to Bianca, who's with Isabel, Adamo, and Blair, and puts an arm around her.

"Take a nice big whiff," Randy says with a laugh. "Eau de unwashed douchebag!"

"Oh yeah, breathe it in deep, Bee!" I say, frustrated that she keeps ignoring me.

Bianca hasn't seen Johnny in a month, but she doesn't seem very excited that he's back. *Is that because she still has feelings for me? Or am I just kidding myself?* All I know is that she's definitely not looking at him like she did the night of the Quicksand show, when I had the pleasure of kicking him in the head. I've never seen the guy drunk before, but he seems to have lost a bit of his lustre, and like Yannis, booze doesn't seem to be a good look on him.

Adamo pats Johnny on the back, casually takes the bottle from him, and hands it off to Martin who happens to be walking by at that exact moment. Martin slides through the crowd and disappears with the whisky, just as Christophe walks by and passes Adamo a bottle of water. Adamo twists off the cap and slips it in Johnny's hand as if it's been there the whole time.

"Holy shit, that was some serious synchronization! Looks like they've done that one before."

"That'll be us with Blair in a year," Randy says.

"Shit, don't even joke."

"Hey, you wanna dip outside for a dart?"

"What about Jules and Vick?" I ask, even though I'm thinking about Bianca.

"They'll be fine in here for now," he says, grabbing a beer off the table and shoving it in his pocket.

"But I kinda want to talk to Bianca quick, and at least thank her and Isabel for snapping me out of my weed funk when they yelled 'We Love You, Marco!' at the start of our set."

"Um, that was Jules and Vicky, bro."

"No way man, it was Bee," I say, but it immediately makes more sense that it was Jules and Vicky. My heart sinks into my nuts. *Ouch.* I stare at Bianca and try to will her to look my way, even for a second, but she's posing for a group photo with Johnny and Isabel and Blair.

*What kind of game you playin' here, Bianca?* I'm starting to have some dark thoughts that I immediately push out of my cranium.

"All right, let's go smoke, Ran."

# JULIANNA

"God, I need this," I say. Vicky scoops a little bit of Rit onto her house key, sticks it under my left nostril, and I sniff it up. "Blair fuckin' looked at me, gave me the *hold on one second* sign with his hand and then went right on talking to some stupid Goth chick!"

"She's probably just doing a quick interview. Seriously, don't worry about it, babe. *I'm* more worried about our mosh pit cuties. I will literally die if I see them again tonight," Vicky says.

"I don't think you will, 'cause I saw them getting dragged out by security with Yannis."

"Oh shit. You did?"

"Yeah."

"Damn. I mean, I definitely don't wanna see them again, but I feel shitty they got kicked out because of me!"

"What the heck made you cry rape anyway?" I ask, rubbing at my nose.

"I dunno. I panicked. I saw Yannis and I could just tell by the look on his face that he was about to do something crazy, and I wanted to stop it," Vicky says, not looking at me.

There's something in the way Vicky says this that makes me think she's not telling the truth. My heart starts beating fast.

"Wait a second, he never tried any shit like that on you, has he?"

"No . . ."

"Are you lying?"

"Not really. I mean, like, we were too young for it to be called that."

"Wait, you said you guys never slept together—"

"We didn't, but we did lots of other stuff, and some of that stuff I wasn't ready to do, but he kinda like made me do it anyway," Vicky says. She serves herself a keyful of Ritalin and snorts it up. "It's not a big deal—"

"What d'you mean? Of course it is!"

Someone jiggles the handle on the bathroom door.

"Be out in a sec!" Vicky says. She makes eye contact with me. "It was a long ass time ago, Jules, okay? And it wasn't until way later that I even realized that what was going on was maybe like unacceptable or inappropriate or whatever." She puts her hand on the knob. "So just forget it, okay? It's all good," she says, as she pushes open the bathroom door.

Tank's standing there, bouncing from one foot to the next. "Oh, hey!" he says. "What's going on? You guys all right?" he asks, after he sees the look on my face.

"Yeah, yeah. Jules is just ticked that Blair's ignoring her."

"Well, what else d'ya expect when you're dating a rock star?" Tank says. I can't tell if he's being sarcastic or not, even though I'm usually hyper-intuitive about stuff when I'm on the Rit. He smiles at me and is about to say more when Vicky points at Blair coming our way.

"Here he comes," she says.

"I gotta piss. Been holding it since before the show," Tank says with a laugh. "You're both looking super hot tonight, by the way," he adds, locking eyes with me for a second. "Even more when you smile," he says just to me, before going into the musty bathroom.

I don't have a chance to process Tank's comment or Vicky's story, because Blair runs up and gives me a hug and a kiss.

"Sorry Jules, I just got mobbed over there," Blair says. I kiss his cheek a few times, and it tastes like Diet Coke.

"It's okay," I say, my bitterness immediately vanishing now that I'm in his arms. "Are you all right, babe?" I ask, as he and Vicky slap five. "I can't believe you didn't go absolutely nutso up there!"

"To be honest, I am fuckin' mortified, Jules," Blair says. "When I opened my eyes right after it happened, all I saw was a hundred fucking cellphones in the crowd recording everything, and so even though all I wanted to do was burst into tears, I knew I had to somehow keep my shit together."

As has happened many times before when I'm frustrated with Blair, he goes and says something so unexpected and vulnerable that it's all I can do to stop myself from blurting out: *I LOVE YOU and am obsessed with you and think about you almost every minute of every day! And in those odd moments when I'm not thinking about you because I have to think about school stuff and other useless nonsense, I feel shitty and small and sad and less like my actual self . . .*

"Well, you were amazing!" I gush. "Flipping the lyrics around like that in the heat of the moment was incredible! How'd you think of it?"

"Yeah, I gotta say that was pretty impressive, Blair!" Vicky adds.

Blair shrugs, and he scans the crowd of hipsters he's just left. "It just came to me, ya know? It was like absolute survival mode kicked in. And even though I hate to admit it, I feel like I was channeling The Blade. I've seen some crazy stuff happen to him on stage, like one time . . ."

Now it sounds like Blair is practicing his interview reply on us, trying to find that perfect quotable moment with just the right mix of humility and pride.

He suddenly sounds so inauthentic and phony that I can't even listen to him. I take a deep breath and close my ears, and I already know that he's going to finish his mock interview with us and then leave and go say it all over again to someone he thinks actually matters.

Blair pats my ass and says: "So um, there's a couple more people over there that want to talk to me, and I need to try and salvage this mess and plug our next show at Le Ritz." Tank comes out of the bathroom and walks over to the table with all the beer. "But did you see who did it?" Blair asks. "Bianca says it was that Yannis asshole. I'm gonna fuckin' kill him."

The two names bring me back into the moment and I frown. Blair's about to say more, but Johnny Temple yells his name, and motions for him to join him. He's standing next to a woman in a short skirt and some bald guy with a scraggly beard who look like they actually matter.

"I'll try not to be too long, okay?" Blair says, pecking me on the cheek and slipping back into his crowd of fans so quickly I don't even have a chance to protest.

"Um okay, see ya later, Blair," I say to the empty space next to me. Tank watches Blair leave and then swipes three beers off the table and hands one to me and Vicky. It looks like he wants to make another comment about Blair, but after he sees the pissy look on my face he decides against it. I open my beer, flick the cap across the room, and take a sip.

"So honestly girls, how did we sound?" Tank asks instead.

I tell him they sounded great, even better than they usually do in the basement, and that a few times when I looked up at them on the stage, they seemed larger than life, like updated versions of their usual selves, more badass, more hardcore. And even though I'm mainly talking about Blair, I can tell Tank digs my compliments.

Vicky tells him how intense the energy was on the dancefloor and in the pit, and then starts to recount the story of our experience with Dreads and Buzz Cut and the Mentos explosion. And am I crazy, or does Tank seem kinda happy that Blair got blasted in the face with Diet Coke?

While Vicky rants, I sip my beer and watch her, as she casually talks about Yannis, and I wonder what else has happened in Vicky's life that she's neglected to tell me. Like, I was under the impression that we told each other everything everything everything.

And then I find myself wondering if we ever really truly know anyone? Like for really reals? Like inside, outside, brightside, darkside?

I fight off a shiver and shift my gaze to Blair. And I watch him, my boyfriend, from afar, laughing and smiling with other girls, hugging and taking selfies with other girls, and I can tell they all want him just as badly as I do. They want to kiss him and hug him and rub their bodies against him, smell his sweat, lick the salt and Diet Coke from his skin. They want him like I want him, but they want the *idea* of him – Blair Matthews, the name, the cred, the fame.

When I just want the boy.

The boy who loves Slim Shady and The Beatles. The boy who's read Jack Kerouac and Jane Austen. The boy who can fold himself into a perfect downward dog. The boy who has mastered the art of the sleeper hold. The boy who will play his guitar like he's in a trance until his hand cramps and his shoulders go stiff. The boy who wants to get high on shrooms and stay up all night and talk about death and birth and every dumbass inconsequential moment in between. The boy who makes me feel so rapturously happy and so profoundly miserable all at the same time.

*Oh c'mon, just give me the boy please!*

Blair disappears from my view, his bright sun eclipsed by the dark moon of people surrounding him. I crane my neck and stand on my tiptoes, trying to catch a glimpse of him through the crowd. But he's gone. And I fight the urge to run after him and stand dotingly by his side while he gives his "interviews", because it seems pretty obvious that he doesn't really want me there. Blair Matthews wants me when he wants me and that seems to be less and less as of late. And I bet he knows that I'll take the less and less because I am pathetic and stupid and blindly in love with him.

The shiver I've been fighting finally takes over, and I shudder and feel a deep pain in my stomach that I'm not sure any amount of booze will be able to dull.

# MARCO

Randy and I stay outside for a while, sitting on a bench across the street from The Sala. It's cold, but we chain smoke, and sip the beers we have hidden in our coat pockets to stay warm, as we dissect every single minute of our set. I'm feeling kinda drunk off the Jameson and giddy at the release of all the nasty butterflies I had flapping around in my stomach before and after the show. *Fly away little papillons de nuit, fly away!*

We talk about how we played much faster than usual, and how our nervous energy actually made the songs sound even more intense than they do in the basement. Randy raves about how awesome the guitars sounded when we kicked into the heavy part of "Aurora", and how hearing a crowd of people clap and cheer gave him major goosebumps.

"Do you think anyone noticed when I dropped my stick during 'Delusional'?" Randy asks.

"I doubt it, man. Especially since you kept bloody-knuckling the crash cymbal until you were able to pick it back up."

"*Badum-crash!* Yeah, my hand is still stinging," he says.

"What about when I turned my amp up too high and it started farting?"

We make fart sounds and giggle like children as two girls walk by and give us weird looks.

*"Bonne soirée, les filles!"* Randy shouts after them, and we laugh some more, not caring about what anyone thinks of us, because we're feeling pretty hyped about the fact that we just played a concert at a cool venue on The Main on a Friday night.

My phone buzzes in my pocket and I grab it.

It's Blair:

> Where u at? FWD about to start. We'll
> be at front by right speaker.

I show the message to Randy and he makes another fart sound and mimics getting splashed in the head with Mentos and Diet Coke.

"Ka-*blammo!*" Randy says, and I can't help but laugh, thinking of the gif on Twitter of Blair getting hit over and over. "Obviously, I feel bad about it happening to him, and you know I fucking hate Andre and Yannis with an insane passion, but c'mon Marco, you gotta admit that was some funny ass shit!" We giggle and make stupid explosion noises.

"Totally unexpected!" I say, laughing so hard I'm practically crying. "I still can't even believe it!"

"Me either," Randy says. "But as bad as it may seem, Blair'll come out of it on top, 'cause he handled it like a total boss! Sincerely."

"Yep, you're probably right."

Randy checks his phone and there's a text from Vicky. "Vick's near right speaker too," he says, and we flick our smokes and walk across the street.

"How drunk d'you think Johnny Temple is now?"

"Oh, we're about to find out," Randy says, as the bouncer opens the door and we head back inside.

Full Watt Drug have already started by the time we get back upstairs, and even though there's a ton of free booze backstage, Randy wants to order drinks at the bar, because he never has before.

"What d'you want?" he asks.

"Whatever you're getting!"

Randy leans over the bar and shouts his order to an absolutely gorgeous bartender wearing an open-backed silk top so she can show off a tattoo of a giant phoenix running all the way down her spine.

"Oh my Lord, she is phenomenal!" Randy screams, his eyes following the phoenix while she slinks down the bar to make our drinks.

We peel our eyes off her tattoo and turn around to watch Full Watt Drug. They sound moody and loud, and Johnny seems fine up there. He's really going for it. If I hadn't seen him chugging the whisky, I'd never know he's hammered.

The song ends, the crowd cheers, and Johnny starts talking about their east coast tour, but I tune him out, because the beautiful bartender has returned with two vodka tonics and three shots of Jagermeister.

"You guys are in The Bad Luck Nickel, right?" she asks with a cute French accent.

Randy and I both nod at her stupidly, like dumb high-school kids, and I stare at a tiny tattoo of a keyhole she has above her heart.

"You guys kicked ass!" she says with a grin. "I loved it! But is Blair all right?"

"Yeah, yeah, he'll survive," Randy says. "His ego's a bit bruised, though."

"It shouldn't be. He was amazing up there! And he handled it so well," she says. She's about to say more, but Johnny Temple starts going off on a rant about how hard it is to actually get up on stage and perform in front of people, especially when there's so many assholes who have no respect. *OK, now he seems drunk.*

"So show some fuckin' respect and give it up for Blair Matthews and The Bad Luck Nickel everyone!"

The crowd goes wild and more girls scream: *We love you, Blair!* and Johnny starts introducing the band's next song.

We turn back to the bar. "See? Everyone loved it!" the bartender says. "When's your next show?"

"Um, it's at Le Ritz in April on Friday the 13th," Randy replies.

"Awesome. I'll be there," she says, pushing the shots of Jagermeister towards us. "These are on the house," she says, grabbing one and raising it in the air.

"Seriously? Wow, thanks, that's super nice of you!" Randy says.

Full Watt Drug start up their next song, and me and Randy grab our shots off the bar, clink glasses with the bartender, shout cheers, and fire them back.

"Thanks!" we yell. I wish we could keep chatting with her forever, but now it's too loud to speak properly. Randy pays for our vodka tonics and she blows a kiss at us, and then slides down the bar to captivate the next customer. I imagine all the other tattoos she might have currently hidden from view as I take a big sip of my vodka.

"Goddamn, she's fine!" Randy says, bobbing his head to the music. "I think I just tipped her almost ten dollars and I don't even care!" He tilts his head to the ceiling and howls. "I can't wait till I'm eighteen!" he hollers, and he starts dancing his way through the crowd towards the right speaker.

I'm about to follow him, but I look up at the stage and the whole scene looks perfect. I need to take a photo of this moment. I put my drink on the bar and pull my phone from my pocket. The lights are bright on stage, and just as I snap the picture the couple in front of me turn towards each other and kiss. I capture them in silhouette in the foreground and it's a perfect accidental composition. I take a few more, but the first one is by far the best. I had asked Jules to record our set, but I have a pretty strong feeling she completely forgot.

As I'm putting my phone back in my pocket it starts buzzing like crazy and a string of text notifications from Yannis pop up on the screen.

> Tell that fuckboi Blair to cash me
> outside right now.

> He's got ten mins before I start
> fukking up his whole life.

Lol lol lol about that mentos bomb
bro!

This is my big day Marco. I'm coming
4 all u bitches.

Been waitin on this for a minute, but
tonites the nite! Wooooooeee!

I read the texts as they come in one after the other,
and I'm about to stuff my phone back in my pocket and
ignore it all, but he writes:

Think I'm playin? Check ça:

and then he sends a photo of Blair kissing some girl. My
breath hitches in my throat. The picture's a bit blurry,
and I can't tell who the girl is, but she has a short blonde
pixie haircut, so it sure as shit ain't Julianna.

Sneak peek! Want more??

And another picture from Yannis pops up on the
screen. This time it's Blair kissing a black girl with long
braids. Again, definitely not my twin sister . . .

*What the fuck, Blair? Are you kidding me? If Jules sees these pics she is going to lose her goddamn mind!*

I can hear Yannis' maniacal laugh squealing in my head and a new swarm of ugly moths hatch in my gut. I glance at the second picture and my heart starts to twist and churn. Blair's hand is on the girl's cheek, blocking a clear view of her face, but I don't think I've ever seen her before.

I wonder what the heck I should do? I wish Randy was still with me. I turn to the bar to grab my drink, but it's gone. The beautiful bartender is walking by, so I flag her down and motion for another vodka-tonic.

She shakes her head. "Nope. Can't do it," she shouts. "I forgot you guys are still in high school! My manager just gave me shit for serving you the first round!" She turns to the guy next to me, gives him her killer smile, and has already forgotten about me.

I try to say sorry, but I'm dead to her. Just some stupid high school kid, an underage loser who shouldn't even be in the bar in the first place.

Full Watt Drug hit a quiet part in the song, and Johnny is growling: *This ain't no club, this ain't no party,* over and over. I'm grinding my molars and vice-gripping my phone in my hand. Another message from Yannis comes through. I'm afraid to read it. Full Watt Drug stomp on their pedals and blast into the heavy part of the song. It's aggressive and the crowd has turned into a giant mosh pit. My thoughts feel exactly like the bodies being shoved around in the pit.

*What the hell, Blair? This ain't good, man. This ain't good at all. Who are these fuckin' chicks? Jules idolizes you, man! She's gonna flip the fuck out! And I don't think Yannis' gonna let this one go. Shit. Shit. Shit. Shit. Shit.*

I wait for the song to end, and as soon as it does, I beeline it through the crowd towards the right speaker.

# JULIANNA

I'm super drunk and high now and am actually feeling pretty numb. Me, Tank, and Vicky are standing at the front of the stage by the right speaker, waiting for Full Watt Drug to begin. Blair said he's going to join us, but at this point I really don't care if he does or not. My thoughts about him have flipped back and forth so much tonight that I'm starting to feel bi-polar. My heart literally feels like it's being squeezed in Blair's fist, and even though he's ignored me all night, I know that if he looked me in the eyes and said something even remotely sweet, I'd melt in his arms all over again, like the totally whipped girlfriends I enjoy making fun of.

*What the hell is wrong with me?* I feel like I have no self-control when it comes to him. And even though I'm up'd on the Ritalin and lull'd on the booze, I have a very vivid feeling that being in love isn't supposed to feel like this! But then again, music has taught me that love hurts and love bites and love is a battlefield and love will tear us apart and love makes people go absolutely fuggin' nutso, so what the hell do I know?

The crowd seems even more packed than it was before. Vicky is next to me and Tank is standing behind me. He puts his hands on my shoulders and gives me a little neck rub, and then he starts playing drums on my back. Vicky was paranoid that Dreads and Buzz Cut would be let back in, but Tank convinced her to forget about them and to come watch FWD's set, but not before he did a bunch of Ritalin with us in the bathroom.

Because of Vicky's blue contacts, Tank could see how dilated her pupils were, so he knew we were high.

"What are you guys on? Did you take molly or something?" he asked.

Vicky told him everything and a few minutes later we were all squished in the bathroom and Tank was snorting his first and second and third ever bump of drugs. Vicky and I did another couple too. Then we went back to the table of booze and Vicky grabbed a bottle of vodka that was half empty and started making us drinks.

"I highly recommend that you chug that can of Coke," Vicky said to Tank, who seemed to be flexing all his muscles as tight as he could. "It'll kick everything up a notch for ya."

Tank grabbed the Coke, opened it, and drank the entire thing.

I tried to recall the sensation I had of knowing every-thing that first time at Vicky's house, and how powerful and serene and buoyant it made me feel, but I couldn't quite capture it. It's dulled at the edges now and there's a dark slant to it. But I could tell Tank experienced that same initial reaction like I did, because after he chugged the Coke and burped triumphantly, he grinned at me like a little kid. All teeth and gums. There was pure wonder on his face.

His tongue was lolling out of his mouth, he looked just like a giant Golden Retriever, trembling with boundless energy, ready to roll over, lie down, shake a paw, race through the fields, howl at the moon, and play fetch forever. *Good dog, good Tanky, woof woof woof!*

He picked me up under the arms and swung me around, laughing wildly.

"I feel so . . . *interesting!*" he shouted, for lack of a better word, his eyes blazing.

"You're cracked! Put me down!" I said with a big grin, which reminded me of his earlier comment about my smile, which also reminded me of another night back in the fall, when he'd made a similar remark . . .

We were all supposed to meet up at The Tunnels, but somehow it ended up being just me and Tank. Marco and Randy got sidetracked trying to buy weed, Vicky bailed because she was Netflix and chillin' with this guy Navin that she dated for like three minutes at the beginning of the school year, and Blair still hadn't become a part of our gang yet – even though he'd started practicing with the band, and we were all sort of infatuated with him.

So it was just me and Tank, and he'd bought a bunch of beer using his brother's ID, and we wound up getting pretty drunk.

It always felt special hanging out in The Tunnels. Being in the dark with no phone and no wifi, made it feel different, as if we were temporarily removed from our regular lives or something. And it made it easy for us to open up to each other. It was like a vault, a safe space that was all ours, where we didn't feel weird or awkward about letting our guards down and being a bit vulnerable, because we knew no one would judge us down there.

I remember going off about my crush on Blair that night, and bugging Tank to tell me anything he might have heard Blair say about me, because whenever I asked Marco, he'd just laugh at me and call me a loser.

"He thinks you're a super cool chick," Tank said.

"That's it? What else? Does he think I'm hot?"

"Of course! Everyone does. You're a total babe, Jules, and if you don't think so, you're crazy. Maybe if you didn't have resting bitch face, you'd hear it a lot more," Tank said with a laugh.

"Hey!" I shouted, dribbling some beer down my chin.

"You're super cute, Jules, but when you smile, WOW! your entire look changes. It's like your face is a flower, but it isn't until you smile that it blooms and shows the world how beautiful it really is, ya know what I mean?"

That was pretty poetic stuff for Tank. He made eye contact with me for a second and then a subway train went by next to us and the noise made my head spin. Thinking back on it now, it's clear that Tank was being all sweet and flirty with me, I was just too obsessed with Blair to even realize it . . . but Tank was being more than just big brother nice to me that night, he was giving me a hint, *un petit indice,* and he did it again tonight.

Tank and I have been friends for so long, I've never really considered him as anything more than that, ya know? But right now, at this moment, where I'm feeling way too overly sensitive, I think if he spun me around and kissed me, I'd really like it. So I rest the back of my head on his chest and sort of sink into him.

"You're a comfy couch, Tanky Poo," I say, but he doesn't say anything back. Vicky is absorbed in her phone texting Randy, so I sink into Tank a little more, and gently rub my butt up against his legs in the process.

It's exciting, and my skin tingles as I try to sense his thoughts. I'm way too messed up to sense anything very clearly so I ask: "What'cha thinking 'bout, Tank?"

He stops massaging my shoulders and slowly says: "I can't stop visualizing all these football drills in my head."

It's not the reply I was hoping for, but it's his first time on the Rit, and he's lost in the swirl of the speed, so I get it.

"And I can literally smell the fresh cut grass on the field and the dank sweat from inside my helmet," he says.

"Wow, that's cool. It's crazy how it messes with your senses, huh?"

He doesn't reply, but I hear him inhale deeply and breathe in the smells of the football field.

After a few deep breaths, he adds: "I'm also thinking about how much I want to punch my brother in the face for not showing up tonight."

Tank and his brother Sandro are each other's worst enemies. They have that love-hate sibling rivalry thing going on like mad. But where Tank rests more on the love side, it seems like Sandro just doesn't give a shit at all. He's always so hostile and quick to put Tank down, instead of raising him up. He finds fault and rips on Tank for practically everything he does. I seriously wouldn't know how to deal if Marco treated me like that.

"It's just . . . I practiced so hard for this show, ya know? And he said he'd fuckin' be here."

"Oh man, I'm sorry Tank, but try not to be bummed right now. You have so much to be happy about."

He bounces up and down on his heels and I feel his body go tense like he's flexing all his muscles again.

Tank's brother Sandro is a gym rat, with bad tattoos, and a man bun. He works security at a douchey club downtown, wears too much cologne, and only listens to EDM and hip-hop. He truly is the stereotypical Montreal-Italian Gino. And as much as I hate to admit it, I had a huge crush on him when I was a kid, mainly because he was older, had tons of confidence, and seemed to never wear a shirt all summer long. He's super hot, okay? But overall, he's a total jerk who seems to get some sort of cheap thrill from letting Tank down or screwing him over.

What makes matters worse is that Sandro moved out last year and since then he rarely visits. It's like he abandoned Tank and his mom, and Tank really resents him for that, especially since their mom has MS, and sometimes it's not so easy for her to move around.

*Oh! Poor Tanky Poo! You're a real sweetie, a sensitive giant, a sexy six-footer, and I should probably kiss you hard on the mouth right now!*

Haha. OK, yep, it's official, I am five sheets to the goddamn wind, and I really wanna suck on Tank's rather full bottom lip, so that he'll forget about his dickhead brother, and maybe I'll forget about No-Care Blair too.

"Forget about Sandro, Tank, we're your fam," I say, blatantly pushing my ass against him. As I start to turn around, unsure if I'll have the balls to do it once I complete my 180, the lights go up and start flashing chaotically. Full Watt Drug walk on to the stage. The crowd screams, someone next to me whistles really loudly, and my moment with Tank dissipates faster than a vape cloud. Vicky grabs our drinks from off the lip of the stage and hands me mine. The band strap on their guitars, and all the people that were hanging out backstage are now standing in the wings to watch their set. I scan the group for Blair, but I only spot Isabel and her goddamn legs for days. I sip my vodka, the lights go black, and Full Watt Drug start their set.

And holy shit, it's LOUD! And sooo heavy! I would never tell the guys this, but Full Watt Drug's sound is fuggin' full watt indeed! Two dudes next to me jam Kleenex in their ears, but I like how the music seems to be ripping right through me. Vicky is banging her head up and down so fast it looks like she's having a seizure. Tank yells something at me, but all I feel is hot breath in my ear, and when I look back a few seconds later he's gone. *Tank pulled a Houdini on me! Where the hell'd you go, yo?*

I don't have time to care because Full Watt Drug somehow get even louder, their guitars riff even heavier, and Johnny Temple is completely wildin' out. His stage presence is intense and his voice sounds like it's going through a paper shredder. I can see why people dig this band. They're fucking tight and Johnny's energy is wildly compelling.

The lights on stage start to strobe and they reflect off of something by my feet. I look down and frown-laugh as I spot one of Blair's bad luck nickels. I pick it up, and grip it tight in my hand like a talisman, wondering where the hell he is?

*He's not coming to join us. Let's fuckin' face it Julio, he's not coming to join us. Even though Blair says he hates the limelight and all of the fawning admiration, and even though he says he feels more like himself in Montreal than he ever did in L.A., he's been in the spotlight his whole damn life, and it's obvious he misses it. Tonight's his night and sadly you just ain't a part of it . . . so fuckin' forget Blair! Now where the heck's my Tanky Poo? And why'd he ditch me? I was gonna suck on his face! And where the heck's my brother when I need him, goddammit? Oooh, I've got some more ugly pent-ups rising to the surface . . . push 'em down, girl, push 'em down deep.*

I feel like I need another sniff, but I think I've done more tonight than I ever have before. I already know

I'm not going to be able to sleep, and tomorrow I'm gonna feel anxious and cruddy all day unless I do a line to level me out, maybe even more if Blair keeps fucking ignoring me tonight. *Thank God, I have my secret stash to get me through,* I say, tapping my jean jacket pocket to make sure it's there.

I clench the bad luck nickel in my fist until my nails cut into my palm. I take a few deep meditative breaths, and Full Watt Drug rock out a blast of melodic distortion.

"You know what? Who gives a shit?" I shout and flick the coin into the crowd. I slam back my drink and start head banging with Vicky. Johnny Temple is on his knees in front of his pedals and I don't know what the hell he's doing, but his guitar sounds like a mewling cat getting chewed up by a lawn mower.

Vicky puts her arm around me and I kiss her cheek and we tilt our heads to the flashing lights and howl like she-wolves in heat.

Me and Vick till the ends of the earth. Fuck everyone else.

# MARCO

I push my way through the packed crowd towards the right speaker, trying to get to Jules as fast as possible, because if Yannis sent her those pics too, she will go absolutely fuckin' nutso! Just thinking of them on my phone makes me dizzy with dread and anger. I'm seeing Blair in a way I do not like at all. It's making me panic.

On stage, Johnny Temple is drunkenly ranting about American politics. *Oh, just shut the fuck up and stick to the music, Johnny.* I'm halfway to the speaker, when a hand reaches out and grabs hold of my bicep.

It's Tank.

I'm relieved to see him, until I see his squirrely eyes. He's sweaty and clenching his jaw and definitely high on something.

"Where you been, Marco?" he yells. "I was in the pit during the last song and it was like I was runnin' drills on the football field. It was fuckin' awesome!" Tank rubs at his nose and blinks like twenty times in three seconds.

"What the hell are you on?"

"Oh dude, I snorted some Ritalin with Jules and Vicky. It's got me airborne, Marco! Such a wicked buzz, and my mind is a clear blue sky right now."

"Ritalin?"

"Yeah bro, you don't know about it?"

I shake my head and feel even more fat angry moths hatching out of their cocoons and creating a vicious tornado in my gut.

"They get 'em from Edwin, and it sounds like they've been doing it on the down-low for a while now."

If Tank wasn't so fucked up and could actually see my face, I think he'd be concerned, because I'm sure I look like a lunatic.

*Whaaaaaat? Jules snorting Ritalin? This is not cool. And how the hell did I not know about this? Double not cool. Fuck. I mean, I guess I've noticed that Jules seemed a little moodier than usual and maybe a bit more paranoid too, but I would've never guessed she was snorting fuckin' prescription drugs . . . it just ain't her style. Does Blair know about this and not fucking told me?*

"You should try some, Marco! You'd dig it," Tank says, squeezing my bicep again.

I feel like my entire being is shaking. *Does Jules not fucking remember our Ma being hooked on sleeping pills after Dad left? Has she selectively deleted that from her fucking head? Has she forgotten how anxious and depressed and freaky she was? And how hard it was for her to actually quit taking them?*

My phone buzzes in my pocket, another text from Yannis:

> Don't make me send those pics to
> Jules. I'm waiting . . .

I quickly tap out a reply:

> Calm the fuck down bro be there soon

I need to get to Jules and I need to find Blair stat. Like post haste. I start to write a text to Blair, but two girls push by me and one of them spills her drink on my arm and doesn't even say sorry. On stage, Johnny stops talking about the New World Order and the lights fade to black.

"This one's brand new. It's called 'Fight Scene,'" he says.

Adamo two counts and the lights go up in a flash. The song starts with a rolling bass line that's both dark and peppy, and Adamo taps out a stuttering beat on the snare. Tank is bouncing up and down, already anticipating the kick, and I'm getting nudged and bumped from all sides, so I jam my phone in my pocket. Johnny and Christophe join in with muted feedback and distortion, and as it builds in volume Adamo hammers on the ride cymbal and Johnny shouts: *"Watch out, I'll fuck you up, hands up, knuckle up . . . FIGHT SCENE!!"* and then they crash into the refrain and it sends the mosh pit into an immediate frenzy. Their guitars are angry and thunderous! They sound like Rage Against The Machine! If I wasn't so stressed out, I'd definitely be loving it.

*"MOTHERFUCKIN' FIGHT SCENE!!"* Johnny hollers over top of everything, as he flails around the stage, swinging his fists at imaginary foes. Tank smashes his way into the eye of the pit, while I try to safely push my way out of it. As I'm doing so, I spot Blair heading towards the bar, phone to his ear. The crowd seems to part like the Red Sea for him, but when I try to follow all I get are these Brick Wall Dudes bigger than Tank stubbornly blocking my way.

"Yo, BLAIR!" I yell, but it's pointless because I can't even hear myself. He walks by the bar and heads towards the exit instead.

*Where's he going?* I squeeze my way through two of the Brick Walls and then ungracefully push by a bunch more people, so I can hopefully catch Blair. I rush out the exit doors and he's on the landing halfway down the stairs, talking on the phone. He looks upset, but I don't give a shit. I meet him on the landing, grab my phone and stuff it in his face, the picture of him kissing the blonde pixie girl burning bright on the screen.

"Eh! Who the hell is this, man?" I say. "And who's this?" I ask, flipping to the second photo.

"I'll call ya right back," he says to whoever he's talking to. His face is pale, and he looks totally shook.

"Who are these chicks, Blair? How could you do this to Jules?" I shout.

"Get your phone outta my face, Marco," Blair says, angrily smacking my hand. "I ain't got time for this shit. Who the hell sent you those? They're from an art project I did for one of my classes last year."

"Huh?"

"They're from an art project I did last year called '100 Kisses'. I kissed a hundred girls and shot it all on 35mm film."

*Oh my god, seriously? Only Blair Matthews would do a project where he takes pictures of himself kissing one hundred girls and call it ART.*

Once again, I hear Yannis' maniacal laugh go off in my head like a tommy gun.

*Well played, Yannis. Have you turned into a goddamn evil genius or something?*

I take a long, deep breath. Man, everything felt like it was unravelling there for a second, so I'm actually really glad to find out it's just Yannis fucking with me. Jules jammin' Ritalin up her nose is a whole other can of gummy worms, but I'll have to deal with her later.

"Who sent you those pics?" Blair asks again.

"Yannis."

"Man, is that guy a fuckin' psycho or some shit?"

I'm about to say yes he is and he's outside, but Blair's phone rings and he answers it with a frown.

"Gimme a sec," he says to me. "I can't talk right now, Dad, okay?"

*Oh damn, The Blade is on the line!*

Blair turns his back to me and keeps talking. Even though, he's trying to be quiet, I do my best to listen in, because I'm nosy as hell, and because he's talking to Thee Mother Fucking Blade!

"I'll call you once I get in my Uber . . . I'm so fucking pissed off with you right now, I can't even breathe. I had her on my side, Dad, I was taking care of it, and you fucked it all up with this interview, man. Like seriously, what in the fuck? Listen, I'll call you back in five minutes, all right? I'm leaving right now."

"Wait, you're leaving?" I ask.

"Yeah. Some shit's gone down at home in L.A. and I have to leave right now," Blair says, his voice shaking.

"Is everything all right?"

"No." He looks down at his phone and taps on the Uber app. I wait for him to give me more info, but he doesn't say anything. *Like what the fugg happened, Blair? Did someone jump off a bridge? Drown in a bathtub? Gimme the skinny, dude!* His face looks grey and that blaze that's always burning inside him seems like it's been pissed on. He's clenching his jaw super tight, and he looks tired.

"Is there anything I can do?" I ask.

"Actually yeah, can you pack up my gear for me and bring it to your place? My mic, all my pedals, and my guitar. Will you do that for me? Just bring everything to your place and leave it in the basement. And please don't try to mess with the pedals that got wet on the board, okay? Promise me you'll take care of my shit, Marco."

"Yeah, of course, Blair. I got you, man. But can you tell me what happened?"

"I uh . . . fuck Marco, I can't talk about it. No one died or anything, but there's been a family emergency and I have to go asap."

"For how long?"

"I don't know. Probably like a week or so."

"Well, you gotta say goodbye to Jules before you jet."

"I don't have time, man. I have to leave right now. I'll text her from the Uber."

"Dude, c'mon you can't just text her, she'll be gutted."

"Have you seen her tonight? She's a fuckin' mess. I can't deal with that shit right now, Marco."

I shake my head at him, but then remember she's jacked on Ritalin and has been doing it for a while now and hasn't told me about it, even though we usually tell each other everything everything everything, which makes me wonder what the heck's up with her? Inside the bar, the song ends, and the crowd hollers.

The exit doors open, and a few people head downstairs to go outside and smoke. Bianca comes out, looking flustered, her phone to her ear. Her face lights up with relief as she sees Blair, but when she sees he's with me, her eyes flicker with surprise and worry. In fact, she starts to look like Bambi after his mom got shot.

"You need to seriously chill, Yan!" she says angrily into the phone, as she joins us on the landing. Quietly she says: "You've won tonight, Yannis, okay? Please just leave it alone. We don't have time for this stupidity. So please just promise me you won't . . . seriously? He just hung up on me."

"That piece of shit's harassing you too?" Blair asks. "He's been sending Marco old pics of me off the internet, trying to start some dumb drama. Did you get my text?"

"I didn't get a chance to read it because of Yannis."

"Well, I really need to talk to you for a second . . ."

"And I really need to talk to *you* for a second." Bianca says this in a way that makes it clear that whatever she wants to talk to him about she doesn't want to say in front of me.

And like, she won't even look at me. Something is not right. And I can't be certain, because she's blocking my view, but it seemed like she just flashed him a quick view of her phone. I hear one of Jules' warnings going off in my head. *She's a shady bitch, Marco, and I don't trust her. She keeps giving you jusssst enough to keep you hooked. But she broke your heart, and she won't even blink when she does it again.*

"Please just read my text," Blair says to her. He sounds weirdly desperate.

"What the hell's going on, guys?" I ask, an edge to my voice.

There's a pause. Bianca glances at her phone and then at Blair. Chews on her bottom lip. The muscles twitch in Blair's jaw.

"Are you serious?" she asks Blair. "Why? What happened?"

"What is going on?" I ask again. They both ignore me. My pulse is thumping in my neck. My Spidey-Sense is going off like mad. All the air seems to be getting sucked up around me.

"I gotta leave right now, Bee, my Uber will be here in like two minutes."

"Well, I'm coming with you," Bianca says.

"OK good. Let's go, babe," he says reaching for her hand, as they begin running down the stairs together.

I'm literally trying to compute everything that's happening as my phone buzzes in my pocket. I grab it. There's four new text notifications from Yannis.

The first one says:

> And finally, la pièce de fuckin
> résistance bruh

The second one is a picture of Bianca pressed against Blair in a tight embrace, her hands riding up the back of his shirt, their lips locked in an open-mouth kiss.

The third one says:

> Oups already sent to Jules too lol

And the last:

When I finally look away from my phone, I'm woozy, and I grasp the railing on the stairs as my vision goes spotty and grey and then I don't see much else after that.

# BLAIR

Everything had been going so great for me, I guess the universe felt like it just had to go and fuck my shit up.

Yannis was waiting for me outside The Sala Rossa and I knocked that piece of trash out with two quick shots to his dumb head and was still able to open the door of the Uber for Bianca. Everyone on the sidewalk outside the club was screaming and hollering and going ape-shit as we drove away.

"What the hell happened, Blair?" Bianca asks. "Why'd she post it?"

"My Dad forgot about an interview he did for *Brave New Waves* a while back and the episode just came out today for fuck's sake."

"And what did it say?"

"More shit about Rainbow," I said, my voice cracking.

The Blade had done so many interviews for the new album, he had forgotten all about a podcast he did with *Brave New Waves* that got pushed back to coincide with the day tickets were going on sale for Hesher's European Tour.

And short story long, it was one of the interviews where he shot his fat mouth off about Rainbow.

Just as Bianca pulls up the photo on Rainbow's social, I get a text from her.

> Srry Blair, but yr dad left me no choice. Still hasn't amended interview with Distortion and now calls me a slut on Brave New Waves? Fuck his bullshitt.

> He's done.

Bianca looks at my phone, and I look at hers, and then we gaze at each other.

This girl.

My twin flame.

I can smell her vanilla-flavoured lip gloss mixed with alcohol. For a few seconds I breathe her in and everything's all right.

Except it's not. I can already feel her slipping away.

"Jesus. This is not good, Blair—"

"I know. I'm seriously fucked, Bee."

I can feel my heart hammering in my chest. We stare at each other silently for a moment before we toss our phones aside and reach for one another longingly, desperately, not giving two shits if our Uber driver is watching.

# JULIANNA

—I'm one with the music my mind a spiral going round and round 'cause everything's connected everything's a circle even love and pain it's all one all the same and I can't see too clear 'cause my eyes have lace curtains over them and my high-speed brain can't process what it sees but my heart *my heart knows only too well and it shrivels and it sizzles and it blackens and the rest of me is numb numb numb but that blackness sears right through my brittle chest and I'm murdered but instantly reborn into something ugly and vandalized and broken and there's no more music it's all quiet now and I—*

# PART III

# MARCO

Blair Matthews came in like a whirlwind and left a giant shitstorm in his wake . . .

After Yannis sent me and Jules the photo to end all photos (at least we thought it was the photo to end all photos, until Rainbow's baby bump pic went viral a few hours later), Blair ran outside of The Sala and cracked Yannis in the head so hard he knocked him out cold, and then he and Bianca hopped in an Uber and drove right out of our lives.

I was still standing on the stairs, looking at the picture, and the way Bianca's hands were riding up Blair's shirt and rubbing his skin. They were next to his stepdad's Prius, and it was parked outside of Bianca's house. I was stunned, but somewhere deep inside me it felt like all my suspicions were confirmed, suspicions I didn't even know I had until I was shown the proof.

And I just could not fucking fathom how the two people I was most obsessed with in the entire world could ice cold betray me like that.

It meant they didn't give a shit about me at all – not Bianca, not Blair – and that harsh realization cut me to the motherfuckin' quick.

I started crying and I rushed back into the venue to find Jules, but by the time I finally pushed and shoved my way through the crowd to the right speaker she was gone.

# JULIANNA

"Gimme more—"

"No Jules, you've had enough."

"Please! Fuck. I need more."

"No you don't, babe."

"How could he, Vick? How could he? How could he? And with *her* of all people, *FUCK!*"

"Shhhh! OK, OK, here, take this. It'll help you relax."

I dry swallowed the pill Vicky gave me and continued to lie on her bed, shivering, and sobbing, while she stroked my hair and whispered softly in my ear. She did this for a while, but whatever she gave me was strong, because it was already pulling me down into the bed, sinking me into her mattress and making my eyes super heavy.

"Wha'd you gimme?" I mumbled.

"One of my dad's Ambien's."

I let out a long sigh and my body calmed and I started to drift off, but my legs twitched and I opened my eyes. Vicky was gone. I cried out her name, and she was back in a flash, comforting me, *Shhh, you'll be asleep soon, babe,* she whispered, *verrrry soon, you're almost there, just concentrate on your breathing and relaxxx and try and get some ressssssssst . . .*

# VICKY

I woke up on the floor, next to my bed, and my face was all sticky and wet. *What the heck? Ewwwww, fuggin' guh-rosss, man!* I got a whiff of what was all sticky and wet and realized I was lying next to a puddle of vomit. The rank ass raunch of my own stomach acid had me rushing to my bathroom and trying not to barf all over again.

I slurped a bunch of water from the tap and gripped the counter as a wave of nausea swept through me. I snuck a quick glance at my face in the mirror. There was crusty blood under my nose, dried puke on my chin, and angry purple circles under my eyes.

*Holy shit, I look fucking terrible!*

My head felt like there was a pencil slowly being sharpened right in the middle of it. My body temperature flared up in a hot flash and then immediately dipped to freezing. I slunk down on my knees next to the toilet and barfed up the water I just drank. Sweat popped out on my forehead and my whole body started vibrating with a sense of foreboding.

I remembered taking one or two of my dad's sleeping pills, and then saw flashes of myself lying on the floor listening to music on my phone and texting with someone, probably Randy, and then trying to pull myself up into the bed with Jules, but falling down like three or four times before I passed out on the floor.

More chills hit me as I imagined passing out on my back instead of on my side and puking, and then choking on my own vomit, and low-key dying in my sleep like a total fucking wastoid.

*What the hell were you thinking, Vicks? Jesus Christ, girl, you coulda fucking died, dude ...*

I dry heaved into the toilet, a thin stream of spittle hanging from my lips. *Never again, Vicks! You hear me? You're done with this shit. Second time you've got a bloody nose from snorting that nasty ass crap? Fuck it. Fuck it. Fuck it. It makes you feel like absolute trash and you are so fuckin' done!*

I pictured an overhead view of the whole scene: Jules asleep in my bed, me sprawled out on the floor, a trail of vomit trickling out of my mouth, my eyes rolled back in my skull, grey, blank, and dead done dead. I shivered uncontrollably.

*What the hell was I thinking? Jesus Christ and Santo Niño, I sure got lucky ...*

I thought of Jimi Hendrix mixing sleeping pills with booze and dying in his fucking sleep. I thought of John Bonham from Led Zeppelin choking on his own puke and dying in his fucking sleep. I think of poor, broken

MJ, hooked on prescription drugs and dying because of them. I lay on the bathroom floor, my stomach a tight knot of dread and fear, my forehead crunching with regret, but thank big baby Jesus I was actually awake right now, I was still alive. It could have so easily gone the other way. I pulled a towel off the rack and wrapped it around me, closed my eyes, and forced myself to go back to sleep.

# MARCO

Maybe part of the reason why I got so hung up on Bianca, is because she's the only girl that I actually ever like, went for, ya know? I'm not very good at flirting or making moves on girls. I get all shy and freeze up in the actual moment. There's been a bunch of times where I've noticed a girl smiling at me in the halls at school, or checking me out on the metro, and I want to go up and shoot my shot, but then my heart starts beating super fast, and I get so stupidly nervous that I can barely even manage to smile back. Instead, I end up making some weird face at them, and then I'm sure they think I'm even more of a loser than I actually am.

It makes me feel so lame.

My Dad hasn't given me too much advice (you kinda actually have to be around to do so, eh boss?), but one thing he did tell me was that girls like it when guys make the first move. And the one and only time I actually went through with it was with Bianca, when I grabbed her and kissed her on top of the empty boxcar as the train raced by – and it worked, because we fell in love, and for a while there, I was living the teenage dream.

When I was dating Bianca, I began to see the world

in a different way. It was weird. The perception I had of a school day was no longer a normal school day, and weeknights seemed so much more meaningful. Going home after school, playing Xbox, watching TV, sending her silly text messages, maybe doing some homework, it was all completely transformed. Everything seemed different. New. Exhilarating. Even dumb stuff like brushing my teeth or putting on deodorant felt exciting. Why? Because I felt like I was doing it all for her. My life was no longer my own, it was hers too. And it felt like she was everywhere. I could feel her sitting next to me on the couch while I played video games, smell her in the autumn breeze coming through the window, and hear her laugh in the lull of the refrigerator humming in the kitchen.

Knowing that someone, besides my mom and Jules, thought I was special, actually made me special, it actually made me a better person, ya know? Or at the very least, made me feel like I was . . .

Until she dumped me for Johnny Temple.

And goddammit did that ever suck! I've never felt pain like that before in my life. My entire *essence* hurt. I'd whisper her name when I was alone and as soon as I'd say it, I'd sob uncontrollably. Everything was gloomy and depressing. But then, still in the weepy throes of trying to get over her, Blair Matthews whirled into my life, and we somehow became friends, and he even wanted to join my shitty band, and the Teenage Dream was reborn even bigger and better than before, with a capital T and a capital D! Bianca would see me playing in a band with Blair fuckin' Matthews and want to be with me all over again! I'd get to be with the amazing girl and be in the cool rock band and everything would be oh so perfecto yo . . . haha, yeah, well, insert a big fat past-tense ironic sad-face emoji right here please. 

**X**

So yeah, things went from total crap to absolute dog shit when Rainbow posted her very pregnant photo with the headline: *The Blade's about to be a grandpa because I'm about to have Blair Matthews' BABY!* and tagged it with *#rapebaby #strippermom #hesher #heshersucks #MeToo #sodasplash #reallybadlucknickel.*

The picture was only up for about six hours before she took it down, but by then it had been screen-capped and re-tweeted a thousand times over, and the internet had already done its research and come up with its own scandalous conclusions.

Snowballing on all the #sodasplash memes, as well

as Bianca's Instagram video of Blair knocking Yannis out into a dirty snowbank outside The Sala, Blair had never seen so much online action before.

Dude was totally trending, as was his dad, but not in a good way.

A sampling of some of the nutso headlines:

*Blair Matthews sexually assaults actress, gets her pregnant, defects to Canada*

*Hesher frontman The Blade pays woman to get abortion, keep her mouth shut about rape*

*Son of Hesher's The Blade knocks up band groupie during violent, coke-fueled romp*

*Another Teen Heartthrob soon to be Another Deadbeat Teen Dad*

After the night of our show, shit went from the local level of gossip (how Blair apparently had flings with several girls in Montreal), which was bad enough, to the entire freakin' internet saying he'd raped a 25-year-old woman after a Hesher show in San Diego, while they were both super high on blow.

*What in the actual fuck? OK, let me try and get*

*this shit straight: not only was Blair hooking up with Bianca, but he apparently had other side chicks too, and not only did he sexually assault some poor woman named Rainbow, but he also got her pregnant, and now, even though everyone thought she had an abortion, she was about to give birth to Blair's baby any goddamn day?*

I couldn't possibly believe that Blair was a rapist, but the thought sent ice cold terror down my spine. It was literally too much for me to handle. So you can only imagine how bad it was for Jules . . .

# JULIANNA

You know that feeling of total relief you have when you wake up from a nightmare and realize it was just a dream?

Well, switch that around.

Instead, you've just woken from the most wonderful dream and you find yourself trapped in an awful nightmare – except it's not a nightmare, it's your actual fucking reality . . . that's what being cheated on and lied to feels like.

It's literally the worst pain somebody can inflict on another person.

It's gut-wrenching.

Callous.

Horrendous.

I locked myself in my room for two days, lay in bed, snorted almost all my Ritalin, listened to sad emo music, and wished I was dead. I texted Blair a thousand times. I filled up his voicemail with messages either incoherent because of tears or incomprehensible from rage. My bones felt cold and damp, and my stomach felt like it was rotting from the inside out. I sobbed pretty much non-stop.

When I *was* able to fall asleep it wasn't for very long, and after I'd wake up, I'd forget about everything for a couple seconds and actually feel kind of good – but then it would all come flooding back, and my whole body would tense up, my stomach would turn, and I'd immediately go back to feeling like complete trash.

I realized that sleep was my only escape from this waking nightmare, but I couldn't really fall asleep because of the drugs, and so then I'd just lie there and sigh and cry and try to ignore all the notifications that kept lighting up my phone, but still checking them every time with the hope that maybe it was Blair.

But nope, no care from fuckface Blair.

All day Sunday, Marco kept knocking on my bedroom door, but I'd tell him to screw off, leave me alone, and turn up the music loud enough to drown him out.

But on Monday morning, after our mom left for work, Marco jimmied open my door with his debit card and brought me water, green tea, and fruit, and told me how worried he was about me, and that no matter how crappy I felt, I needed to stop snorting the fucking Ritalin. He even went as far as to try and find it so he could flush it down the toilet, but I had it hidden in my bra, close to my busted heart. He lifted up my mattress and looked there, went through my backpack, dresser, and desk drawers, and when he tried to look under my pillow I bit his arm, forced him out of my room, and pushed my desk in front of the door so he couldn't get back in.

He threatened to tell Mom about everything, and I screamed so loud that he just swore under his breath a few times, told me he loved me, and then I heard his feet stomping down the stairs and out the front door as he took off to school. A few minutes later he texted:

I'm hurting too Jules.

My mom was too busy with work to notice anything was up. She thought I was sick on Sunday and let me stay home from school on Monday, but then on Tuesday morning even she saw the picture of this fuckin' Rainbow woman on the internet and the awful allegations against Blair. After I wailed through the door that there was no way in hell I was going to school, and swore to her that Blair never raped me, she let me stay home again, but I wouldn't let her in my room, and wouldn't let her talk to me about anything. I sniffed up the last of my Ritalin and stared at the photo of Rainbow and her baby bump and her huge boobs, and her arms covered in tattoos, for practically an hour straight. I was dumbfounded by the whole thing. *So this was why Blair came to Montreal? To hide out from a baby and a rape charge? Seems like he'd need to go way the heck further than Canada to get away from all that noise, doesn't it?*

Blair was never rude or rough with me during sex. And even though, yes, he did pressure me to do it faster than I originally wanted to, he never forced himself on me or treated me disrespectfully . . . but, he also didn't have a bunch of cocaine up his nose when he was with me, so I really didn't know what to think. All I knew was that the picture of Rainbow made my stomach ache even more than the one of him kissing Bitch Face, and my entire body would not stop pulsing with anxiety.

But there was also this underlying feeling that Rainbow and her big preggo belly stole my fuckin' thunder. Blair cheated on *me*. Blair stabbed *me* in the heart. Blair screwed *me* over. Blair spit in *my* face. How the hell could my feelings matter now, when there was a pregnant chick in L.A. saying that Blair raped her and that she was going to be his baby mama any day now?

Vicky texted and said she was skipping math class and coming over, so I asked her to bring me some Rit, but when she showed up and told me she didn't have any, I stupidly decided to use all the anger I'd been brewing on her and I said some really rude stuff.

"Oh, you like suddenly quit cold turkey even though you were doing it way more than I was? Leave me the hell alone then. I'll get some from Edwin. And you know what, Vick? You're a total bitch, and I feel like I don't even know who you are anymore. I thought we told each other everything? I thought there was no secrets between us? Ya know, maybe I should tell Randy that apparently you're the type of chick that would let an asshole like Yannis take advantage of you . . ."

She was standing there with her mouth open and hand up, trying to cut me off, until my dig about Yannis . . . that one made her leave. She told me to screw off and slammed my bedroom door. And of course, the instant she was gone I wanted her back with me, and all my dumb anger melted away. I sent her a text saying I was sorry, but she didn't write back, and I cried until I was choking and couldn't breathe except in ragged gasps.

Finally, after fifteen long minutes she texted:

> I didn't tell you anything on Sunday
> because you were a hot mess, but I
> almost fucking died on Saturday night
> because of that shit, Jules! THAT's
> why I'm done! And I'm gonna make
> damn sure Edwin doesn't hook you up
> with any more either.

*What is she talking about? Almost died? How?* I shivered and sighed and pulled the covers over me and tried to close my eyes and sleep. But the notifications on my phone kept buzzing: the pic of pregnant Rainbow with my face Photoshopped over top. The pic of pregnant Rainbow with Blair's face smiling in her belly. A screen cap of Blair getting hit with the Mentos bomb with the caption: *And he thought this cumshot was bad! Dayum!* And girls from school who I *thought* were my fucking friends sending me messages on Instagram like:

> Oooh, didn't know you liked it rough, Jules?

And:

> 2 for 1 pregnancy tests at Pharmaprix, u can grab one for Bianca too LMAO!

And:

> TFW u just the bland bitch he hooked up with for his public image.

At some point later in the afternoon, I woke from a brief nap, and I was shaking and sweating like crazy and all I could see were spots in front of my eyes and everything else was dark. I started having a panic attack. I screamed for help. Marco broke in again, and he and my mom grabbed me, and brought me into the bathroom.

I coughed up bile in the sink and started babbling: "Why'd he do it? Why'd he do it? Why does Blair hate me? Is it because I'm ugly? I hate my body, I'm so fucking ugly, and Bianca is so pretty. And so is Rainbow. Goddammit. I'm a FAIL. A fucking *fail*, Mom. *Why?* Why Mom, why, I just don't . . . I just don't understand, I just can't comprehend anything right now . . . and why did he leave me without saying goodbye, Mom, why?"

During my rant, my mom gently shushed me over and over and then undressed me like I was a three-year old and put me in the shower. She sat on the toilet, while I sat in the tub, and she placed her hand on the small of my back and just kept it there, as the water scalded my skin.

We stayed like this for probably ten minutes until I stopped crying.

And my mom told me she'd be here for me, just like she's always been here for me, and that no matter how bad I felt in this moment it was all going to fade away, and before I knew it I'd start to feel okay again, and she was going to make it her mission for me to feel as good as humanly possible as fast as humanly possible.

She turned the water off, kept her hand on my back, and very quietly told me a story about how when Dad left us she had never felt so betrayed and alone. Even though they were no longer in love, she couldn't believe that he would cheat on her and start a relationship with another woman while he was still sharing a life with her.

"It was the hardest time of my life, trying to keep it together for you and Marco. I was falling apart in every way, and it got even harder once I was hooked on those damn sleeping pills. I felt like they were my only escape, ya know? I don't know if you were too young to really remember, but I had a heck of a hard time getting off those things. So, no matter how crappy you feel right now in this moment, you are done with the pills, Julianna."

*Did Marco rat me out?*

I tensed, tried to get up, but my mom kept her hand firmly on my back.

"Even if ya ain't ready to accept it, it's non-negotiable, hon, okay? 'Cause the sooner you stop, the sooner you'll get it all outta your system, and then you'll be able to think a lot more clearly. And I know you're panicking right now and probably telling me to eff off in your head, but I don't care, 'cause it's the only way you're gonna actually start to feel better."

I started crying again. I clenched my jaw and my fists and screamed. My mom just kept firmly patting my back as I hollered.

"I think you should take a bath right now and try to relax a little, Jules." She plugged the drain and turned the water back on to fill up the tub. "Listen, being cheated on by someone is the worst feeling in the world, believe you me I know it, and no matter how charming Blair Matthews may have pretended to be, he sure as hell ain't worth it, Julianna. And if he *ever ever* did anything to you like what he's being accused of, you need to tell me right now, because if he did, I will be on the next flight to L.A. and I'll be coming home with his balls in my fucking carry-on luggage."

# TANK

I stood on the stairs as Marco and his mom grabbed Jules and dragged her into the bathroom. She looked like she was having a fit she was shaking so badly. It tripped me out seeing her like that. Her t-shirt was riding up so high I could see her bra, so I averted my eyes and looked at Marco instead. He had a big frown on his face.

"Hey Tank, can you turn her music off?" he asked, as they brought her into the bathroom.

I went into Jules' room. It was messy and smelt kinda bad. I turned the volume down on her stereo and heard her sobbing from down the hall. It made my heart hurt. She just sounded sooo sad. I glanced at the cover of the album she'd been playing: *Disintegration* by The Cure. I never heard it before, but it seemed pretty damn gloomy.

"Yeah, she's been playing it on repeat for the last two days," Marco said from the doorway.

"Is she okay, Marco?"

"I dunno, man. She's all messed up right now. My mom's gonna try and get her in the shower, and while she does, I'm gonna ransack this place for her fucking stash." He flicked on the lights.

"Vicky told me she doesn't have any left," I said. "She skipped math class to come here and I guess Jules bitched her out when she didn't bring her any."

"Well, I'm gonna look around regardless," Marco said, going to the corner by the window and pulling her dresser away from the wall. "She has a little hideout spot under the carpet here," he said, lifting up the corner of the carpet to expose a hole in the floor. "She doesn't know that I know it's here, but it's the perfect . . . oh shit, what do we have here?" he said, pulling a little plastic bag out of the hole. "Damn, it's just some weed," he said, throwing it to me.

I opened the bag and sniffed it, while Marco continued going through Jules' stuff. "It smells kinda old," I said, remembering that the first time I smoked weed was actually with Jules, after a football game in Grade 10.

It was the end of the regular season, and we made the playoffs for the first time in three years, so we were celebrating at our backup quarterback Alex Gouin's house. His parents were out of town a lot, so he was always having parties. I think that was a big reason why he was our backup QB, but anyway, even though it wasn't really their vibe, Jules and Vicky were there, because Vicky was crushing on Alex at the time.

Marco and Randy had started smoking weed earlier that summer, but I always said no when they asked me if I wanted to smoke because I was afraid it would turn me into a burnout like my brother and his friends. But that night, after a couple keg-stands in Alex's kitchen I was feeling pretty lit, so when Jules asked me to go outside for a smoke and pulled out a joint instead, I was like, "Sure, why not?"

I've often thought back on that moment and wondered if it had been Randy or Marco who asked me to smoke would I have said no? Was it just because it was Jules that I agreed?

A lot of kids say they don't get high the first time they smoke, but that wasn't the case for me . . . goddamn, I got so baked! I only had two or three tokes, but I held each one in as long as I could, and the last one made me cough really bad. At first, I wasn't sure if I felt anything, but on our way back into the party, Jules asked me a question with this silly look on her face, and I just started cackling. I got the giggles so hard you could literally say anything to me and I would burst into hysterics. Jules kept trying to trip me out and at one point she made eye contact from across the living room and simply mouthed the word: "Potato" and I nearly pissed myself.

I felt like a better version of myself that night – a little lighter, a little deeper, a little kinder, a lot wittier, and a hell of a lot more prone to fits of wild giggling. Everyone and everything, including myself, was more intriguing and magical. And man oh man, music sounded so fuckin' amazing! I feel like that was the first time I actually heard bass for real. Some shitty hip-hop was playing on the stereo all night but I was hooked on the sub levels. I heard frequencies I never knew existed until that moment. It was trippy and made me bob my head and chuckle to myself and dance around the living room as if I was the only one there.

The next day, my abs hurt more from laughing than a trip to the gym. And I couldn't wait to do it again . . .

I heard Jules crying again from the bathroom and I started to get angry.

All of this was Blair's fault. Every inch of it.

I imagined what I'd do to him if he had the balls to walk into Jules' room right now.

*I would lay him out so fuckin' hard, bro.*

Me and that guy had a weird relationship, because he realized that as soon as I got to know him, I saw right through his bullshit. I didn't trust him, and knew he would burn us one day, and I didn't like how he just swooped in and took control of us all. Marco and Jules were absolutely obsessed with him. I used to tell Marco he had more of a crush on Blair than Jules did.

Marco tried to tell me that my hostility came from being the Big Dawg Alpha Male of our group, and sure, I will admit that some of that is true, but most of it comes from the fact that Blair Matthews is a total fucking worm. I mean, look at all the shit he's caused in both Montreal and L.A. He's nothing but a selfish douche bag, and I sooo wish I would've called him on it sooner.

I'm seriously just so thankful he never did anything to Jules like what he's being accused of by this Rainbow woman. I don't know how I'd be able to live with that fact. I mean, I already have to deal with all the chatter at school that I was quote-unquote friends with a fucking rapist. And it's crazy how fast opinions changed at school, because Blair went from top shit to rock bottom in like an hour, with kids starting up mad gossip about him. Bianca's been very vocally blasting down all the rumors, and I heard she's started a "We Support Blair" group on Facebook and Twitter.

But I want absolutely nothing to do with any of that noise.

Marco flipped back the sheets on Jules' bed and found an empty lip balm container under a fleece blanket.

"Hey, I think that's the same little jar Vicky had her stash in when I tried some at The Sala," I tell him, remembering how it burnt the inside of my nostrils, and how crappy my head felt the next day because of it.

"It's empty."

"See, I think she's out, dude."

"Good. But now we gotta make sure she keeps it that way." Marco said. He grabbed the weed from me and gave it a whiff. "Yup, this shit smells like it's from 2015. Still get us high though. You wanna go to Randy's? He downloaded *Zombie Stomp 3* and says it's super fun."

"I dunno, I've got a big math test tomorrow—"

"Yeah, I've got a ton of homework too, but I just need to zone out for a bit, kill some fucking zombies, and try not think about anything else. C'mon, just come with for an hour."

We walked out of Jules' room. I heard the shower running in the bathroom. I kind of wanted to stick around and see if talking to Jules might help her.

"Do you think there's anything we can do for her right now?"

"I don't know. I don't think so. I feel like she needs to detox that stuff out of her, and get a couple days under her belt, before we can really be of much help to her, ya know?"

"All right then, let's go stomp on some zombies," I said.

"Yass! Let me just quickly text my mom about the crime scene investigation in Jules' room, and then we're good to go."

## AUDIO CLIP of The Blade being interviewed by *TMI* outside of Urasawa Restaurant in West Beverly Hills

*The Blade:* C'mon man, the accusations against Blair are 100% false. Completely fabricated and entirely baseless. His accuser is a known substance abuser and has been for years. Here's a woman who's down on her luck, strung-out on drugs, failing as an actress, and looking for her fifteen minutes of fame wherever the hell she can, so she's decided to capitalize on this current #MeToo moment we're having and ruin a young man's life. It's total horseshit.

*TMI:* Are you making light of sexual assault victims?

*The Blade:* No, of course not! Fuck you, man. You know what I'm getting at, so don't try and flip my words against me, all right? Blair is innocent. But to even hint that someone has committed sexual assault these days is enough to destroy his career and reputation. Blair is seventeen years old for God's sake, and this chick is dazed and delusional. A person that would use the hashtag rapebaby, is someone who needs to check herself into rehab and get herself sorted asap, know what I'm sayin'? She's manipulating this story around for her own personal gain and putting an unborn baby in the middle of it. That's some ugly ugly shit, man. Plus, it's highly unlikely the kid is even Blair's to begin with, so—

*TMI:* If the child isn't his, why did your manager make an appointment for Rainbow to go to Planned Parenthood? And is it true you offered Rainbow work in exchange to keep silent about the assault?

*The Blade:* No comment. I've already fuckin' spoken to you people about this. She's twisted things around to make herself look like an innocent victim, which is pretty crafty work for a drug addict. But I ain't gonna stand here and be verbally abused by some potato-faced paparazzi shithead, you feel me? So please, get out of my way . . . (he swears numerous times and pushes past crowd into the restaurant)

# RANDY

Because Blair left town our next show at Le Ritz got cancelled. He was the big draw, and without him we were back to being three high school losers. We tried to jam one afternoon a couple weeks after he disappeared, but we sounded sloppy, uninspired, and lame. The sight of Blair's gear all around us and his microphone stand empty, probably didn't help much either. After about a half an hour, Tank broke a guitar string and we decided to call it quits and play video games instead.

It bummed us out, because me and Marco, we'd started to foolishly dream and believe that The Bad Luck Nickel was actually going to go somewhere. We were feeling like we were right on the verge of something special.

A few nights before our show at The Sala, we were supposed to be studying for a biology midterm, but Marco stole a bottle of wine from his mom, and we drank it and spent the night getting all hyped about the show and imagining our future.

"We sounded really good today. Our whole set from start to finish. We have it down now, don't ya think?"

"Yeah man. We were tight. I think we're ready for Friday."

"If the show goes well, we'll be able to keep building buzz, and who knows, maybe by summer we'll even be able to do a little tour to Toronto or something!" I said.

"With Blair's contacts, we could probably even play in New York City, man! Could you fuckin' imagine?" Marco asked, smiling at me, his lips stained purple from the wine.

We jam really well together, me and Marco, and even if The Bad Luck Nickel is dead, I still need to beat hell on those drums. I still need to go down into that moldy basement and make some fucking noise. Marco's told me it's like therapy for him and I'd say it's the same for me too. It keeps us sane in a world where everything is going completely insane. It's our escape hatch to nowhere. And I've been missing it big time. That's why I tried to get us to jam, but the wound was still too fresh. It made us think of Blair too much, so I guess I'll have to wait a while until all the emotions fully blow over.

It's weird, because it felt like Blair dumped all of us, and not only did we have to get over him suddenly being gonzo, we also had to get over the death of The Bad Luck Nickel too. Not to mention all the drama that came with it. I mean, shit, we all had to completely flip on him overnight and go from being Blair's best buds to full-on hating him because of how he fuckin' iced Marco and Jules so badly.

Not to mention, having to process the whole Rainbow nightmare.

Poor Marco man, I feel like he kinda idolized Blair in a way, and we all know how goddamn obsessed he was about Bianca. But my dude has handled the whole thing like a champ, mainly because of how worried he was about Jules. He needed to stay strong for her. Jules didn't come to school for like a week, and on the day she came back she had a meltdown when she found out Rainbow had the baby.

That same day she managed to get her hands on some Ritalin from this 20-year-old shit bag with the actual name Romeo – he deals drugs out of his Toyota Camry in the Burger King parking lot on Henri-Bourassa – and then she was out of school again for a while.

It took Vicky two weeks to start acting like her normal self too, because after she quit the Ritalin cold turkey she was hella antsy and pretty much in a shitty ass mood all the time. She looked sick, almost as bad as one of the zombie girls in *Zombie Stomp 3,* like her skin was all pasty, and she broke out with zits on her forehead and chin, and she had bags under her eyes, and looked dazed most of the time. She came to school but was just going through the motions and wouldn't talk to me about anything.

I was sorta ticked off that she hid the whole thing from me. I was like completely in the dark about the whole Ritalin thing. I mean, I knew she'd sold some of Edwin's stash at school a couple times, but I had no idea she and Jules were tootin' it up on the regular. The fact that she kept it a secret from me made me question our whole connection, and I kinda felt like ghosting her. When I mentioned this to Marco he got super pissed with me, and said this is when she needed me the most and to bail on her now would be a total dick move on my part.

"She and Jules obviously hid it from us because they knew we'd be like what the fuck? But that doesn't mean we should judge them now, know what I mean? We need to be there for them and try to help them work this shit out."

Marco pulled two cigarettes from his coat pocket, passed me one, and we stood there smoking in silence for a couple minutes. Then without making eye contact with me, he said: "I know your mom's been hooked on antidepressants ever since Nicole died, and I know you don't like to talk about it, but I know what it's like, bro. I've been through similar shit with my own mom, and I swear I'm not trying to tell you what to do or anything, but you shouldn't run away from her, or Vicky – you need to try and be there for them."

At first, I got all defensive, and told Marco to screw off and stay outta my business, but he was totally right.

So even though Vicky was all grumpy and sullen, I did my best to be her little ray of sunshine. I sent her goofy texts and memes all day to try and make her smile, bought her snacks from the dep at lunch time, and walked her home from school every day.

Marco's words kept running through my head, especially about my mom. Vicky didn't know anything about my home life, and one afternoon as we were walking home through Chopin Park, I decided fuck it and just let my guard down and be vulnerable. I made her sit on the frozen bleachers by the baseball diamond, and I unloaded on her.

I told her how my mom was a mess and been addicted to prescription meds for over a year.

"She's like totally lost right now. Off on a Lexapro and Xanax vacation. It makes her numb to everything, she's comatose to any sort of emotion, except just being there. She's never happy, never sad, she's just . . . there. So she still hasn't properly grieved for Nicole, because she's pushed every single one of her emotions out. It's really awful, Vick. And my dad said she was going to get help soon, but that was like three months ago. And one other time, he told me he'd flushed all her pills and was gonna make her stop, but then she wouldn't get out of bed, and she cried for like two days straight. And as heartbreaking as that was, hearing her actually *feel* things, even though they were shitty, made me feel *good*. Is that weird? I think that's weird. And that's why I'm like, in denial or some shit, and try to act as if nothing is different at home even though my mom's like a fucking robot. And my dad's constantly at work, and I don't want to be home alone with her, because she just sits there watching home renovation shows, so I hide out in my room playing video games, or I do the same thing as my dad and pick up extra shifts at work or hang at Marco's so I won't be home as much. And I feel guilty for not doing enough for her, and I think it's time I tried to do more, ya know? And so I promise, I'm gonna be there for you, Vicky Santos, okay? Because I think you're like, absolutely amazing . . ."

And yes, at some point during this, I started crying, because I miss Nicole so goddamn much, and I miss my mom from before, and just wish things could go back to the way they were . . . and then Vicky started crying, and we kissed and hugged each other, and it felt so goddamn good to finally tell someone all that. And

Vicky was so sweet to me, she kissed away my tears and made me feel like everything would eventually be okay. And we kept sitting on those cold ass bleachers, because my rant turned Vicky's rant button back on too, and she told me everything about the Ritalin.

"It's amazing, Ran, how your brain can like, convince you that something is right, even when you know damn well it isn't. But I was doing it every night there in the days leading up to your show at The Sala, to the point where I got nosebleeds! And then almost choking on my own vomit? That was the turning point for sure, but it's really only been the last couple days or so where I'm starting to feel like my old self again. Ya know, I feel so bad that Jules had a relapse, because now she has to start all over. I don't think I could do it. But knowing that you've got my back really means a lot to me, Randell Hill."

I smiled. Something about calling each other by our full names was exciting.

We were gazing at each other – like really making eye contact, and seeing each other in a brand-new way, stripped of all the bullshit and the games. It was like we were feeling this whole new level of trust between us that we didn't have until that very moment. We shivered and held each other tight on the bleachers. My heart was fluttering so fast, and the word 'love' popped up like a cartoon thought bubble above my head. It scared the crap out of me, but I just smiled and kissed Vicky Santos again and again and again.

# JULIANNA

I stayed home from school for a full week after Blair left town, and of course, on the Monday I went back, Rainbow had her goddamn baby. She posted a photo to her Instagram of a tiny hand resting inside her palm, and Blair's hand was wrapped around hers (I knew it was his because of the chipped black nail polish on his fingers that I'd painted on them a couple weeks ago).

The photo had the caption: *it's a boy! he gave us a scare for a minute but lil dude is happy and healthy in his mom and dad's arms! we're going underground for a while, so please respect our privacy during this special time. xoxox*

Vicky sent me a text about ten minutes into first period with the news, and then my phone started blowing up with notifications. I turned it to silent mode and sat in a stupor in the back of the classroom.

*Blair's hand!*

It was the picture of his hand that had me in a daze. Did that mean he really actually *was* the father? And that he was there during the birth? Of his son?

*Omigod, Blair has a son.*

*Omigod, Blair is a dad.*

I gasped quietly as if it took that long to sink in. These two girls in front of me, both named Alessandra, turned around, gave me weird looks, and smiled knowingly to each other.

*And so, what about the rape thing? Was that all just complete bull? What the heck is going on?*

I was so confused.

I irrationally started imagining that the reason why I felt so shitty last week wasn't because I'd been detoxing off the Rit, but instead, because I was pregnant and having morning sickness. Sweat jumped out on my forehead and all the blood drained out of my face. It wasn't true because I had my period two weeks ago, but it didn't matter because I was about to have a full-blown panic attack in class.

"Holy shit," I said too loudly, stuffing my textbook in my bag, and rushing from the back of the class towards the door. My teacher, Mr. Ellis, said something to me and he sounded concerned, but all I could hear were people laughing, so I just booked it out the door. I ran to my locker, grabbed my jacket, and walked straight out the front doors, fighting the urge to puke. The cold spring air helped me fight off the anxiety and calm down a little bit.

I decided then and there to skip the rest of the day and go hide out in Tim Horton's until I was sure my mom would be gone to work. And because fate is a crazy biatch, of course I was gonna see Romeo the dealer in the parking lot, standing in the cold with no jacket on, having a smoke next to his car. I'd never spoken to him before, but I walked right up to him and asked what he was holding.

"Watchoo lookin' for, girl?" he asked.

"Ritalin."

"You sure you don't want Adderall? Shit's way better."

I shook my head.

"You old school, I like that," he said with a douchey leer.

Five minutes later, I'm dry swallowing a 15mg pill of generic Ritalin and ordering a hot chocolate at Timmy's with a broken smile on my face.

After my relapse, everyone tried to help me in their own misguided way.

Initially, Marco had been super supportive, but this time around he got upset with me, mainly I think because he was having a hard time dealing with the whole Bianca and Blair thing himself. So he tried to use tough love, barging in my room and saying shit like: "We've all got problems, Jules, but you gotta snap out of it, and stop taking those stupid pills. They're not doing anything to fix how you feel!"

*Yeah, not very helpful, bro.*

Vicky blamed herself for making me try the Rit in the first place, and in doing so, she just turned it around and made the whole thing about her. I know she was still going through her own withdrawals at that time, but yeah, strike two on the helpful list, Vick.

And my mom, well she just got scared, so she called my dad.

*And strike three, you're out, game over!*

He showed up on a Saturday morning with a bunch of records under his arm. I was surprised. He actually took a flight from Toronto and left his other better family behind to come deal with my bullshit. We hadn't seen each other in probably six months. We didn't even see each other last Christmas because he went to Florida with the other better family.

"Hey Ju-Jube," he said, walking into my room and sitting on the edge of my bed.

He looked older. It tripped me out. I'd never noticed him aging before. He was still his handsome self, but he had lines under his eyes, needed a shave, and he looked a little thicker around the waist.

He put his hand on my shoulder, and gave me his charming smile, the one that would usually melt my bitterness, but this time it bounced off me and dropped dead to the floor.

"What's going on, Jules? Your Mom's really worried about you and so am I."

I laughed sourly. "And what? Just because you show up, I'm supposed to suddenly feel better?" I brushed his hand off me and rolled away from him in bed.

He sighed. "You can talk to me. C'mon, tell me what's going on—"

"How's Jasmine?" I asked.

Jasmine was his other better daughter.

"Yeah, she's fine. She's turning eight at the end of the month."

"Well, good for her," I said into my pillow. I turned back towards him and said: "What gives men the right to be so goddamn selfish and just leave whenever the hell they want, huh?"

This caught him off guard. He started to reply but I cut him off.

"Like, I want to know what makes men think they can do whatever they want and not even consider or seem to care about any of the consequences."

He rubbed a hand over his beard stubble. "I have a feeling that this isn't really about me, and that you're simply projecting your anger, Jules."

"It's absolutely about you! You fucking left us when we needed you the most!" I yelled. It actually wasn't about him at all, but I didn't care, it felt good to call him out on being a deadbeat.

"Look, I know you're upset, Jules, but I'm not here to rehash old issues right now. I'm here to help you figure out what to do about Blair Matthews. Maybe talking to a therapist might help you work through the, um, trauma you're suffering because of that little prick."

"Oh, and now you're diagnosing me?" I shouted. "Blair didn't rape me, Dad! He just broke my fucking heart, okay!"

At this point, Marco stormed into my room and also started yelling at Dad.

"Oh, the big man shows up with some records and thinks he can save the world! Get the hell outta here, bud, we don't fuckin' need you!"

"Don't talk to me like that, Marco, I'm your father—"

Marco clapped his hands and started laughing like an insane person, and I wrapped a pillow over my head and tuned them both out with thoughts about Blair.

He was gone from all his social media. And except for the one photo of his hand on Rainbow's Instagram, he was completely incommunicado, off the grid, allegedly living in a beach house somewhere near the Mexican border with Rainbow and their new baby.

*And I hope to God that baby wails and cries and screams and never stops, so that Blair doesn't sleep for an entire year.*

After the baby was born, and no one could find Blair or Rainbow, The Blade was left to deal with the reporters and paparazzi. They were relentless. And I, obviously, became obsessed with following the story online, hoping for some answers and updates . . .

*What's the deal? Did Rainbow and Blair reach a settlement out of court? What's happened to Rainbow's allegations of sexual assault?*

*Now that the child is here, can you tell us what really happened between Rainbow and Blair? Because the story just doesn't add up . . .*

*Is there any truth to the rumor that you're the one who impregnated Rainbow, and this is all just a giant smokescreen?*

*How is it possible that they're suddenly a happy couple?*

*You've called Rainbow "a liar", "delusional", and "extremely ugly" on record. But if she's the mother of your first grandchild, do you still stand by these insulting terms?*

*Is Rainbow still using drugs?*

*In past interviews, you've mentioned owning a beach house south of San Diego near the Mexico border. Is that where Blairbow are hiding out?*

*Can you at least please tell us your grandson's name?*

*If the allegations were fabricated, how can you and Blair so calmly move on and get over them? And if they aren't, how can Rainbow?*

There were hundreds of questions just like these, but The Blade stood tall, and smugly smiled them all off – not unlike the grin his own son had perfected in that Tim Horton's commercial from a million years ago.

And for a week, he calmly answered every one of them with a firm "No Comment", until finally, when he could take it no longer, he said the following to a dozen or so reporters, while standing outside the gates of his mansion in Santa Monica:

"Listen guys, I'm sorry, but my tinnitus has really been acting up these days. Way too many loud gigs over the years, can barely hear anything, man. So like, I'm not going to even acknowledge any of your questions, all right? But, with the hopes y'all will leave me the hell alone, I'll tell you a couple things. So listen up, 'cause I'm only gonna say this once. First and foremost, The Blade is super stoked to say that hell yeah, he's a granddad to a healthy, happy, and super fuckin' cute baby boy, God bless . . . and secondly, I've just released a formal statement with *Distortion* and *Brave New Waves* and *TMI* and *Needle Drop* amending all of my earlier negative statements about Rainbow, and you can be damn sure, she'll also be releasing her own statement about Blair soon enough, she's just a tad busy at the moment, okay? Life can be complicated sometimes, ya know? And sometimes people do things without the best of intentions, myself included. But the three of us have started slowly working through our piles of shit together—"

The reporters started yapping questions at him, but he just closed his eyes, did yoga breathing, and waited until they were quiet again.

"Yeah, Rainbow and I talked, real talk for a change . . . and I saw it from her point of view, and man, she's totally right. I was able to drag her name through the mud, just like I did with Blair's mom all those years ago, mainly because of who I am. And I'm ready to admit that the stuff I said was rude, misogynistic, and straight-up not true. No one likes to be called names, it's the crudest and cheapest way of dismissing someone, and when I did it, I was just feeding my own ego, ya know? I thought I was protecting my family, but I was just making everything worse, and I feel terrible about that, for real, man. I'd like to be able to stand here and tell you that I've come a long way and have grown and evolved from the guy I was fifteen years ago, but shit, it looks like I still have a bunch of work to do.

Rainbow's my family now too, know what I'm sayin? She deserves respect and I hope at some point she'll be able to respect me too. But I'm gonna have to build that up over time. So for now, I'm gonna keep on keeping on trying to do just that. As is everyone else in my fam-jam, all right? And th-th-th-that's all, folks! End of fuckin' story. Now, if you wanna ask me any questions about Hesher's upcoming sold out European tour, fire 'em at me. Otherwise, y'all can kindly get the fuck off my lawn, thank you very much . . ."

Like The Blade, I had to stop it all too. The whole thing still made me so confused, and I was pretty sure there was a heck of a lot more to the story than he was letting on about, but it didn't seem like we'd be getting the facts any time soon. Maybe eventually the truth would come out, but it had all begun to feel so Bizarro Hollywood, I wouldn't be surprised if they tried to turn the whole story into a bad reality show.

So after a week of detoxing for the second time, and lying in bed and internet obsessing, I decided it was time to think about myself for a change – time to leave the shitstorm in California, and give myself a break from everything everything everything related to No Care Blair.

Because he didn't deserve the attention.

So I started double detoxing off of both him and the Rit.

And I'm not sure anyone would believe me, but the weird part was that getting all strung-out again actually made it easier for me to truly quit the second try. It was like I needed to go to that ugly place one more time, to feel like I didn't have to go back there ever again. I was chasing that first high, that initial fuck-yeah moment that felt so goddamn good, but now I knew I couldn't get there ever again. The glitter and wonder was long gone and I could now honestly see it for how shitty it was.

Like I said, I know it kind of goes against all the talk about addiction and what not, but as I lay in bed, listening to Marco and my dad and now my mom all screaming at each other, I just knew it would be different this time.

I was done.

In the end, Tanky Poo was the one person who was actually helpful. He came over after school one day, knocked on my door, and when I told him he could come in, he sat on the floor next to my bed and started reading *The Great Gatsby* out loud to me. We're in the same English class and I was falling way behind, and so was he, so he'd come over every day after school and read one chapter of the book to me. He didn't ask about my problems or my feelings, instead he brought me into the Roaring 20's, with Nick and Daisy and Gatsby, and helped me escape everything for a little while.

Tank was a good reader. He'd do different voices for the characters, but nothing too melodramatic or cheesy. Like, he didn't do an annoying high-pitch voice for Daisy, he'd just put a slight effeminate lilt to his own voice.

There was something tragic about Jay Gatsby looking so cool in his pink suit while he reached towards the dim green light across the water.

I started calling Tank "old sport", just like Gatsby calls Nick. After Tank would finish a chapter, I'd nod to him and say something like: "Same time tomorrow, old sport?" or "The plot sure does thicken, eh old sport?" or "You know what, old sport? I bet you'd look just as good in a hot pink suit."

I could tell he really dug it.

"Ya know, there's something like ten different movie versions of this book. Once we're done reading it, we should watch every one of them," Tank said with a grin.

"Nope. I'm sorry old sport, but I only want to watch the one with Leonardo DiCaprio," I said. Tank's smile faded a bit, so I added: "But we can watch it ten times in a row if you want."

"Smashing!"

Tank was easy company, he made me feel comfortable, and he was the only one who kept up the illusion that everything was same old same old. And that was exactly the vibe I needed to help get me through those early days off the Rit. After we finished *Gatsby*, I asked if he'd be willing to read an old Stephen King book next, for fun, just as an excuse for him to keep coming by.

It wasn't until I started feeling a bit better that I realized how shitty I'd been looking, wearing the same grubby pajama pants for a week at a time and barely showering. So I started doing regular things again, ya know, like bathing and putting on clothes and going downstairs for breakfast and dinner. I even started wearing a bit of make-up and had the urge to look cute again.

Was I doing it specifically for Tank?

I'd say, yes and no.

Occasionally, I'd think back to that night at The Sala when I was all messed up and rubbing my ass against him in the crowd and wanting to kiss him, but I was also still pretty numb and broken and confused over the whole Blair debacle. So I couldn't possibly think about romance, unless it was fictional and doomed to fail, like in *Gatsby*.

But I did really enjoy and even crave Tank's company during that time. I felt like he was the only one who got me, and maybe it's simply because unlike everyone else, Tanky Poo didn't push me to say a goddamn thing. And when I finally was ready to talk about everything, he just listened, he let me vent, and slowly work through all my shit.

And it helped, so take notes, fellas.

I started seeing a therapist about two months ago and she's super chill, she also lets me vent, and it's nice to talk to a woman that isn't my mom. I thought I was going to hate it, but I actually like going to the appointments. I drink green tea, rant like Vicky for an hour, and then lie on the Persian rug in her office and try and do some meditation.

She says that it's possible to move on from a relationship without getting any closure, you just have to close the door by yourself. But that can be tough, when it's also your first broken heart, because at the same time you're shutting the door, locking it up tight, and tossing the key in the Saint Lawrence River, you also need to be stitching up your heart wound with a needle and thread and slowly make it *lub-dub lub-dub* all strong and steady again. So you need to be patient. Get some days and nights under your belt and gain a little perspective.

I gave up thinking that Blair would ever contact me again and wondering if he was still talking with Bianca, and after a couple months his face started to blur in my mind jusssst a bit, his essence began to get hazy, and at times he started to feel really distant, just a shadow in the shadows. I found myself thinking about Tank more often instead and our vow to have a Sober Summer together. I was excited about our plan. Tank got the whole crew on board, and we were going to rediscover the fun of summer without relying on getting drunk and stoned.

So, I was actually pretty surprised when I got a text from a random number with a California area code a day before my birthday. There wasn't much too it, but it read:

> Hey Jules, I know u prob think I'm the
> world's biggest dick, but I just wanted
> to say I'm sorry, and happy birthday to
> u and Marco! Hope it's great.
> U totally deserve it.

Reading a text from Blair didn't make my heart go crazy like it would have before, I felt oddly calm, more so than I had in months.

Surprisingly, his half-assed happy birthday text was the goodbye I needed.

I could shut the door.

Throw away that key.

Pull out them stitches.

And summer was almost here.

# MARCO

"All right, Ran, you and Vicky create a diversion," Tank says, the corners of his eyes crinkling with excitement.

"We're on it!" Randy says, as he and Vicky run off hand in hand towards the Fitting Rooms in the Women's Clothing section. "Give us like five-ten minutes!"

"Make sure it's a good one!" he yells after them.

We're at the Value Village thrift store and Tank is about to sneak through the Employees Only area and out the back exit into the hallway that leads to The Tunnels.

"It's time to reclaim our chill spot!" Tank says, as he tosses an old velvet suit jacket at me. "Here, try this on!"

"I will! As long as you try these on too," I say, handing him a pair of enormous lime green corduroy pants. Tank puts them up against his waist and starts swaying his hips wildly back and forth. I put on the velvet jacket, and we crack up when we notice it fits me perfectly.

"Dude! You gotta buy that thing! You look fantastic," Tank says, as he steps into the giant cords. They're so big he pulls them on over the pants he's already wearing. "Oh my Lord, these have to be the widest wide leg pants I've ever seen!" Tank says, doing a little shimmy.

"Sooo wide!" I say, laughing. "All you need are some glow sticks and a soother and you could instantly bring back the 90's raver look."

Unlike the thrift stores closer to downtown that are all picked over or too expensive, no one seems to come to this Value Village, so it's like a weird time capsule of the Montreal-Italian community. The closets of dead Nonno's and Nonna's no doubt. And some *Mamie's* and *Pépé's* too.

So much polyester.

I throw a green paisley tie at Tank. "Here's a wide-ass *cravat* to go with your wide-ass pants!"

"Nice!" he says, putting it around his neck and trying to tie it, even though it's clear he has no idea how to tie a tie. "Oh my God, soooo wide! Soooo perfect!"

We giggle uncontrollably. I rub the arms of the velvet jacket and it feels super soft and comfy.

"Whoa! Pimpin' jacket, bro. How much does it cost?" Jules asks, coming towards us in a frilly old black dress with hilariously over-sized shoulder pads.

"$14.95," I say, looking at the price tag on the sleeve.

"OK, I know we said no birthday presents, but I will buy you that ridiculous jacket if you buy me this widow's dress, and we'll wear them all day today and hopefully they'll be in tatters by morning."

I put my hands on her puffy shoulder pads and grin. "Ya know what, Julio? I think these could be the greatest birthday presents evahhhh!"

Jules laughs. It's really nice to see her smile. I didn't see too many of them for a while there, and we were all pretty worried. Thankfully ever since the weather pulled its head out of its ass and finally turned to spring, Jules' spirits have begun to warm up too.

However, it hasn't been easy for her.

But it's supposed to be nice and sunny all weekend, school is almost out, and today is Jules' and my 17th birthday. So things be lookin' up, yo. And last night Jules told me she's finally ready to leave the shitstorm that was Blair Matthews firmly in the past.

And I am sooo here for that!

"All right, all right, everyone! How y'all doing today?" Randy yells from the Furniture section. "We're super happy to be here and we hope you are too!" He and Vicky are standing on top of an old dining room table and they're both wearing tight pink dresses. Randy has a massive blonde wig on, and his lips are painted bright red. Tank and Jules burst out laughing at the sight of him.

"This first one goes out to the Birthday Twins!" Vicky screams, as a cheesy 80's hand-clap drum beat starts up really loudly from Randy's portable speaker. After a few seconds, I realize it's "I Wanna Dance With Somebody" by Whitney Houston.

Tank slips out of his giant pants and throws them at me. "Buy these! And meet me outside The Bat Cave door in exactly twelve minutes!" He drops down and slinks away like a ninja through the Men's Clothing section towards the Employees Only door.

Meanwhile, Jules and I run over to the Furniture section for a close-up view of Randy and Vicky. *Oh mon dieu, they have a choreographed dance going on!* Spinning, and dipping from side to side, and slapping each other on the ass! *Ahh-mazing!* The employees working the cash registers are all sort of just standing there watching, but as Randy turns up the volume as high as it can go, two middle-aged men wearing red vests come out from the back to see what's going on.

I look at Jules. Her face is a sparkling grin. She grabs my hand. "Let's join 'em!" she says, and we jump up on the arms of an old plaid couch next to the table and start dancing with Randy and Vicky.

We all shout-sing the chorus, as Jules and I get up on the table with Randy and Vicky. I cackle as I get a close look at Randy in his pink dress and blonde wig. He looks really good.

*"Eh! C'est quoi cet osti de merde, la?* Stop what you're doing right now!" one of the Red Vests shouts to us.

We ignore him, clap our hands above our heads, and sing the lyrics even louder.

"Come on, *joindre la fête, messieurs!"* Vicky shouts at the Red Vests, who are standing with their hands on their hips.

A handful of shoppers have formed a little crowd around us, and I notice an older lady singing along, and then two little kids jump up on the plaid couch, and there's no stopping our dance party now!

"We'll leave after this song, we promise!" Randy shouts to the Red Vests and blows them each a kiss. And then we turn our backs on them and dance like no one and everyone is watching.

It's barely noon on a sunny day in June, and the four of us are getting kicked out of Value Village for being too damn joyful. We paid for our outfits with the Red Vests hovering over us, and then we burst out into the parking lot, laughing and hyped from our morning dance party/wicked diversion. And as far as we know,

Tank has ninja'd his way through the office and out the door into the hallway that leads to The Tunnels.

"Omigod guys, I seriously almost lost it when those two kids started dancing with us! That was epic!" Vicky says.

"I know, right! Those little kids had some moves," Randy says.

"And Ran, you look amazing!" I say. "I just wish you were wearing high heels instead of Yeezy's."

"I know, what a *faux pas*, right? Sadly, I didn't have any time to learn how to dance in heels."

Vicky grabs Randy's hand. "Please tell me you'll stay in drag all day, because it's really turning me on."

"I feel sexy and comfy and fierce, girl!" he says, kissing Vicky, and leaving a big lipstick stain on her cheek.

We walk by the hair salon, turn the corner into the alley, and I remember that the last time I was here I was with Blair, and we had just jammed together for the first time, and things were so goddamn different.

I can't help but get all up in my feelings for a second, and I try to shake 'em off, but it's hard. Maybe it's because Jules and I had been talking about him last night after he sent her the birthday text, but I can almost feel his presence, like he's smoking a joint behind one the dumpsters or already waiting for us down in The

Tunnels. I get the same sort of feeling sometimes after scrolling through someone's Instagram that I haven't seen in a while. I'll look at their pics, catch up on all the stuff they've been up to, and afterwards that person feels closer to me in my mind, as if we've been texting all day or just hung out, even though we haven't seen each other in months.

And despite the fact it's been almost three months now since our big gig with Full Watt Drug, it all still feels like yesterday to me.

But today's the start of a whole new year. Seventeen! I can't believe it!

So, like Jules said, it's time to move the funk on. And I'm ready, but I also can't help but kinda miss how things were going for a minute there with The Nick, ya know?

We're going to start jamming again as soon as school is out and try to get things moving again, write some new songs, maybe even have Jules and Vick do some vocals . . . and just try to have fun.

Seconds after we arrive outside The Bat Cave door, Tank pushes it open.

"Damn! You're one boss-ass-ninja, Tank!" I say, but he's not smiling. "What is it?"

"See for yourself," he says, looking back at The Blue Door.

The four of us walk in the hallway and see a new heavy-duty deadbolt lock has been added to The Blue Door.

"We're never getting into The Tunnels again," Tank says.

Randy goes up to Tank and tries to hug him. "C'mere, honey bun, let me give ya a big hug and a smooch."

Tank bursts out laughing.

I look up and see a new surveillance camera in the corner. "Well, if you do, it'll be on video, because this place has gone full spy mode," I say, pointing up at the camera.

"Damn, I was really hoping to get The Tunnels up and running again."

"Well, it looks like you really *can't* repeat the past then, eh old sport?" Jules says to Tank.

He smiles at her. "Guess not. It sure didn't work out for our man Gatz."

"What the heck are you two cuties flirting about?" Vicky asks, but then the exit door to the Value Village bursts opens and the two Red Vest managers come rushing out, yelling at us in French about private property, trespassing, the police.

And we're gone, outie 5000, through The Bat Cave door and racing down the alley, scared but laughing at the same time. The Red Vests don't chase after us, but we keep running until we're almost two blocks away, and Randy's begging us to slow down.

"Hold on! I lost my wig!" he shouts. "Could you imagine if I had been wearing heels?" he sputters, hands on his hips, as he gasps for air. "And hot damn it's hard to run in a dress. Am I right, ladies?"

"You gotta hike that skirt way up, girlfriend," Jules says. She has her funeral dress pulled up above her thighs.

"Or just always wear a mini skirt," Vicky says, going up to Randy and smacking his ass.

"So, where the heck should we go?" Tank asks.

"Do you all have your Metro passes?" I ask. Everyone nods. "I've got just the place then."

A half an hour later, we're walking on a bike path next to the train tracks just south of Rosemont Metro station. I take off my new velvet suit jacket and stuff it in my backpack, because the sun is shining bright and feels good on my skin.

"It's a gorgeous day! And to tell you the truth, I'd much rather be outside enjoying the sun, than be underground," I say.

"RIP dem Tunnels!" Tank shouts.

"I hear dat, honey!" Randy shouts back.

The entire metro ride over here, every time the train started moving and we left a station, Tank, wearing his ultra-wide lime green corduroys, would yell: "RIP dem Tunnels!" and Randy, still in his giant blonde wig and dress, would turn to him and say: "I hear dat, honey!" and then they'd start grinding on each other.

Made me and Jules and Vicky crack up every time. Sure, they were acting like idiots, but they were so fearless. I only wish I had the balls to act like such a goof in front of strangers and not give a shit about what people thought about me.

"Are we almost there?" Randy asks.

"Keep your skirt on, we're just about there."

I'm taking everyone to this secret spot that Bianca and I used to go to when we started dating.

We discovered it by accident on our first real date. We'd gone out in group hangs a few times, but this was our first date just the two of us, and I had a whole big thing planned. I'd heard that *Donnie Darko* was playing at some park in the Plateau and I thought it would be romantic to watch a movie outside on a summer night. But we got off the metro one stop too soon, and then Google Maps lead us to a bike path, and we couldn't find a way to get across the train tracks because it was blocked by a fence, so we just started walking down the path, hoping there'd be a spot where we could cross over.

We walked down the path for about five minutes, when Bianca spotted a hole that someone had cut in the fence with a pair of wire-cutters. This part of town by the train tracks is full of abandoned warehouses and factories. It's a bit desolate but there's also something kind of cool about all these old buildings, now overgrown with weeds and covered in graffiti.

"Let's cut across," Bianca said, pulling back the fence and slipping through. I hesitated for a second but followed. There were two sets of tracks, but also a stretch of unused ones veering off to the left next to a big old red brick building, and there were a bunch of empty boxcars, stacked two on top of each other, resting on the unused tracks. Most had the CN logo on them, and others said Canadian Pacific Railway or Hapag-Lloyd, and pretty much all of them were tagged up.

"Hey cool, let's go check out those old boxcars," Bianca said, totally taking the lead on turning this into an adventure. I'm glad she did, because I was too stuck on the fact that this was screwing up the romantic date I had planned to be chill.

"But the movie starts in ten minutes," I said lamely.

"Well, maybe this will give us a view of how to get there," she said, starting to climb up a ladder on the back of one of the cars.

"Be careful, it's getting dark," I almost said, but heard Tank's voice in my head, telling me to just be cool and go with the flow and see what happens. So, I took a deep breath and decided to let the summer night take us wherever it may.

When we got up on top of the boxcars, Bianca had a grin on her face. "I feel like we could be in some crazy action film, where the characters get into a fight on top of a moving train. This is totally cool, Marco!" she said. "Can you take a picture?"

"Sure," I said. She put her hands on her hips and posed. She looked so pretty in her forest green tank top and tan short-shorts. I almost couldn't believe we were standing on top of a train together. I snapped a few pics. "Let's get one of the both of us," she said, and I happily jumped in the frame with her.

"If you want, I can take a video of you running towards me, and you could like, even jump over top of me and make it seem like you're leaping from one car to the next," I said.

"Yes! That'd be dope!" she said. We did three takes, and with each one Bianca's grin grew. "I love how we're always getting into these random adventures, Marco," she said. "I mean, why bother going to see the movie when it feels like we're in one!"

"Well, let's have a toast then," I said. I pulled a bottle of wine out of my backpack and handed it to Bianca. "A lovely Pinot Noir, stolen from my mom's extensive collection," I said. Then I pulled out two plastic cups and a corkscrew.

"Wow, you sure come prepared," Bianca said. I opened the wine and poured us both a glass.

The sun was just about to set, and the sky was a pastel pink colour. The first stars of the night were starting to twinkle above us. A million crickets and cicadas were chirping and buzzing. There were a few mosquitoes, but they weren't really biting us too much. The air smelt like freshly cut grass and a little bit like weed. I felt the rumble of a train heading our way on the tracks next to us. We were sitting so close to each other our legs were touching, and as I passed Bianca her wine, she put her hand on my knee. My heart started going nutso and I knew it was now or never – I had to make a move and tell her how I felt.

I raised my glass, looked right into Bianca's eyes and said: "To many more random shenanigans with you, Bianca Marcuzzi . . . the most beautiful girl I've ever known!"

It was the grandest statement I'd ever made in my life and after saying it, my head felt like it does on a plane during take-off, filling up with so much pressure it seems like my skull's going to crack open like a watermelon, until finally, when I think I can't take it a second longer, my ears pop.

"You're so sweet, Marco," Bianca said, blushing. "And ya know, you ain't so bad yourself."

She glanced at me with those big Bambi eyes. The train blared its horn and began to rush by us, making so much mechanical noise, and before I could change my mind, I pulled her close and we kissed . . .

We ended up hanging out on top of the boxcar for a while, drinking our wine, kissing some more, and getting to know each other. It's as if it took that first kiss for us to actually feel comfortable around each other. It was almost fully dark now, and I was joking around doing an impression of our French teacher, Madame Bernard, when we heard voices heading towards us on the abandoned tracks. I was kind of scared for a second, until we saw it was two couples.

"I hope they don't come up here," Bianca whispered. But they walked past the boxcars, and over to the old brick building. I heard one of them shout, "Be careful!" as they started climbing up a rusty fire escape on the side of the building that went all the way up to the roof.

We watched the four of them climb the ladder and disappear on top of the roof.

"I wonder what's up there?" I asked, and then we saw fireworks begin going off above the downtown skyline.

"Oh man, we gotta go up there too, Marco! The view will be incredible!"

"*This* is the secret spot you used to bring Bianca to so you guys could make out?" Jules asks, as we veer onto the unused tracks. "Sooo romantic, bro!"

"Hold on, we ain't quite there yet," I say. "We have to get up there first." I point to the top of the old warehouse.

"How?" Vicky asks.

"Rickety old fire escape," I say.

"Let's do it!" Vicky says.

We jump off the tracks and walk through the weeds towards the brick building, and one by one carefully climb up the metal ladder.

"Who's afraid of heights?" Randy yells. "Oh, just me? Perfect!"

"Better not look down, Ran!" Jules says.

Once we're all safely on top of the roof, I tell everyone to check out the city. The view is wicked. To the west, we can see a big old church and the mountain with its cross on the top, and to the south there's the downtown skyline and an old steel bridge crossing the Saint Lawrence River.

"At night, that bridge over there is all lit up with lights, and every weekend in the summer, there's fireworks."

"OK, OK, I see it now, Marco!" Jules says. "This could be pretty darn *romantique*, especially at night. Ya know, I'm actually surprised that you're finally sharing your secret spot with us. You were always so hush-hush about it."

"Well, it's like you were saying yesterday, Jules, it's time to move on. This place is special to me, but I am totally ready to create some new memories, with all you silly muthafuckas!"

"Even me?" Randy says, pouting his red lips.

"And me?" Tank asks, swinging the legs of his giant pants back and forth.

"*Et moi, aussi?*" Vicky asks, flipping her blonde wig off her shoulder.

"Heck ya, my dudes," I reply.

I put my arm around Jules and grin. Jules gives me a big smile back. Vicky runs over and gives us both a hug.

"Happy born days, you sexy ass twins!"

I grab my phone, put it in video mode, and prop it up on one of the big metal vents that are scattered across the rooftop. I tap the record button.

"All right, all right, my friends! It's time to crack open this Mountain Dew, and celebrate this random, fleeting moment of our lives, right here, right now!"

"Well, you better get that sweet new jacket of yours on, Marco, because the first annual Birthday Dance Party is about to begin," Vicky says, as she connects her phone to Randy's Bluetooth speaker.

Randy hikes up his dress, puts the bottle of Mountain Dew between his legs, and crudely *pops* off the lid like it's a cork. It goes flying into the clear blue sky above us, and we all cheer. Tank hands everyone little plastic cups and Randy fills them up.

"Are you guys ready for another round of Whitney Houston? Me and Randy will show you our choreography!" Vicky says.

Jules laughs. "Totally! I want in on some of those smooth butt-slapping moves of yours!"

"No problemo, Julio!" Vicky says, as she presses play on her phone, and "I Wanna Dance With Somebody" starts up in the background.

"Aww yeah, let's do this!" Randy says.

And we all raise our cups in the air and strike a pose for the camera – Randy and Vicky in their hot pink dresses, Tank in his jumbo cords, Jules in her frilly widow's gown, and me in my blue velvet suit jacket – just five teenage weirdos, sipping neon green soda on an abandoned rooftop in Montreal, tilting our heads to the bright sky, and dancing dancing dancing.

# ABOUT THE AUTHOR

**MATTHEW LESLIE** grew up in Windsor, Ontario, where he played in bands during high school and university. He reckons himself a writer, musician, and lover of lovely things. He lives in Montreal where he teaches his favourite books to teens with the goal of inspiring a love of reading.

Find him online at: mattleslie.org/the-bad-luck-nickel/

www.ingramcontent.com/pod-product-compliance
Lightning Source LLC
Chambersburg PA
CBHW030927120726
47906CB00002B/514